THE
RED
DOVE

D1507336

THE RED DOVE

Derek Lambert

STEIN AND DAY / Publishers / New York

First published in the United States of America in 1983
Copyright © 1982 by Derek Lambert
All rights reserved, Stein and Day, Incorporated
Designed by Judith Dalzell
Printed in the United States of America
STEIN AND DAY/*Publishers*
Scarborough House
Briarcliff Manor, N.Y. 10510

Library of Congress Cataloging in Publication Data

Lambert, Derek, 1929-
  The red dove.

  I. Title.
PR6062.A47R4   1983   823'.914   82-42837
ISBN 0-8128-2913-1

For
Frank and Marsha Taylor,
friends and advisers

The dove descending breaks the air
With flame of incandescent terror.

T. S. Eliot (1888–1965)

ACKNOWLEDGMENTS

My thanks to the following for their help in researching this novel: the NASA authorities at John F. Kennedy Space Center, Florida, U.S.A.; my agent, Julian Friedmann; Colin Murray of Sphere Books; my old colleague Ronnie Bedford, Science Editor of the *Daily Mirror* and *Sunday Mirror* (through his publication *Space Mirror*); Arthur Smith, Science Correspondent of the *Daily Mirror*; Frank Taylor of the London *Daily Telegraph*'s Washington Bureau, and his wife, Marsha, and Dick Beeston, chief of the same bureau. Any mistakes are my copyright.

THE
RED
DOVE

SCENARIO

1

THE absurd possibility that he, a Hero of the Soviet Union, could ever become a traitor, occurred to Nicolay Talin when he was 150 miles above the surface of the Earth.

The absurdity—it was surely nothing more—was prompted by an announcement over the radio link from Mission Control:

"We know that you will be proud to hear that at 0500 hours Moscow time, units of the Warsaw Pact Forces crossed the Polish border to help their comrades in their struggle against the enemies of Socialism attempting to subvert their country."

Proud? Involuntarily, Talin shook his head. Such timing! While he was acting as ambassador of peace in space the Kremlin had perpetrated an act of war on Earth.

"So they finally did it," was all he said.

He felt Oleg Sedov, commander of the shuttle, *Dove 1,* on its maiden flight, appraising him. Sedov, forty-seven years old and as dark and sardonically self-contained as Talin was blond and quick, had been appraising men all his adult life.

Sedov, separated from Talin by a console of instruments, leaned forward in his seat, cut the radio, and smiled at Talin.

"You didn't exactly glow with patriotic fervor," he remarked.

Talin gazed at Europe, bathed in spring sunshine, sliding away below them. There was a storm gathering over the sheet of blue steel that was the Mediterranean. To the north lay a pasture of white cloud; beneath that cloud was Poland, beneath that cloud, war. In ninety minutes they would be back, having orbited the Earth. How many would have died during that time?

He tried to relax, to banish the specter of treachery that had suddenly presented itself. True, he had often doubted before, but his doubts had never been partnered by disloyalty. He unzipped his red flight jacket and said, "You know better than I do, Oleg, that what goes on down there," jabbing a finger toward an observation window, "doesn't have much impact up here."

"So you're suppressing your joy until we land?"

"*If* we land," Talin said. He was piloting *Dove*.

"Ah, there I share your doubts. But let's keep them to ourselves," Sedov said, reactivating the radio.

"*Dove One, Dove One,* are you reading me?" The voice of the controller in Yevpatoriya in the Crimea cracked with worry. When Sedov replied, his tone changed and he snapped, "What the hell happened?"

Sedov shrugged at the panels of controls, triplicated in case of a failure, and said, "Just a temporary fog-out. Also, I had to use the bathroom."

The controllers had long ago learned to accept Sedov's lack of respect: Not only was he the senior cosmonaut in the Soviet Union, he was a major in the First Chief Directorate of the KGB.

"Is everything still going according to schedule?"

"Affirmative," Sedov replied.

"We were worried about Comrade Talin."

Sedov frowned. "He looks healthy enough from where I'm sitting."

"His heartbeat went up to a hundred and twenty just now."

Again Sedov's dark eyes appraised Talin as he said to the controller, "Maybe he was thinking about Sonya Bragina."

"That," the controller said, "is a remarkable observation, because it so happens that we have Sonya Bragina here waiting to talk to Comrade Talin."

This time Talin himself felt his pulse accelerate as he anticipated Sonya's voice, pictured her at Mission Control, wearing her severe, dark blue costume to make her look more like a Party member than a dancer, blonde hair braided and pinned—remembered her the last time he had seen her, naked on the bed in her apartment in Moscow.

What was happening was obviously the dream-child of a Kremlin publicist. Bolshoi ballerina converses with lover in space; as subtle as a *Pravda* editorial but more effective. And if *Dove 1* crashed into the Siberian steppe, then the Russian people would always remember this last, space-age conversation and weep delightedly.

"Hello, Nicolay, how are you?"

"I'm fine," he said.

"Where are you now?"

"Right above you."

"Your mother sends her love. And . . ."

"Yes?"

"I love you."

Talin guessed that someone had prompted her, because although she was by nature passionate she wasn't demonstrative in public, certainly not for the benefit of the millions watching and listening on television and radio.

Now he was expected to respond, "And I love you," but he rebelled because the whole exercise was so gauche. There was nothing they could do about that, and she would understand.

He said, "Do you know what I would like now?"

A nation held its breath. Sedov raised an eyebrow.

Talin said, "A plate of *sakuski,* salted herring, perhaps with a pickled beet salad, followed by a steak as thick as a fist, washed down with a bottle of Georgian red."

He thought he heard her laugh, but he couldn't be sure. The laugh would be surfacing all right, but she had the discipline to fight it back. Anyway, their audience would appreciate the remark: A man wasn't a man unless he indulged his belly.

She hesitated, the Kremlin script in tatters. "Aren't they feeding you all right up there, Nicolay . . . ?" Her voice faded as she realized that she had made a mistake, implied criticism.

He came to her rescue. "I was only joking. The food's fine." Well, not bad, if you liked helping yourself to rehydrated vegetable soups, *blinis,* and coffee, in slow motion to combat weightlessness.

"I miss you, Nicolay."

Another cue. He ignored it.

"Ten more orbits," he said, "and we'll be down."

"Goodbye, Nicolay."

"Goodbye, darling." *Sweet compromise.* "Don't forget the *sakuski.*"

And she was gone.

"Well," Sedov said, "I didn't realize I was in the presence of a great romantic."

"I'm not a ham from Mosfilm," Talin told him.

Even that was a perversity—Mosfilm made good movies. Perhaps space had got to him. It could cause disorientation, which was why cosmonauts underwent so many psychological examinations.

That would explain his aberration when he heard about the invasion of Poland. A side effect of the transition into space, awareness of the curve of the globe below and the void above.

The Soviet Union occupied a sixth of the world's land surface but up here he could see nothing of it. The pendulous sack of South America, oceans scattered with fragments of land.... Space and freedom had become one, the breeding ground of fantasy.

Beneath them now was the cutting edge of the United States. In eleven minutes thirty-eight seconds they would have crossed the North American continent. *Dove* had reached the Midwest when another irrational notion presented itself unsolicited to Talin: What would happen if, because of a malfunction, they were forced to land in America?

Far away in the Crimea one of the scientists monitoring the shuttle reported that Talin's heartbeat had increased to 125.

When darkness returned to Earth, that is, when the globe was between *Dove* and the sun, the disturbing specters fled, the reverse of the norm on Earth when the fantasies of night vanish with the dawn. And Talin and Sedov began to prepare for their return to Mother Russia.

Both shared one doubt about the shuttle. They feared that, like the spaceship destined for Venus that had exploded on the launchpad in October 1960, killing Field Marshal Mitrofan Nedelin and scores of technicians, it had been put into production too quickly.

The Kremlin was obsessed with firsts. The first satellite into space, *Sputnik I* in 1957, the first man in space, the late Yury Gagarin in 1961. They had been mortified when, in 1969, American astronauts had made the first landing on the moon, paranoic when, in April 1981, the Americans had soft-landed their shuttle Columbia in California.

That achievement had heralded the dawn of an age when man could commute in space, when passengers could visit floating hotels and return home in a winged ship that looked like an ordinary jet airplane—a ship that could be used time and time again.

It had also heralded the possibility of a titanic power struggle. With a shuttle, a superpower could deposit in orbit convoys of spy satellites equipped with beam guns and telescopes that could sight a kopek coin 400 miles away.

The Russians had been poised to launch this new age, but they had been beaten to it by the Americans—who had also had the gall to make the launch on April 12, 1981, the twentieth anniversary of Gagarin's first orbit.

So they had postponed the launching of their prototype and concentrated on another first: building a fleet of space trains modified to construct, rather than merely deposit, stations in space.

Fears that the Kremlin was dangerously obsessed with the race to overtake the U.S. initiative were realized when the first, unpublicized launch aborted on blast-off.

There were two more trials, one successful, one not, before *Dove I* finally went into orbit with Sedov and Talin at the controls. Not all the refinements had yet been incorporated, but the Kremlin could boast that it possessed the command ship of its construction fleet in space.

The military potential of the Dove shuttles, including some of the refinements, was the responsibility of the commander, Sedov. Talin accepted that it would have to be armed—you had to defend yourself. But, projecting the dreams of his youth into the firmament, he saw himself as a pioneer of peace in space.

And the Kremlin backed him. Having accused the Pentagon of building *Columbia* to lay a trail of nuclear mines in orbit, they assured the world that their aim was the peaceful exploration of the heavens.

Dove not Hawk.

The red and white ship looked much the same as its American sisters. It was 190 feet long, with swept-back wings and brutally large and powerful engines in its tail. On its back it bore a cargo bay with a capacity of forty tons, ten more than *Columbia*. In its inquisitive-looking nose there were three decks— storage area, living quarters, and flight deck.

It was to the living quarters, as *Dove 1* orbited at 18,000 mph on this May day, that Talin now walked with ponderous, weightless steps to prepare for reentry.

On one side was a bathroom, on the other bunks and lockers, in the center a table. From the dispenser Talin took a small tray wrapped in plastic and marked *Day 3, last meal*. He squirted water through a hollow needle attached to a faucet into the dehydrated food inside; then he removed the plastic, clamped the tray to the table, and slowly began to eat the cold beef and potato salad.

He drank a glass of synthetic orange—it was impossible to rehydrate natural orange because water and crystals don't mix—took off his flight jacket, and put on an antigravity suit with inflatable trousers. The pressure of the oxygen on legs and belly in these stopped the blood from plunging to the lower extremities. Puncture those pants and you blacked out.

Back on the flight deck, Sedov had prematurely begun the pre-burn checkout. It was only Talin's second trip into space, but he had spent 300 hours in a simulator, and he knew this was unusual for a veteran such as Sedov. Talin shivered and glanced into the star-strewn darkness for comfort.

Sedov was sitting on his high-backed seat, one hand on the rotational hand controller, staring at the computer screen. He was frowning.

"What's wrong?" Talin asked.

"I wish I knew. She just doesn't feel right. Maybe space is getting to me." Sedov stood up. "You take over the checkout while I get into my antigravity gear."

As he plodded away, Talin strapped himself into the seat next to Sedov's and examined the indicator lights, computer readouts, dials. Nothing wrong there. And yet. . . . Sedov's concern was contagious.

Sedov who had circled the moon, Sedov who had spent ninety-six days on a SALYUT space station, Sedov the laconic cosmonaut/intelligence officer who had been personally chosen by Nicolay Vlasov, chairman of the KGB, to represent the MPA, which maintained Party control over the military in space. Hardly the sort of man to be fanciful.

What worried most cosmonauts was their reliance on computers. If a computer could foul up your home electric bill, then it was perfectly capable of abandoning you with only manual glide control over the Pacific Ocean.

Figures on the screen in front of Talin danced with blurred speed.

Sedov returned, strapped himself into his seat, and slipped on his white helmet and headset. His lean Slav face was expressionless as he spoke to Control.

Turning to Talin, he said, "We're just halfway around the world from touchdown."

Green light shone below them, gaining strength by the second. They were over the Atlantic, which was just emerging from a night blanket of cloud.

Again Sedov disconnected the radio link. "Stop thinking about Poland," he said. "They had it coming to them."

"I wasn't thinking about Poland." Although his doubts had begun with the announcement of the invasion.

The trouble was that Sedov, his mentor, knew him too well. Read his thoughts. Sedov had known him when he was a young rebel, and because he admired Talin's talent for space navigation, because he had no son of his own, had taught him to quell—not kill—the rebellion. He had also per-suaded Military Intelligence, GRU, even then little more than an arm of the KGB, that he was politically acceptable.

In a way Sedov's insight into his own reactions was another conscience. To betray Communism, even in thought, was to betray Sedov.

At 0600 hours, one hour before the scheduled landing, Sedov, having recontacted Mission Control, nodded at Talin and said, "It's all yours."

It was the crucial moment, no abort possibilities after this. Forget Poland, forget Sedov's doubts.

First Talin had to reduce the impetuous speed of *Dove*. He turned her around and ignited the retrofire engines. She quivered, slowed down, and, with the two small engines thrusting forward, began to descend backward toward the Earth's atmosphere. A dozen dangers now lurked in her straining body. If, for instance, the skin of ceramic tiles protecting her from heat peeled off, she would explode into a ball of fire.

20

After the retroburn that took *Dove* out of orbit, Talin turned her around again and pulled up her nose. Inconsequently, he remembered pulling the reins on a recalcitrant horse he was riding as a boy on the steppe.

Their altitude was now seventy-five miles. The temperature on the outside of *Dove* was between 2,000 and 3,000 degrees Fahrenheit. As the melting point of aluminum, from which her body was made, was 1,200 degrees, they couldn't afford to lose many ceramic tiles. In front of them the air glowed with heat.

As *Dove* dipped toward the land masses of Europe and North Africa and the Earth's gravity began to pull, Talin's arms felt heavier, and he became weighted to his seat.

He checked the instruments. They were 3,000 miles from the landing strip, which was itself 100 miles north of the launch pad at Tyuratam in the Soviet central Asian republic of Kazakhstan.

Talin spoke to Control to reassure them. Not that there was any real need, because every reaction of *Dove* was monitored on forty-eight consoles. Even my heartbeat, he remembered.

"Everything under control," he reported. "I think I can see Russia ahead and that's always a beautiful sight," which it was. He only wished that, being a Siberian, they were homing down from the east coast, over the Sea of Okhotsk with the fishlike body of Sakhalin Island beneath.

He glanced at the digital clock. In less than half an hour they would touch down on the established flight path. Sedov had been wrong: There was nothing wrong with their beautiful red and white bird. Talin gave a thumbs-up sign to Sedov.

Which was when the radio link with Mission Control went dead.

Don't panic. Talin's preparation for any emergency in the simulated shuttle on the ground asserted itself. Controlled panic. His arms felt even heavier than they should, a rivulet of sweat coursed down his chest.

He glanced at Sedov. Sedov was smiling. Smiling!

Sedov spoke into his mouthpiece, "*You* can hear me?"

Talin nodded, remembering as Sedov spoke.

"The blackout we anticipated," Sedov said. "You were prepared for it?"

"Of course, the heat . . ." The lie stood up and took a bow. Sedov ignored it because that was his way and said, "It won't last long."

When Control returned, Talin suppressed the relief in his voice. At 250,000 feet he began to fly the ship a little, using elevons, brakes, rudders, and flaps, correcting the flight path and speed.

At 80,000 feet over the Sea of Aral, the engines cut, and, as planned, *Dove* became a glider. From Control, "Perfect ground track."

They were wrong. At that moment the shuttle veered sharply away from the runway laid out like a white ceremonial carpet. Talin quickly took over completely from the autopilot and tried to correct the flight path. Nothing. Panic returned but was instantly disciplined, a wild dog on a leash.

Beside him, Sedov was also struggling with the dual hand controller and rudder pedals. But the Dove had become a wilful bird of prey that had sighted a far-off quarry.

Sedov's face was a mask, a single muscle dancing on the line of his jaw. He said, "This is crazy," and Talin knew what he meant: Rockets, computers, all the most sophisticated technology that man could devise had worked, but elementary controls used by any weekend glider pilot had failed.

They were below 50,000 feet, supposedly descending for the final approach and landing on a twenty-two-degree glide slope.

Sedov finally was able to take over and raise *Dove*'s nose. As they headed away from the strip in a wide arc he said, "I once had a car like this."

His voice calmed Talin. "A car?" He peered down. A ten-mile radius around the strip had been leveled in case of a forced landing. Beyond this circle of black earth and shale lay the desolate steppe still patched with snow.

"Sure, a car. It wasn't much of a car, an old Volga that looked like a tank. And it developed this trouble—it would only steer in one direction."

From Mission control came a hoarse voice, "What's going on up there?" Talin could picture the consternation as screen monitors and visual trackers reported *Dove*'s deflection.

"A minor technical fault," Sedov said.

"At this stage?"

"This bird doesn't want to return to its cage," Sedov said.

Talin noticed that he was no longer trying to correct the flight path of the shuttle.

"What the hell are you talking about?"

Sedov cut the radio link.

He said to Talin, "About that old car of mine. I was lecturing at Moscow University in those days, but I lived in a boarding house off Russakouskaya Street. Now as you know that's on the other side of the city but in a direct line . . ."

"I don't see . . ."

"You will, you will." The lack of noise was eerie and Talin wondered again if space had at last affected Sedov. What sort of impact would 100 tons of spaceship make on the steppe? They could always eject—but only to disgrace. In any case, Sedov would never permit it. "You see," Sedov was saying, "all I did was to drive in a semicircle around the city until I arrived at the university." He leaned back in his seat. "There," he said, "now you take this old Volga back to base."

Talin took over. There was no maneuverability to the left, only to the right.

That meant that, although he was committed to a curving glide, he could bring the ship right around again to the strip.

He tightened the circle. *Dove* completed its northward arc and began to return on a southward curve toward the runway.

"Just tell me one thing," Talin said. "How the hell did you get home again after you'd lectured at the university?"

"Easy. I just continued on around the other side of the city."

"If I miss the strip this time, I'll have to go around again."

"I wouldn't advise it," Sedov said. "You should have touched down at 235 mph. By the time you get there on this lap you'll have lost so much speed that we'll probably land like a spent meteorite."

"You should have been a doctor," Talin said. "You have a perfect bedside manner."

"Take her down a little," Sedov advised.

Talin began his approach at 12,000 feet. He could feel *Dove* straining down. She didn't want to glide anymore, she wanted to answer the call of gravity.

The great tail engines, the heaviest part of the ship, tipped back, jerking the nose up. Talin grappled with the hand controller, the tendons on his wrists standing out like cords. Fleetingly, he saw himself again as the boy on the horse, a gray, pulling on the reins as, mane flowing, it galloped through a copse of silver birch. He summoned Sonya to him, Sonya, naked on the bed. Loving her, determined to keep that last picture with him. But he discovered that such pictures don't stay, only survival stays.

Dove's nose leveled. Below, to the right, Talin could see the strip. To one side, scattering, were the spectators. No massed crowds like those who swarmed to the launch and landing of the first American shuttle, *Columbia*. Fatalistically, the Kremlin always anticipated failure.

Sedov was staring ahead, private as always. What picture had he tried to lock in his mind? Even as he wondered, Talin knew: Sedov had seen a blond teenager from Khabarovsk in Siberia, who wanted to become a cosmonaut.

The strip was almost beneath them. Air speed too slow, descent speed, which should have been about three feet a second, too fast. Talin lowered the undercarriage.

The tail was sagging again. With one last effort, Talin fought the earth's magnetism.

Tail up fractionally. A little more. The strip directly below.

They bounced. Hit again. Bounced. *Dove* was veering away once more, out of control, a beautiful bird hellbent on suicide. Tarmac raced past. Then they were onto the hard black soil, chasing the fleeing spectators.

Brake, brake . . .

Dove shuddered, stopped.

Talin closed his eyes, kept them tight shut for a moment.

Sedov said, "As a matter of fact I've still got that old Volga. You just qualified to drive it."

Three hours later in the debriefing center, Talin switched on the radio to pick up the news:

"*Dove One,* command ship of what will one day comprise a fleet of space shuttles, today completed its maiden flight without a hitch."

Talin switched off the radio.

2

HE was seventy-two years old, and he enjoyed chopping down trees.

You could almost feel his enjoyment, his companion thought, observing the play of muscles on his naked chest, hearing his grunts of satisfaction as the blade of the ax bit into the young redwood.

Feel it but not share it. The axman's companion had never enjoyed physical exertion, although to keep fit he exercised, working out as thoroughly as he did most things he put his mind to. He didn't enjoy dispatching men to their deaths but he did it competently enough.

With awe he watched the veteran take another swing at the redwood that was shading his ranch house. His sun-reddened torso was slicked with sweat and his breathing had accelerated, but there was no evidence of real stress. God almighty! He would be an octogenarian in eight years, yet his muscles, except perhaps around the neck, had none of the stringiness of old age, his hair was still shiny dark—possibly doctored to stay that way—and his skin was smooth.

And as if all that wasn't enough, he talked between swings. They say I'm a hard man, mused the observer, who was fifty-four, but, hell, I'm a lightweight beside this guy.

The lightweight was George Reynolds, director of the Central Intelligence Agency. His companion was the President of the United States.

Wood chips flew, the tree trembled. Reynolds wondered if it would eventually fall on the small, red-roofed ranch house.

The President smiled and said, "Don't worry, George, it won't," and prepared himself for another swing.

Patiently, Reynolds waited for the dénouement: The reason for his summons from his headquarters near Washington, D.C., to the presidential ranch in California, high in the Santa Ynez mountains, 160 miles northwest of Los Angeles and six miles off Coastal Highway 101.

While he waited, he surveyed the terrain the way he had been trained to as a young man. He noted the lemon and avocado groves below, the glint of the Pacific, the ranch fences hewn from old telegraph poles (show the man wood and he reached for an ax), the cattle grazing in the heat of this August day.

But Reynolds didn't observe with aesthetic appreciation. For him the woods behind the ranch were cover for an assassin who could easily outshoot the two guards standing fifty yards from them. In the expanse of ocean he pictured a gunboat. The President had been shot once: It must never happen again. And it was with relief—although security was the responsibility of the Secret Service, not the CIA—that he heard the clatter of a surveillance helicopter.

The President leaned on the ax handle, polished by his hands, as though the helicopter had disturbed his rhythm. One hand strayed to the puckered scar on his chest left by the bullet fired by the would-be assassin. He pulled it away as if the scar had burned his fingers. From the pocket of his blue jeans he took an orange bandanna and wiped his forehead.

Grinning, he said to Reynolds, "How about a few swings, George? Could do wonders for your golf. In any case, you look far too neat for this kind of country."

Reynolds became aware of his gray lightweight suit, black Capitol Hill shoes, red and blue striped tie, button-down collar. With his prematurely silver hair, as fine as a baby's, his disciplined features, and his jogger's physique, he looked like any Washington bureaucrat who had almost made it. But Reynolds could adapt. He took off his jacket and tie, rolled up his sleeves, and he was a countryman.

The President handed him the ax and he swung it, efficiently but without pleasure. The redwood swayed—in the direction of the ranch. As Reynolds swung, as the helicopter slanted away, the President began to talk.

"Thought I'd get you out here, George, because it's a place where a man can talk, where the air is clean—and free of your kind of bugs." He shaded his eyes and stared at the branches of the redwood with their hemlocklike leaves. "You know it's a real shame to cut down a young tree like this. Did you know one of them once grew to 364 feet?"

"It looks like a sequoia to me," Reynolds said.

"If it was I sure as hell wouldn't cut it down, George. They're pretty damn rare." And then, "Hey, I didn't know you knew anything about trees. Did you read it up on the jet?"

"I like to be prepared," Reynolds admitted, "for every eventuality."

"You're a wily old bird, George, and a rare one."

Reynolds paused before lifting the ax. He was pleased there wasn't any ache in his muscles. "Rare?"

"You enjoy your profession in an age when it's fashionable to be masochistic about it. Do you ever read about happy spies these days?"

Reynolds considered this. Was he happy? He'd never really thought about it. Perhaps that indicated happiness. No, a more neutral condition, at best contentment. What ensured that contentment was the knowledge that he was the only man to do his job, the only man in an age of doubt to acknowledge that to help your country to survive you had to be devious and ruthless.

In his devious and ruthless way, Reynolds was the ultimate patriot and his life was littered with sacrifices. No wife and children, no real home. No social life to speak of. He had dispensed with these in the interests of efficiency.

A warm breeze ruffled Reynolds's baby-silk hair. "I never read about fictional spies, Mr. President." He swung the ax.

"But you *are* human and you *are* wondering why I brought you here." The President's voice became more incisive. "My term of office comes to an end in just over a year."

"But not necessarily your presidency."

"Don't you think I'm a bit long in the tooth to stand for reelection?"

"Not you, Mr. President."

"I'm glad to hear you say that, George. I intend to run. But before I do that, I want to rejuvenate my image."

"How?"

"By giving the United States a boost. It's sad to see what's happened to U.S. strength. The Russians have been calling the shots lately, I think its time we changed the tune."

"What do you have in mind?" Reynolds asked cautiously. He leaned on the ax. The wood at the apex of the triangular wound made by the ax groaned as the tree swayed.

"First there was Afghanistan," the President said softly. "Then there was Poland. Then they threw out twenty of our diplomats from Moscow. All your men, George."

"We reciprocated."

"Reciprocation is diplomatic bullshit for playing second fiddle."

The conversation was being honed into an attack. But what, Reynolds wondered, was he being set up for? The helicopter returned. The two guards looked up, hands instinctively moving toward the guns. One of them spoke into his radio-set, they both relaxed.

Reynolds waited.

The President said, "Here, let me finish the job, put the tree out of its agony." He reached for the ax. "What we need, George, is a spectacular." To the two guards he shouted, "Better move your asses, she's about to go."

The two big men, one bald, one heavily moustached, moved away looking ruffled—their vantage point had been carefully calculated and falling trees had no part in their scheme of things.

"A spectacular?"

"Before the election," the President said. He examined the wound in the tree, stared calculatingly at the ranch house. To Reynolds, who was only a rustic by default, it still looked as though the tree would smash through the roof. "Three more strikes should do it."

The President walked to the other side of the leaning redwood and measured his swing. The blade sliced into the hinge of wood still holding the trunk.

Reynolds joined the President, who was spacing his last blows. "What sort of a spectacular?" he asked.

"Think like a Russian," the President said. "Think what they'd like to do to us—then do it first."

The second blow thudded into the tree.

"How long did I invite you for, George?"

"Three days," Reynolds told him.

"Then that's how long you've got. I'd like an outline of your project before dinner on Saturday."

"And if I can't make it by then?"

"The atmosphere over dinner will be strained."

The President wiped the sweat from his forehead with the back of his hand. The muscles on his arms and chest tensed. He had said the third blow and the third blow it had to be.

Steel met wood. The tree creaked. Swayed. Leaned into space and crashed to the ground twenty-five yards to the right of the ranch house.

As it happened, the idea came to Reynolds just before dinner that night. He wondered if it had occurred to him before, only to be rejected by his subconscious because of its sheer audacity.

He was drinking a martini with the President and his wife in the living room of the ranch house, a long, beamed room stamped with the President's personality. There were islands of skins on the tiled floor, historical bric-a-

28

brac from the Wild West on the walls and shelves. A stone fireplace that still smelled of winter fires occupied one corner; through an open window the great outdoors breathed indoors.

The President's wife, slight and blonde and astute, with a smile that was both practiced and genuine, held up the cocktail shaker, "Another, George?"

He shook his head. One on working days, two on vacations. Today, like most days, had developed into a working day.

The President had turned on the television set a few minutes before so that they could watch the fourth space train to be sent into orbit land at the Kennedy Center in Florida. The first shuttle had landed on Rogers Dry Lake in the Mojave Desert. Now Florida was geared to take most of the traffic.

Shots of the approach to Florida, taken by cameras inside the shuttle, appeared on the TV screen. But the crowds waiting for the landing were nothing compared with the great concourse that had assembled for the first touchdown. Commuting into space had been accepted more casually than the first railroad engines.

While they were watching the TV, it was a remark made by the First Lady that launched a possibility in Reynolds's brain.

The President and he had been discussing the military significance of such shuttles and the possibility that the Russians might be thinking of equipping theirs with CPB, or charged particle beams. These were rays capable of traveling at the speed of light, far more sophisticated than conventional lasers. The effective use of such a weapon could give either side command of the heavens.

"You're talking about real Star Wars, in our time," murmured the President's wife. The Columbia was straightening out over the runway at Kennedy, and pointing at the screen she said, "If there was such a war, that could be a crippled Soviet shuttle landing in the United States." Like a depth charge, the remark projected inspiration up from the depths of Reynold's subconscious.

As he watched *Columbia* touch down, he imagined red stars on its wings. From the cockpit he heard Russian voices. At the head of the stairway he saw a cosmonaut emerge, wave wearily, and depart for the medical center, leaving behind at the end of the runway the greatest military prize ever deposited in the lap of the United States.

But why do I only see one cosmonaut? he wondered.

He heard the President's voice trying to penetrate his distraction. It seemed dinner was served.

After dinner, Reynolds excused himself and went to his room. For a time he lay on the bed fully dressed, hands behind his head, thinking. Why only one cosmonaut? There should have been two on board. At least two.

He closed his eyes. He was back in Moscow in the early seventies when he was counsellor and CIA coordinator in the U.S. Embassy. And he was at a rendezvous in Sokolniki Park with a double agent from GRU.

It was sweaty hot, he remembered. In front of the bench where he was waiting, a group of children on bicycles and tricycles were learning road drill on a mock-up street complete with traffic lights.

The man who joined him was well cast for the meeting. The park had once been a hunting ground for the tzars—Sokolniki was a derivation of *sokol,* meaning falcon—and Vadim Muratov looked like a bird of prey. Lean, graying, and greedy.

The exchange was a cliché but still the way they did it. One crumpled copy of *Pravda* containing Muratov's payment, 300 roubles-worth of coupons that he could spend in the *beryozka* shops; one crumpled copy of *Trud* containing the information Muratov was selling.

Each picked up the other's newspaper and, after watching the children for a few moments, went their respective ways. The mock-up traffic lights, Reynolds recalled, had jammed at red as he left.

In his office in the embassy, Reynolds studied Muratov's 300 roubles-worth of information. It wasn't calculated to set either the River Moskva or the Potomac on fire. Not then.

According to Muratov a young cosmonaut named Nicolay Talin, quite brilliant apparently, a future captain of space, had been investigated by GRU because of his outspoken views. He was a bit of a rebel, not a totally unacceptable attitude—the Soviet Union had been founded on rebellion—but his views were idealistic and if idealism didn't conform with the Communist dream then it was criminal.

But Talin was getting away with it for two reasons: He was an exceptionally gifted candidate for aerospace travel; and he was being protected by a senior KGB officer named Oleg Sedov.

And that was all. Reynolds instructed a junior CIA officer to check out Talin and then, because it wasn't that urgent, sent the details to Washington by courier and forgot them. Until today.

Suddenly Reynolds knew why, in his vision, only one cosmonaut had emerged from the Russian shuttle; the others were either dead or wounded. Nicolay Talin had been persuaded to defect and had overcome the rest of the crew. The President just might have his spectacular. Reynolds reached for the bedside telephone and called CIA headquarters.

The two computer print-outs were flown from Washington to Los Angeles within six hours of Reynolds's call and brought by car along Coastal Highway 101 to the ranch.

The first was a routine assessment. The second and more interesting document was the result of an intensive and prolonged exchange between operator and computer.

The assessment was based on the investigation Reynolds had authorized on Nicolay Talin in August 1971, which had been revised annually.

Sitting in the sunlit bedroom, Reynolds read the assessment first. From outside he could hear the lowing of cattle.

NICOLAY LEONID TALIN.

BORN 10 OCT. 1950, NEAR KHABAROVSK, EASTERN SIBERIA.

ATTENDED WORK-POLYTECHNICAL SCHOOL 14 AT AGE 7 (NORMAL SCHOOL STARTING AGE IN SU). BY GRADE 2 SINGLED OUT AS POSSESSING EXCEPTIONAL ACADEMIC POTENTIAL.

AT AGE SEVEN JOINED LITTLE OCTOBRISTS, AT AGE NINE YOUNG PIONEERS. GROUP LEADER REPORTED TO PARTY COMMITTEE THAT TALIN WAS BOTH HIGHLY INTELLIGENT AND QUOTE UNUSUALLY ADVENTUROUS UNQUOTE. LATTER POSSIBLE EUPHEMISM FOR EARLY SYMPTOMS OF REBELLION.

EMOTIONALLY AFFECTED AT AGE 12 BY DEATH OF FATHER THROUGH RADIATION SICKNESS CONTRACTED IN COBALT MINE NEAR YAKUTSK, REPUTEDLY COLDEST PLACE ON EARTH. MOVED WITH MOTHER TO NOVOSIBIRSK AND ENTERED FOR ELITE PHYS-MAT SCHOOL NO. 5

The climatic observation, Reynolds reflected, pinpointed the fallibility of computers: the feed-in. The operator, probably working on a sweltering day in Washington, had been unable to resist this totally irrelevant morsel of information about Yakutsk.

AT SCHOOL EARLY COMPUTER ASSESSMENT CHANNELLED POTENTIAL TOWARD AVIATION. THIS SUBSEQUENTLY AMENDED TO AEROSPACE. PLACE RESERVED MOSCOW STATE UNIVERSITY.

Early computer! As if the sophisticated brain machine spewing out Talin's life was sneering.

CAREER ENDANGERED BY OUTBREAKS OF DEFIANCE DURING YOUNG PIONEER INDOCTRINATION. SAVED BY SYSTEM SO RIGID THAT, HAVING FILED SUBJECT AS

FUTURE HERO, IT COULD NOT QUESTION ITS OWN JUDG-
MENT.

SYSTEM CONCENTRATED ON WIDOWED MOTHER,
BRIBED THROUGH USUAL CHANNELS AVAILABLE TO
SOVIET ELITE, TO REASON WITH SON. PLOY LARGELY BUT
TEMPORARILY BRACKET SEE LATER UNBRACKET SUC-
CESSFUL.

Why the hell did this computer write commas but not brackets and quotes?

AT AGE 16 JOINED KOMSOMOL BRACKET YOUNG COM-
MUNIST LEAGUE UNBRACKET. AT UNIVERSITY IN MOS-
COW REBELLIOUS SPIRIT AGAIN NOTICED. ANTI-STALIN-
IST ATTITUDES COMMON TO YOUNG PEOPLE EXPRESSED
IN HIS CONVERSATION.

APPROACH MADE AT THIS STAGE BY OLEG SEDOV,
COSMONAUT AND KGB OFFICER, WORKING IN CONJUNC-
TION WITH DOSAAF RESPONSIBLE FOR INDOCTRINATION
OF YOUTH BEFORE MILITARY SERVICE.

UNDER INFLUENCE OF SEDOV, MARKED CHANGE
NOTED IN OUTWARD ATTITUDE OF TALIN. RELATION-
SHIP SEEMS TO HAVE PROGRESSED BEYOND MENTOR-
PUPIL NORM. POSSIBILITY OF HOMOSEXUAL TENDEN-
CIES INVESTIGATED BUT REJECTED IN RELATION TO
TALIN ON GROUNDS OF HIS UNDOUBTED HETEROSEXU-
ALITY.

FROM UNIVERSITY SUBJECT TRANSFERRED TO NEW
YURY GAGARIN COSMONAUT TRAINING CENTER AT
STAR TOWN, ZVEDNY GORODOK, IN EASTERN SUBURBS
OF MOSCOW. THERE TO TYURATAM, BETTER KNOWN IN
WEST AS BAYKONUR COSMODROME, IN KAZAKHSTAN.

INTENSIVE TRAINING CONTINUED IN PREPARATION
FOR SPACE SPECTACULAR ...

Was Washington inhabited totally by movie buffs?

... INVOLVING SOYUZ AND SALYUT CRAFT. AT SAME
TIME, ROMANCE FIT FOR FUTURE HERO ARRANGED
WITH DANCER AT BOLSHOI DESTINED TO BECOME PRIMA
BALLERINA. LUCKILY FOR SOVIETS, TALIN AND GIRL,
SONYA BRAGINA, WHOLEHEARTEDLY ENDORSED AR-

RANGEMENT PRESUMABLY ASSUMING IT HAD BEEN FORTUITOUS.

TALIN'S SPACE FLIGHT CONSUMMATELY SUCCESSFUL. SUBJECT ELEVATED INTO SOVIET ELITE, COMPLETE WITH RED PASSBOOK. BECAME YOUNGEST HERO OF SOVIET UNION IN HISTORY. ACCOMPANIED BY OLEG SEDOV, PILOTED FIRST SOVIET UNION SHUTTLE DOVE I.

CONCLUSION: TALIN REPRESENTS POSSIBLE MATERIAL FOR MANIPULATION. BEHAVIOURAL PATTERN INDICATES CONTINUED EXISTENCE OF REPRESSED RECALCITRANCE. FACT THAT SUBJECT IS IDEALIST SUPPORTED BY EVIDENCE THAT SOVIETS HAVE NOT INVOLVED HIM IN MILITARY ASPECTS OF SPACE PROJECTS. PRINCIPAL OBSTACLE THAT WOULD HAVE TO BE OVERCOME—UNDOUBTED PATRIOTISM OF SUBJECT.

Reynolds called the kitchen and asked for coffee. Through the window he could see the President, who had abandoned his ax and was digging a posthole. Beside him stood his wife in jeans and shirt, carrying a basket of flowers. Reynolds envied them their togetherness.

The cook brought the coffee. He drank it black and began to read the second print-out.

This document wasn't as crisp as the Talin assessment. Questions and answers hadn't yet been synthesized because Reynolds had emphasized that the priority was speed. But the direction of the conversation between man and machine was easy enough to follow.

Relentlessly, the operator had picked the computer's brains to find an agent capable of subverting a young Hero of the Soviet Union. Into its electronic intelligence he had fed Talin's age, background, sexual inclinations, aerospace career details, ambitions, pastimes, IQ, character estimate . . .

The operator had then fed his machine with the specialized qualifications needed by the CIA agent. Knowledge of Russian, ability to mix—here the computer had been very much taken with the word *simpatico*—unswerving devotion to country, fatalistic attitude to death. . . .

The computer had then responded with the shattering conclusion: NO SUCH AGENT AVAILABLE.

Which was hardly surprising, Reynolds brooded. What sort of agent was it who would be able to travel undetected through the Soviet Union to Leninsk (known in Russia as Rocket City), where the cosmonauts working at the Tyuratum space center lived, and single-handedly persuade a Hero to defect?

But the operator hadn't given up. The conversation between master and machine—or was it the other way around?—had continued.

Reynolds guessed where it was leading. He should have known all along. He stopped reading and opened an envelope marked PHOTOGRAPHS: WITH CARE that had accompanied the print-outs.

There was Nicolay Talin descending the steps from *Dove 1*; thick blond hair brushed back in timeless style, keen features, slight cleft in the chin. Triumphant—and yet the eyes seemed to be searching for someone, something. A Viking, Reynolds thought. No, a Siberian.

He looked at the second photograph and came face to face with a man who had once briefly obsessed him. Had the mug shot been taken before or after that obsession? After. The experience had drawn lines from nose to mouth, pouched the eyes, changed the expression.

Nevertheless, there were still traces of youthful appeal in the face staring accusingly at him. The mustache that made him look like a cop, the aggressive features, the slant of the brown eyes that softened the aggression. Also discernible was the intellect that had earned him a *summa cum laude* BS in physics at Rice University, Houston. The casual observer might also suspect that the face in the photograph had been supported by an athlete's body, and he would have been right—both the Dallas Cowboys and the Los Angeles Rams had tried to sign him as a quarterback, only to discover that, for him, sport was only a diversion from his real purpose.

And that purpose had been to fly. First with the USAF, graduating to F-15 Eagles, but always viewing the Earth's atmosphere as a stepladder to space. He had subsequently been selected for training with the National Aeronautics and Space Administration (NASA), and that selection had been a mistake.

Reynolds returned to the print-out, speed-reading because he knew the details and he didn't enjoy them, returning finally to the abridged service biography.

MASSEY, ROBERT S. (B. 14 APRIL 1939). PILOT USAF. SELECTED NASA DEC. '65. COMMAND MODULE PILOT FOR APOLLO MOON LANDING 1972. TRANSFERRED SHUTTLE EXPERIMENTS, DESTINED FOR FIRST TEST OF ORBITER 101 SHUTTLE IN 1977 BUT WITHDREW: DIVORCED. IN-ACTIVE.

Inactive! A euphemism of the space age.

But it was all there in the extended print-out. Every requirement for the plan that had been evolving in Reynolds's brain since the computer had told him to forget trying to find a trained agent. Right down to aerospace experience, right down to "fatalistic attitude to death."

34

Now all he had to do was persuade Massey. All? After what I did to him? Sometimes Reynolds wondered at his own icy optimism.

He locked the print-outs and photographs in his attaché case and left the room. Outside the President was leaning against a fence, drinking root beer and talking to his wife.

Reynolds told him that he was leaving. "But I'll be back for dinner Saturday," he said.

"That's fine, George," the President said. "Just fine."

In Moscow that day, it was even hotter than in California.

But, unlike capital cities such as Washington and London, Moscow wasn't adversely affected by the heat; her summer was a luxury and a sweltering day encouraged energy rather than torpor.

Sightseers thronged the Kremlin grounds. Ice cream and *kvas* sellers sold their wares as chirpily as street vendors selling hot chestnuts in winter. At the packed beaches on the outskirts of the city, bathers swam energetically. In Gorky Park, love blossomed feverishly while young men in black-market jeans strummed their guitars.

In a walled garden near the memorial erected to mark the line where the Russians halted the German advance on Moscow, the heat collected like soup. Two men in open-neck white shirts played chess in the shade of a birch tree. Despite their age, despite their infirmities—one had been fitted with a pacemaker, the other with a steel plate in his skull—they displayed no discomfort. That would have been an admission of frailty.

The garden, crowded with flowers trying to beat the ax of the executioner winter, was attached to a dacha belonging to the minister of defense, Marshal Grigory Tarkovsky. Unlike the other members of the Politburo who chose weekend dachas in a sylvan setting twenty miles to the west of Moscow, Tarkovsky preferred to spend as much time as possible in the city that, as a younger man, he had helped to save from the Germans. Tarkovsky's favorite record was the *1812 Overture* but when the cannons fired it was Hitler, not Napoleon, who was on the run, and the steel plate in his skull that had replaced the bone removed by a German bullet seemed to throb with triumph.

Tarkovsky, sturdy and bleak-faced, gray hair clipped as short as an army recruit's, leaned forward, moved a pawn one square and said, "So what do you think, Comrade President?"

The President of the Soviet Union—his real power lay in the leadership of the Communist Party, not the presidency—didn't reply immediately, because he had been stunned by Tarkovsky's previous words.

After a while, he moved a knight and reflected that a few years ago he would have reacted with tigerish speed to both Tarkovsky's move on the chessboard and his cataclysmic suggestions.

But I am an old man, brooded the President, who was seventy-six, three years older than Tarkovsky, the leader of a pack of old Kremlin wolves whose decisions are all affected by their years. Some, like myself, move ponderously with elaborate caution. Others, like Tarkovsky, act with rash impetuosity seeking acclaim before death.

In fact, if you accepted that it was governed by Moscow and Washington, the world was in the hands of old men.

"Well, Comrade President?" Tarkovsky stared at the President across the chessboard.

"I'll grant you this, Grigory, if you'd put such policies into practice in this game I would have resigned half an hour ago. Now if you'll excuse me for a few moments . . ."

As he crossed the lawn a yellow butterfly danced in front of him. It made him aware of the weight of his big body. He raised his head and straightened his back. Sweat trickled down his chest, and he masochistically longed for winter.

Inside the yellow-walled mansion where Tarkovsky, a widower, lived alone, attended by a cook and housekeeper, the President paused in the lofty hall adorned with military memorabilia, and gazed critically at an oil painting hanging above the fireplace. It was a portrait of a man staring defiantly into the future; a middle-aged man, glossed with youth by the artist, with black hair and powerful, shaggy features that had the look of a buffalo about them.

We picked them younger in those days, thought the President as he turned away from the picture of himself painted nearly twenty years ago when he first came to power. He headed for the bathroom.

As he washed his hands he could see through the barred window the figure of Tarkovsky bowed over the chessboard. What disturbed him so deeply about Tarkovsky's plan was that, despite its horrendous potential, it might just work.

Because today, despite the furor they always created, conventional disarmament talks were really academic. The answers to the future of the Earth lay in the space surrounding it, not on its crust. And it was into space that Tarkovsky's ideas were directed.

As he returned to the chessboard on the white-painted table, a thrush sang blithely on a branch of the birch tree. Little did it know. Tarkovsky had made his move, a singularly unenterprising one in the circumstances, and was sipping iced tea.

The President sat down and studied the board. An end game and a dull one at that. Without looking up, he could sense the tension in his companion. At last, he said, "Your proposition is intriguing."

"Anything that envisages bringing the United States of America to its knees must be."

36

"I foresee sacrifices."

"Perhaps, but not great ones. Not in relation to the benefits we would enjoy."

"*We,* comrade?"

"Yes, Russia."

Precisely. The President studied the chessboard. The prospect of Communism's world-wide triumph was not so exciting as it would have been when he was young. But Russia! That was different, and about Tarkovsky's patriotism he had no doubts at all. The President's hand settled down over his remaining bishop, and, with a fine show of confidence, he swept it across the board. Then, looking up, he said, "Are you really sure this would work?"

"Yes, if the aerospace industry can meet the challenge."

"If they're equal to it, when would you be ready to act?"

"Early next year."

Six months. The President put his hand to his chest; sometimes he imagined he could hear the pacemaker.

Tarkovsky moved one of his foot-soldiers and added, "Naturally, I would only recommend such action in the event of hostile action by the United States."

The President grunted. He did not actually believe that. He knew Tarkovsky was the personification of Russia's national fears. Who could blame the defense minister? The Motherland had lost twenty million of her children as a result of German treachery in 1941. He would certainly interpret the flicker of a presidential eyelid as "hostile posturing." Yes, give Tarkovsky a position of indisputable superiority, and he would advise a preemptive strike.

And what a strike.

The President advanced a pawn with minimal hopes that he might be able to queen it. Perhaps Tarkovsky, too, was tiring. Pacemaker versus metal plate.

"It is obvious," Tarkovsky said, eyeing his depleted black army, "that whoever commands space commands the world. Soon we will have space stations and gunships armed with beam weapons. The Americans, in spite of their blunders and hesitations, are not far behind. If we don't take command, they will."

"I agree that we should exploit our advantages while we have them, comrade, but its ironic that your proposition involves the fleet of *Dove* space shuttles that we're building."

Tarkovsky's gray eyes appraised the President across the checkered board. "Not ironic, Comrade President, deliberate." He moved his rook. "Check."

The President blocked the threat with his bishop, at the same time putting the black rook in jeopardy. It was also ironic that he, who, after the bloodstained reign of Stalin and the eleven erratic years of Khrushchev, had brought rest and stability to Russia, should be offered fame of an entirely different order. As Tarkovsky withdrew the rook, he said, "I suggest,"—and by this he meant order—"that you personally draw up a plan of campaign and present it to me. Have you discussed this with anyone else?"

Tarkovsky shook his head.

"Then don't."

Tarkovsky's hand strayed to the area of skin on his scalp covering the metal plate, a sure sign that he was tired.

The President leaned back in his chair. "A draw, Grigory?" He was tired, too.

"I think I am in a stronger position."

"I beg to differ. There's a long haul ahead, but eventually we'll fight each other to a standstill."

Stubbornly, Tarkovsky brooded over the board. Finally he accepted the President's offer. A gesture, the President guessed, from an old warrior who would never have settled for a draw with the Germans.

"Well played, Comrade President."

"Perhaps we both learned from the game."

"Perhaps. I feel that I played too cautiously."

The President sighed. The lesson surely was that Tarkovsky had played too rashly.

When he got back to his apartment on Kutuzovsky Prospect in the center of Moscow, the President summoned Nicolay Vlasov, the chairman of the KGB, who lived in the same block.

Vlasov, astute and sophisticated, was a schemer. He was also unrivaled in the arts of survival. He was, therefore, the obvious choice—especially as his survival was currently at stake—to produce an alternative plan to Tarkovsky's. A plan that would cripple the U.S. in space without introducing the specter of Armageddon.

But the President didn't tell Vlasov about Tarkovsky's proposition.

By consulting Vlasov, the President was, without realizing it, establishing a neatly tiered battle order between the reigning colossi of the world, the United States of America and the Union of Soviet Socialist Republics.

The stakes: Final victory in a conflict that had lasted for nearly forty years.

Later, as dusk descended on the sweating city, Nicolay Vlasov—silver-haired, with greenish eyes and a skull that looked peculiarly fragile—stood at the window of his study, a glass of Chivas Regal whisky in his hand, watching the traffic far below and digesting the President's requirements.

They were formidable—perhaps insoluble would be a more apt description!—but he welcomed them because they gave direction to his current campaign for survival. Ever since the debacle in 1980 when his plan to debase the American dollar with a disinformation operation at the Bilderberg Conference, the annual get-together of capitalist clout in the West, had failed ignominiously, his star had been in the descent.

To ensure survival without resorting to blackmail based on KGB surveillance, he had to mastermind a sensational intelligence operation. Then he could move on to other things or, at least, retire honorably and explain to his family why he had neglected them. If, that was, you could ever explain to anyone that, if you were born a schemer, your intrigues possessed you.

From one wall of the study, the photographs of his three children, quick with youth then, but now middle-aged, reproved him. He went into the living room where his wife was watching television, poured himself another whisky, and returned to the study. It was dark now, and the cars below were beads of light being pulled on invisible threads. He imagined for a moment that he could control those threads as he controlled the destinies of Russia's people.

But it is *your* direction, that should concern you, Nicolay Vlasov. Sipping his whisky, listening to the ice tinkle like wind chimes, he applied his mind to what, at the moment, seemed an insuperable problem.

But he did not know that a man named Robert Massey was about to be asked to take a hand in his destiny.

3

ROBERT Massey chose to live on Padre Island because it reminded him of space. The skies were wide and deep, the beaches went on forever, the quiet enfolded you.

Padre Island is, in fact, two islands, South and North, that form a scimitar 140 miles long, off the Texas coast in the Gulf of Mexico. It consists mostly of grass and sand, although the smaller South Island, only twenty-five miles long, has been developed and boasts a Hilton in Port Isabel. What is said to be the world's largest shrimping fleet anchors here and a little further down the mainland at Brownsville.

Massey walked up the beach. He was on the south side of North Island, which has its own port, Aransas, and long, lonely stretches of land inhabited by gophers and ground squirrels, below skies where herons and falcons join the gulls.

At the turn of the seventies, Padre Island's tourist industry received two publicity boosts: an army of 200 unemployed, armed with shovels, managed to clear the residue of a massive oil-spill from the beaches; and a local girl, Gig Gangel, was featured as a *Playboy* centerfold. But still the lovely wastes of North Padre, where treasure hunters seeking Spanish gold are prohibited, remain untarnished, protected by the Padre Island National Seashore Trust at Corpus Christi and conservationists such as Robert Massey.

Massey, with a gratuity and pension supplied by "a grateful Government," patrolled North Island, protecting wild life from tourists, clearing jetsam from the beaches, scanning the sea by helicopter for oil slicks, caring for birds and turtles crippled by the oil.

He walked slowly now, watching the sky and the waves. Anyone who saw him would have thought he was a hobo—a stringy, tough-looking man of about forty-five, wearing patched jeans and a tattered black sweater, with two days stubble on his jaw. He was a little drunk and in a foul mood. A few days before he'd gotten into an argument with a muscular, college kid who'd been littering up the beach. Two of his ribs still ached. It was typical. How many fist fights had he been in since they booted him out of NASA? Thirty? Forty? He could take care of himself, but one day someone would smash him up beyond repair.

As he trudged toward his old green Chevy to drive back to Port Aransas, the wind strengthened. The grass on the dunes bent with it, and the ocean was plucked with white feathers of foam; ahead of him scuttled a flock of sanderlings. The sky was still blue, but it had a metallic sheen to it. Massey spotted a marsh hawk flying high. He cupped his hands to his eyes and stared at the hawk; but he peered far beyond the hawk, to a platform in space where, among the stars, he looked on an island far bigger than Padre. The island was the world.

He climbed into the Chevy and drove along the highway to the shack on the fringe of the little port, where Rosa, the woman he lived with, would be waiting for him. Once loving, still comforting, sad for him and herself, the Mexican girl from across the border in Matamoros only reminded him that she had sacrificed her youth for him back in the days when he was a real drunk.

When she heard the car she ran across their patch of yard with its top-heavy sunflowers and bolting lettuces, the only part of Padre Island that he didn't seem to care about.

She reached his side and said, "We have a visitor."

"Yeah? Who?"

"A man called Reynolds."

The green dossier lay on the cracked glass surface of the cane table between them. Reynolds tapped it with one finger and said, "I want to level with you. That's why I want you to read it "

The dossier was marked TOP SECRET and bore the coding SI 202, Massey's name, and, in the bottom right-hand corner, a round coffee stain. Massey picked it up and flipped the pages, 183 of them.

"Didn't you always level with me?" he asked.

"I don't want to discuss anything now. I want you to read that, then we'll talk tomorrow."

"Why the hell would you suddenly want to level with me after all this time?"

"Tomorrow," Reynolds said.

Massey poured himself whisky from a half-full bottle of J & B. Reynolds sipped an orange juice. Rosa had gone into town to buy groceries. The only other occupant of the shack was an old green turtle crippled with oil-tar that two boys had brought him. Outside the wind pushed at the fragile walls of the shack and played music in the bamboo roof.

"Why not now?" Massey said. He sat down opposite Reynolds.

Reynolds was silent for a few moments and then said. "I've come to ask a favor."

"It's considerate of you to ruin my life first and ask me a favor afterward."

"I wouldn't be here if this wasn't important, and you won't believe me unless you read that dossier."

Massey stared at Reynolds. The innocence was still there, just as it had been in 1974 when he had been Deputy Director (Operations) of the CIA, but the innocence was a deception, like everything about Reynolds. It derived, Massey had long ago decided, from that brand of patriotism that is viewed through a gunsight. The silver hair, so soft that it stirred in the draughts creeping through the walls, compounded the illusion.

Massey went into the kitchen and fetched a bowl of water, detergent, and a dishcloth. He knelt beside the turtle and squirted some of the liquid on to its scarred old shell.

"Believe you? Only if you told me you were lying." Delicately, he cleaned the polished, jigsaw patterns on the head of the turtle. "Don't waste your time, Reynolds. Get yourself another lunatic."

"I have no reason at all for thinking you were ever crazy," Reynolds said.

The turtle, who had been enjoying the rhythmic movements of Massey's hand, looked up, head bobbing, when the movements stopped.

Massey splashed more whisky into his glass. Finally, he said softly, "What the fuck are you talking about, Reynolds? Everyone said I was crazy."

Pointing at the dossier, Reynolds said, "It's all in there." He finished his juice and stood up. "I'll be back in the morning. Early."

"What makes you think I'll be here waiting?"

"I know you'll be here waiting."

Massey started cleaning the turtle again. It lowered its head contentedly.

Reynolds opened the door. In the wind-blown dusk, Massey thought he could see another man standing outside, but he couldn't be sure. The wind charged the room. "Until tomorrow," Reynolds said, shutting the door behind him.

A flake of bamboo parchment fluttered around the room before settling on the table beside Massey's empty glass. Massey picked up the dossier, put it down again, and said to the turtle, "I'm more interested in getting you clean than reading this bullshit," which was a lie.

Nevertheless, he finished cleaning the turtle. Then he took the dossier into the bedroom, lay on the big, sighing bed, and, while Rosa, who had returned from the store, clattered about in the kitchen, began to read.

As he turned the pages his hands trembled. The words became pictures and, unable to evade the fearful and vivid past, he rejoined it.

Massey had always known that the perils of space flight were not confined to the obvious—accidents that NASA described as malfunctions. There were more insidious dangers locked inside the minds of the astronauts. The earthbound lives of some of those early, crew-cut pioneers had been totally disrupted; they had parted from their wives, plunged into manic depressions, taken to drink. A happy few saw God in space and became evangelists.

Massey had triumphantly passed the early medicals in which ear, nose, and throat disorders, faulty eyesight, internal diseases, neuro-circulatory weakness, and motion sickness were the most common causes of rejection. His reactions to hypoxia and loss of atmospheric pressure in a chamber simulating an altitude of 38,000 feet had also been excellent.

The tests he feared most were the vestibular checks designed to examine balance and orientation in space. Some astronauts had experienced illusions that could prove fatal. "You might be making a lunar trip, but you don't want to be a lunatic," a scientist trying to be funny had observed. When he had completed the tests sweat was running from his body, but he had passed, according to the electrodes attached to his body, according to his voice patterns.

Then he had gone to school. Space navigation, astronomy, meteorology, geography, and technical preparation—manual control, life-support system, etcetera—for the moon shot in a mock-up of *Apollo*. He had also been prepared for weightlessness, simulated by immersion in water, free-fall parachuting, and, briefly, in a curving flight in a supersonic jet, and introduced to the phenomenon of acceleration on launch and reentry in a flight chamber where scientists monitored fifty physical and mental reactions.

He joined the other two crew members for lunar education—how to operate on the Moon in one-sixth gravity conditions—but, since he was piloting the command module, it was unlikely that he would ever follow in the footsteps of Neil Armstrong, who on Monday, July 21, 1969, became the first man to step onto the moon.

During the final medicals, Massey's mind was reexamined. How would he relate to the other crew members? How would he react to an emergency? How high was his level of emotional stability? To ascertain the latter they isolated him in a soundproof chamber. They also questioned his wife, Helen.

She, having an extremely high emotional stability, confirmed that he was "cool."

It took three and a half years to train Massey, and all the time he sensed that somewhere there was a flaw in the system. A hidden place in his subconscious—his soul?—that no electrode, no voice-stress analyser, no computer, had reached.

In his shack on North Padre Island, Robert Massey turned a page of the dossier. Rosa came into the bedroom, undressed, and stood for a moment, naked before slipping into bed and kissing him. Then she turned away from him, because she knew he was somewhere else.

Massey was in orbit around the Moon. Alone.

On the Moon, on the fringe of the Sea of Serenity, the commander and a geologist were collecting samples in the lunar rover.

So far everything was proceeding as planned except for a master alarm warning that, as far as they and Houston could determine, was without foundation. But every astronaut still remembered the explosion amid the oxygen tanks that had, in 1970, ripped open *Apollo 13*. A warning during testing had gone unheeded, according to Commander Jim Lovell.

But Massey wasn't worried. The reverse, in fact: he was euphoric. Below, the pocked surface of the Moon was silver green, ahead in the darkness another moon was inching over the horizon, only this wasn't a moon, it was the Earth. A repeat of the "Earthrise" photograph that Frank Borman had taken on Christmas Day 1968.

Massey smiled.

Space enfolded him, no—released him. The warring factions on the blue and silver ball that was Earth seemed spiteful and immensely unimportant when you were a privileged spectator to the infinite scheme of things.

Surely the cosmos had to be shared, the earthbound factions plucked from their little planet and given the freedom of the heavens. The idea was so bounteous, so joyous, that Massey laughed.

A sonorous voice from Houston inquired, "You okay up there, Bob?"

"Just happy," Massey replied.

"That's fine," a note of doubt in the voice.

They were probably feeding his voice level into the computer. Petty. Massey stared beyond the Moon, beyond the Earth, into the star-dusted void of time.

When the lunar module redocked and the other two astronauts rejoined Massey, he was still grinning.

"Did we do it that well?" the geologist asked.

"You did it just fine," Massey said dreamily.

"You okay, Bob?"

"Sure I'm okay."

"I guess I'll take over now," the commander said. "You get some rest."

"You're the guys who should be resting."

"I'll take over," the commander said, more firmly.

They completed five more orbits of the Moon before firing the SM engine to start the journey back to Earth.

The trouble started during the descent debriefing, after which they were expected to give a TV press conference from the descending ship.

In answer to questions from Mission Control about two possibly volcanic craters that Massey had reported seeing in orbit he replied, "That's what we all need, space to live in, to breath . . ."

The controller addressed himself to the commander. "I've cut all outside transmission. What is it with Massey?"

"A little stress problem," the commander said. "Nothing to worry about. But," he added, "I guess you'd better cancel that press conference. You never know."

For the rest of the descent Massey remained silent, still smiling, in communion with himself. After splashdown in the Pacific, he was rushed to a private hospital at River Oaks, Houston.

It was there that he suggested sharing all America's space knowledge with everyone, including the Russians.

Massey lowered the dossier, stared across the bedroom, then raised it again. Rosa watched him. It was 1 A.M. and she hadn't slept. But there were only fifty or so pages of the dossier left. She could wait.

As he read on, Massey's breathing quickened. This section was by a psychiatrist:

> After five hours the condition of the subject [not patient, Massey noted] returned to normal, and I formed the opinion that he had been suffering from temporary spatial disorientation aggravated by a vestibular—inner ear—condition. There is no reason to suppose that, if this latter condition was treated by passive methods, linear acceleration etc., the subject's normality would not be maintained.

So I wasn't crazy! And yet . . .

The next passage was by Reynolds.

> In my opinion the subject may, under earlier psychiatric examination, have deliberately suppressed his desire to impart information to foreign agencies such as the Soviet Union. Such a phenomenon was not

unknown among servicemen returning from Vietnam, but whereas, in the majority of such cases, they had nothing of value to impart, Robert Massey is in possession of information—the embryonic plans for a space shuttle is a case in point—that, if divulged, could do immeasurable harm to the United States's aerospace program. In this context it should be remembered that any future war between superpowers will be directed from space.

It must also be appreciated that the fact that the press briefing was cancelled, and that the subject has subsequently been incommunicado, has caused intense speculation in the media, and it is now generally accepted that Massey suffered a stress problem. In my opinion, we should not only support that conclusion, we should embellish it to the extent that any plausibility he might have with representatives of the Soviet Union will be totally destroyed.

Hatred replaced relief.

Next a report from another psychiatrist, after Massey had been flown to a CIA clinic near the Agency's headquarters at Langley, eight miles from downtown Washington.

Acting on instructions, I decided to submit the subject to a course of hallucinogenic drugs that would simulate the required mental attitude for this operation. The appropriate drug was selected with care to minimize the risks of paranoia, chronic anxiety, and other symptoms of psychosis. It was finally decided to administer lysergic acid diethylamide, which has fewer detrimental effects than other halucinogens, although the possibility of some chromosomal damage cannot be ruled out. Within two hours of the initial administration, the desired hallucinations with characteristic synesthesia—crossing of the senses, color being heard etcetera—had manifested themselves. The principal disadvantage in the use of this drug is increased tolerance. As the treatment was to be prolonged, this necessitated increased dosage.

He had believed they were trying to cure him and all the time they had been launching him on a series of LSD trips.

Massey remembered asking the CIA operative, during a period of lucidity, about the silver-haired man who was often in the background. The operative had replied, "That's Reynolds, he's in charge."

When he had first learned that the CIA had leaked the fact that he was crazy, he had despised Reynolds. Now . . .

"The bastard," he whispered. He dropped the dossier onto the bed, twenty pages of conclusions unread.

Massey stared across the room for several minutes as though hypnotized. Then he brought his hands up to cover his face, and his shoulders shook.

When he was finished, Rosa sat up and put her arms around him, long black hair curtaining her face, big soft breasts touching his chest. "I'm scared," she said. "Tell me what it's all about, Roberto."

"I don't know what it's all about. Not yet."

"That man, Reynolds, he frightens me."

"Reynolds is a dedicated man."

"I don't understand." She picked up the dossier. "What is this writing?"

He took the dossier from her and dropped it on the floor. "It's a murder without a death," he said. Before she could question him again, he drew her to him, finding, to his astonishment, that despite everything he was aroused. Then he was inside her, and together they found a little comfort.

When finally she slept, Massey got out of bed and went to the dresser beneath the window. Reynolds had been right: He would be waiting.

He opened a drawer and took out a World War II Colt .45 automatic.

Dawn. Two figures walking on the hard sand beside the gentle waves, their presence emphasizing the emptiness around them.

Reynolds wore a camouflaged windbreaker and gray trousers tucked into rubber boots. Massey, shaved for the occasion, wore sneakers and jeans and an old tweed jacket, leather-patched at the elbow, over a white, turtleneck sweater. He wore the jacket to hide the gun stuck in the belt of his jeans.

The storm had blown itself out, leaving its signature on the sand—driftwood, seaweed, cans, and plastic bottles. The sea was milky calm and pink-flushed. Sanderlings pattered among the jetsam, and in the sky a single, low-flying pelican kept the two men company.

"I understand how much you hate me," Reynolds said. His hands were plunged deep in the pockets of the windbreaker, his stride was measured, his voice rang with sincerity.

"I despise you more than I hate you, Reynolds."

"It had to be done. You were a risk. In war, millions die for their country. Peace is merely a euphemism for another kind of war, an undeclared war, when men are equally expendable in the interests of the majority. In the Soviet Union," he said, glancing at Massey, "they would have eliminated you."

Massey kicked a plastic bottle. Eventually, someone would clear the debris from the beach and Reynold's body with it. Now was the time to kill, while the sky to the west was still cold, while the day was primitive. But he delayed, and once, while Reynolds's attention was distracted by a leaping fish, he slipped his hand inside his jacket and felt the butt of the automatic.

Reynolds said, "We attract a lot of criticism in the intelligence agencies, some of it justified. They talk about our Dirty Tricks Department: It's lily-white compared with its Russian counterpart. Some people," Reynolds continued, an edge to his voice, "would have us haul down our defenses, self-destruct."

"What do you want from me?" Massey asked, thinking, "I have to know before I kill him."

The pelican veered away and headed out to sea. There were a few fleecy clouds in the sky, and the pearl-pink of dawn had strengthened to blood-red.

"I've got a lot to *give* you," Reynolds said enigmatically.

"You should, you took enough away."

"I want to give you a cause. You had one once."

"Sure, to explore space. And to safeguard it."

"Which by definition means keeping ahead of the Russians. When we get to Washington I'll show you the evidence of what the Soviets are up to in space."

Massey stopped walking and stared at the rays of the sun splintering on the water. He said, "Stop crapping around, Reynolds, what *do* you want? I'm not going to Washington or anywhere else with you."

When Reynolds told him, he wondered whether he was experiencing another hallucination.

He said, "You mean you want *me,* who once babbled about sharing our secrets with the Russians, to persuade a *Soviet* cosmonaut to defect?"

Reynolds said, "That's one of the reasons why it has to be you. When you were . . ." Reynolds hesitated, choosing his words, ". . . when you were *ill,* the Soviets discovered that you wanted to communicate with them. Therefore they will be sympathetic now that you are cured, when you make contact with them prior to meeting Talin."

"Why didn't they ever try to contact me?" Massey held up one hand and answered himself, "Because they thought I was out of my mind, a raving, 22-carat lunatic. You made sure of that."

They walked on, more slowly now. Behind them, their footprints had moved a little closer together. Before I kill him, Massey thought, I have to know everything. He picked up a small branch of driftwood scoured bone-white by sea and sun; it was shaped like a hand-gun. He pretended it was the gun in his belt.

Reynolds said, "You see now why I had to let you read the dossier? You would never have believed that I would seriously ask you to undertake a mission like this when I had once dismissed you as crazy."

Reynolds had done more than dismiss him as crazy: He had emblazoned his craziness across the world. As a result, Helen had divorced him. If you were the Vassar-educated daughter of an oil-rich fat cat in River Oaks, it was fine being married to an astronaut; being married to a madman was different.

Massey asked, "What makes you think the Russians will take me seriously now? I presume you mean I would have to pull a fake defection."

"I'll come to that later," Reynolds told him. "First the other reasons why it has to be you."

"Because the computer says so?"

"Of course," Reynolds turned in his tracks. "Let's go back." Massey followed because he still had to know.

A jet flew high over the Gulf, spinning a white thread behind it. Reynolds took his hands from the pockets of his windbreaker—the sun was beginning to warm the day—and ticked off the other reasons on his fingers.

"*One:* in a way you're Talin's twin. You're both idealists and natural rebels. *Two:* you had started training for the shuttle, so you've got a lot of common ground there. *Three:* Talin's stability was slightly suspect, but he had a mentor who covered up for him. Talin will be sympathetic to your experiences, especially when he sees that you're eminently sane. *Four:* you speak Russian."

"I often wondered in the past whether that would be held against me."

"Why should it? I understand that you decided to learn it when the possibility of the Soviet-U.S. joint venture with *Apollo* and *Soyuz* ships docking with a SALYUT space station was first mooted."

"Some computer," Massey observed. "In fact the *Apollo* and the *Soyuz* ultimately docked directly. Any more reasons?"

"A few."

"But you're not telling?"

"That's right," Reynolds said.

Massey, disappointed with himself for trading conversation with Reynolds, said, "You still haven't told me just how the hell you think I'm going to persuade a man like Talin to defect."

"If I explain you'll do it?"

It would be satisfying, Massey decided, to get a concession from Reynolds before shooting him. He said, "I would only consider cooperating with you on one condition—"

"That you are allowed to return to space? Don't worry, that's already in the pipeline. As soon as this operation is completed you are to be allocated a fresh place in a training program for service in the shuttle."

Massey's thoughts blurred. The initiative left him. Without realizing it, he straightened his body. He saw the curve of the Moon, the bright shining globe that was Earth. Infinity beckoned. Everyone had their price.

Reynolds said, "So you agree?"

When he didn't reply, Reynolds took his arm and said, "Don't let that gun in your belt confuse you. You don't want to kill me now. You want to fly to the stars." He increased the pressure on Massey's arm. "Do you want to be an astronaut again?" Astonished by the strength of his own feelings, Massey stared at Reynolds, took in the innocent, cold blue eyes, the pink cheeks, the smooth forehead, and nodded.

Reynolds got back to the President's ranch at 5 P.M. on Saturday. Half an hour before dinner, he handed the President a manila folder containing five sheets of typescript. "The scenario for your spectacular," he said.

4

MANY people imagine the Kremlin to be a brooding mausoleum. Nothing could be farther from the truth. On a fine day the gilded husks of its cathedrals sail majestically in the blue sky, and the sunlight finds gold in its green-roofed palaces. During fog or blizzard it is baronial and snug.

For Nicolay Talin the Kremlin was a joy. Not because it was the fount of an ideology, but because its epic history appealed to the Siberian in him. As he walked through its grounds this November day, almost six months after his return from space, he saw the ice-dust sparkling in the sunlight, the first snow on the ground freshly crisped by frost, and he marveled at its fragile elegance conceived in violence.

Talin knew his Kremlin as well as he knew his spacecraft. Here, in the twelfth century, the natives had built a wooden stockade, a *kreml,* to the protect themselves against the Mongol hordes. Thereafter it was taken, sacked, freed, by Mongols, Tartars, Turks, Poles, Swedes. . . . Here Ivan the Great reigned—demanding the title Tzar (Caesar)—and built the cathedrals of the Annunciation and Assumption. Here was born Ivan the Terrible, who terrorized his own countrymen and was not above stuffing his enemies full of gunpowder and exploding them. To his credit, he built St. Basil's Cathedral, with its cluster of spun-sugar baubles, in Red Square.

Here, in 1613, the Romanov dynasty was born, to last three centuries until, in 1917, it reached its bloody end and Vladimir Ilyich Lenin installed the Supreme Soviet in the Grand Palace.

Napoleon reached the Kremlin, Hitler failed. Both were ultimately beaten by a land and its people whose spirit was crystallized here, in the Kremlin, and both should have known better.

When Talin was on leave, he and Sonya often visited the parts of the Kremlin grounds open to the public. They met beside the silent 200-ton hulk of the Tzar Bell, which crashed from its tower during the fire of 1737. They walked the cobbled squares. They held hands, watched inscrutably by a bronze and granite Lenin.

This morning Sonya wasn't with him, she was rehearsing at the Bolshoi. But he felt her presence. The way he smiled made two fur-hatted militia stamping through Cathedral Square think that the blond, arrogant-looking man in the Western-styled topcoat and sealskin *shapka* was a bit tipsy. How could they know that, later that day, he intended to ask a girl they couldn't see to marry him.

But first he had to meet Oleg Sedov in a bar off Petrovka Street, not far from the Bolshoi. He left the Kremlin and walked across Red Square, heels tapping on the cobbles. Sometimes Talin felt like telling the gawking tourists that its real name was *Krasnaya Ploshchad,* Beautiful Square, and that Red had nothing to do with politics, only its color. Or hauling them off to see the real Russia, outside the Intourist guide books. Siberia, of course, or the bar where he was meeting Sedov for that matter.

The cold crackled in his nostrils. He breathed it deep into his lungs as others inhale cigarette smoke.

On the far side of the Square he climbed into his red Moskvich, an aging but neat little car that butted through the sparse traffic.

He felt lucky to have a car, though as a cosmonaut and therefore one of the elite, like authors approved by the state, officers of the Party and the services, academics, doctors, football players, he was one of the unequals. Privilege didn't bother him. In his view, Communism should be the equal distribution of wealth, not poverty.

Sedov thought otherwise.

You could see it the way he dressed as he leaned against the bar peeling shrimps and small crabs and dropping their shells on the floor. His bruised shoes looked as though they were made from cardboard, his gray suit beneath his blue parka was East German rubbish, tailored to fit a coathanger.

Talin had come to tell Sedov that tonight he was going to propose to Sonya. He told him most things.

"Beer?"

Talin nodded, pointing at the plate of crustacea (prawns on a good day but not today). "And some of those."

Sedov ordered two brown bottles, fluted like barley sugar, of tepid beer, black bread, and more seafood. The bar, as basic as a barn, was crowded with men, cheeks polished by the cold, talking and guzzling. Listening while Sedov ordered, Talin picked up snatches of football—Dynamo's prospects—sex, wages . . . no politics.

They drank. Sedov wiped foam from his lips. "You're looking remarkably cheerful," he said.

"I've got reason to be."

"Good news?"

"I think so."

"I have news, too. From the First Deputy Commander-in-Chief of the Soviet Air Force."

"Really?" Talin refused to look surprised, he was used to Sedov's dark humor. He searched the face of his friend and mentor, eyebrows charcoal black, shadow of a cleft in the chin. "And what does the First Deputy Commander-in-Chief have to say?"

"He wants you to get married," Sedov said, popping a morsel of crab meat into his mouth.

Talin grinned, waiting for the rest of the joke. When it didn't come he began to roll a pellet of black bread between his thumb and forefinger. The sparkle that had been with him all morning faded.

"*He* wants *me* to get married?"

"He's a romantic," Sedov said. "But, to be fair, he's merely conveying a message from the image makers."

"Married to anyone in particular?"

"To Sonya Bragina, of course."

"Supposing I don't want to marry Sonya Bragina?"

"But you do, don't you?" Sedov stared at him over the rim of his glass.

"I did."

Sedov ordered another couple of beers from the headscarved woman behind the bar and said, "I don't know why you're being perverse. Both you and the general want you to marry Sonya."

"What the hell's it got to do with him or anyone else?"

Two men in spaniel-eared fur hats pushed their way into the bar, bringing a gust of cold air with them. "You know how it is," Sedov told him. "You and Sonya are featured in all the magazines. Readers are beginning to think it's time you made it legal. It's quite permissible for husbands to be unfaithful to their wives, but young people living in sin . . . that's a different story."

"I thought," Talin said, flattening the pellet of black bread, "that the Cult of Personality was discouraged."

"Ah, if you're a big wheel in the Kremlin, yes. If you're a young man and a beautiful girl who personify the spirit of Soviet youth, no."

"Some big wheels seem to get their fair share of publicity."

Sedov held up a warning finger.

The sunlight outside had faded. Or was it the grime on the windows? Talin said, "As a matter of fact, this evening I was going to ask Sonya to marry me."

He noticed a fleeting change of expression on Sedov's face. Pleasure? Regret? It was a difficult face to read. Theirs' was a difficult—no, unusual—relationship. It had endured since the university when Sedov, responsible for indoctrination of young cosmonaut hopefuls, had singled him out for special attention. In appointing Sedov for that job the KGB had chosen well. He hadn't been too old—mid-thirties—and he himself was a cosmonaut and therefore a hero. Talin, who had lost his father when he was twelve, had responded to his advice: *Don't kick the system, it kicks back.* And Sedov, whose only child had been stillborn, had responded to Talin.

So here we are, Talin thought, father-and-son, adviser-and-pupil, fellow cosmonauts, friends, discussing my marriage.

"She will accept, of course," Sedov said.

"I said I *was* going to ask her. Before a bureaucratic matchmaker interferred."

A chunky man wearing blue coveralls barged past Talin saying, "Sorry, Comrade, we mustn't spill beer on that fancy coat of yours, must we," but when he noticed Sedov he moved away.

Sedov said, "In three months' time—that will be mid-February—you and I will be flying together in space again, in *Dove II.* May I suggest that before the flight, in December perhaps, you take a couple of weeks off from training and go to the Black Sea for your honeymoon?"

"I wish," said Talin tightly, "that you and the Comrade General would stop trying to market my life."

"Our lives have always been arranged, you know that. And, let me assure you, it's not so different in the West. Lives are regulated just as methodically there, but the people don't realize it. They think they're masters of their destiny, but they still set their alarms for seven, catch the 8:05 at the train station, leave the office at five, switch on the television at eight, and go to bed after the late-night news. Life is a timetable, Shakespeare knew that. All we can do is enjoy the ride in between the stops."

"I've never heard you talk so much," Talin remarked.

"I'm just telling you not to let our version of the timetable interfere with your feelings for Sonya." Sedov zipped up his parka. "Personally, I think I instilled a little humor into the situation. Imagine a general acting as a go-between." He stuck out his hand. "Well, I must be off."

"To report on the success of the mission to the Comrade General?"

"To buy a bottle of vodka to celebrate your engagement," Sedov said.

They shook hands and walked into the street and went their separate ways in the cold, bright sunshine.

The swan died. The curtain fell. The audience erupted.

In his box in the great red and gold well of the theater, Talin watched the audience clapping and cheering. Sedov should have been with him: nothing was arranged here.

Beneath him, a stout woman dressed in gray was crying. Her husband, a balding man in a black suit and open-neck white shirt, put his arm around her.

The Bolshoi, the gold domes of the Kremlin, wooden cathedrals in the countryside, dachas, Tzarist treasures, icons . . . they were all the scourge of the party publicist trying to accommodate the decadent past in the present. The publicist's mistake was in trying. The extremes and contradictions were an entity, part of the exquisite torment of Russia.

In the front stalls they were on their feet, these discriminating judges. If they departed after a mere couple of encores, then the ballerina might as well retire to teach dancing in Archangel. Tonight, Talin lost count of the encores for Bragina who, according to his companions in the box, was comparable with Pavlova. Her arms were full of flowers.

Talin excused himself from the box. Outside, he drank a glass of pink champagne in which a glace cherry bobbed like a cork. Communism! He fetched his coat from the cloakroom and in the street, beneath the Quadriga of Apollo, hailed a cab and told the driver to take him to the Georgian restaurant where he had reserved a table for two.

Three quarters of an hour later, she joined him. She wore a white, gold-threaded dress that was cut low—for her—and her shining blonde hair was loose, which was also unusual. He wondered if she had sensed that this was to be an unusual evening. Worse, if she had been told. Could the whole relationship have been set up from the beginning? Had she known all along? Angry with himself, Talin thrust aside such suspicions. This was a day for gossamer, not cobwebs. He told the waiter to bring the champagne he had ordered.

"You're very extravagant."

But she was smiling. She must know the reason for the extravagance. Stop it!

The cork popped, the champagne fizzed. The waiter, wearing a black jacket and drooping bow-tie, expertly poured it and replaced the bottle in the ice bucket. A few people stared. Talin was rarely recognized alone, Sonya occasionally, betrayed by the mole on her cheek. Together they attracted attention as though they had stepped out of a magazine page. Twenty years ago, reflected Talin, the only couples photographed in the press would have been workers on an assembly line or a combine harvester. No longer—today a few stars were allowed to glitter.

"Would you like to order now?"

She nodded, watching the bubbles spiral to the surface of her glass of champagne. Waiting!

He called the waiter, who handed them a menu. The restaurant's decor was ordinary, its only concession to style a few silk screens, but the food was good, if expensive, prepared exclusively for tourists and the Muscovite elite. Such blatant class-consciousness was part of the unique Georgian approach: even their graft was arrogantly obvious. Talin and Sonya decided to order a dish made out of Georgian grass, lamb shashlik, and Kinzmarauli wine.

The waiter placed a carnation flown from Tblisi onto the table. The set-up! Talin drank more champagne, inwardly cursing the First Deputy Commander-in-Chief and Oleg Sedov.

She said, "You don't seem in a very good mood, Nicolay."

"I'm jealous," he said, "of all the men looking at you."

So they might. With her high cheekbones and her assurance, which was mistaken for aloofness, she looked unattainable, and yet at the same time she exuded sensuality. Talin had a good idea what form the men's fantasies took when they glanced at her. It was not true that he was jealous.

His reactions, however, would have been more extreme had he known what the man on an Ilyushin 62 airliner high above the Atlantic, recalling a photograph of Sonya, was thinking at that moment.

Robert Massey was wondering whether such a girl was capable of forestalling the plot to subvert Talin.

Reynolds had shown him two photographs to memorize, Sonya Bragina and Oleg Sedov. Reynolds believed that these were the two Russians most likely to loosen any hold Massey might obtain over Talin.

Remembering the black and white photograph of Sonya Bragina—like a Hollywood casting photograph from the thirties—Massey could, in her case, believe it. The beauty spot on her cheek did nothing to disguise the strength in the set of her eyes and mouth. Ballet graces cast in steel.

The pictures of Sedov had been more enigmatic. Massey had detected loneliness in his eyes. According to the terse CIA biography, he was married to a woman whose increasingly neurotic behavior had become conspicuous to others. She had seemed less nervous when she became pregnant, but after a child, a son, had been stillborn she swiftly suffered a complete breakdown. She couldn't be left alone, she needed someone in constant attendance, and Sedov was given no choice. He had to let them take her away to a clinic among the VIP's summer dachas to the west of Moscow, where her depression increased. When Sedov visited her, he assured her, as best he could, that he was looking after their son and that, when she was well, they would all be together again.

A stewardess was beside Massey's seat, with a cart bearing Russian champagne, Stolichnaya vodka, Kinzmarauli wine, Long John whiskey, amber beads, lacquer boxes, beaming wooden dolls, and jars of caviar glistening in the cabin lights. Massey had been steered away from hard liquor, but, hell, he wasn't being totally dried out. His hand hovered over the Long John, picked up the vodka.

The woman with the blue rinse sitting beside him bought a jar of caviar, confiding, "I've never tasted it. It looks like blackberry jam." If the woman, a member of the same tour group as Massey, wanted a conversation she was out of luck. Massey had too many thoughts to contend with.

He went to the bathroom and, while washing his hands, glanced in the mirror. He surprised himself. His eyes were clear, his skin, although prematurely lined here and there, was healthy, even his thick moustache seemed to have a gloss to it. His face was . . . jaunty, that's what it was. The face of a man with a purpose who had, for the moment forgotten his doubts about the means to the end.

When he returned to his seat the woman said, "Have you ever been to Russia before?"

Massey said, "Why, is that where we're going?"

Sonya took Talin's hand and kissed it and said, "Of course I will, Nicolay."

Happiness expanded inside him but didn't quite banish the doubt. "Did you know I was going to ask you?"

"I guessed."

"Only guessed."

She frowned. "What do you mean?"

"No one told you?"

She let go of his hand. "How would anyone know?" Enlightenment dawned. "You told Sedov first?"

"I told him this morning." On the defensive.

"Always Sedov," she said bitterly. "You even share your marriage proposal with him. Do you intend to share the marriage itself with him?"

"I see no harm in telling my oldest friend that I'm going to ask the girl I love to marry me."

"It's too late," she said.

"What's too late?"

"Words like that. *The girl I love.* You can't escape under camouflage, Nicolay." With a sudden movement she swallowed the rest of her champagne as the waiter arrived with the wine and the shashlik. "Why don't you marry Sedov?"

"Shush."

"Why should I shush? You ask me to marry you and then tell me you've already consulted Oleg Sedov. What if he had said no? Would you still have asked me?"

"Please." Talin nodded toward the waiter, who had backed away.

Sonya's hand tightened on the champagne glass. The fragile stem snapped, and a spot of blood appeared on her finger.

Both the waiter and Talin reached forward to stem the blood with napkins, but Sonya reached into her purse and brought out a tiny pink handkerchief. "I can manage," she said.

The waiter cleared away the broken glass and lit a candle on the table. Then he served the food and wine. The flame burned without movement in the silence between Talin and Sonya.

Talin began to eat, slowly and without appetite.

Sonya said after a while, "I'm sorry, Nicolay, it's just that I thought this at least would be between the two of us."

"You didn't answer my question," Talin remembered, picking at his food.

"I told you, I guessed you were going to ask me. I felt it."

He drank some of the red wine and began to relax. It was, after all, he who had been clumsy. She hadn't known, merely sensed—feminine intuition.

He held up his glass. "Here's to us."

They touched glasses. She smiled, lips trembling, and he noticed that there were tears in her eyes.

"I wish," Talin said after a while, "that you liked Sedov a little more."

"I wish I did," she said, "for your sake."

"Why don't you?"

"I think he's a poseur. I find his act boring and irritating."

"What act?"

"You know, the dull clothes, the drab little apartment. All perfectly understandable if you are poor, but Sedov isn't. He's the most respected cosmonaut in the Soviet Union. Among other things," she added to show that she understood his dual role. "So what, I wonder, does he do with all his money?"

"That's his business," Talin said. He didn't mind any of this. It was good to have it out in the open.

"And I don't like his attitudes. He acts as though he were one of the old Bolsheviks, as though he were a sage. He's not that old, for God's sake. What's more," Sonya hurried on, encouraged by Talin's good humor, "I don't trust his brand of Communism, it's too cynical."

60

"There," said Talin placidly, "I think you're wrong. True, he seems cynical, but that's only a façade."

"I think his outlook is out of date, but he won't admit it," Sonya blurted out. "He's the sort of Party hack who would like us still to be in the dark ages of Communism when revolution was the only answer. Now that we have so much he finds refuge in cynicism."

Sometimes, Talin thought, Sonya couldn't see far beyond the walls of the Bolshoi. He and Sonya and the like had *so much,* it was true, but millions had very little. Her beliefs were as bright and true as a crusader's sword but confined, the philosophy of the elite.

And my beliefs? he pondered. Essentially they were the same, except that he gazed beyond the perimeter of privilege and saw hypocrisy. The Kremlin vilified colonialism and yet it colonized; it preached peace and waged war. Talin had been into space.

Glimpsing the obstacles that lay ahead of them, Talin poured more wine and said, "Let's forget Sedov for today." The flame of the candle wavered, then found strength.

"I do love you," Sonya said.

In the background, a violinist with a brigand's face began to play music from the mountains of Georgia.

Later, in Sonya's apartment in the Arbat, they made love. Their lovemaking was more acutely satisfying than it had ever been before, the lovemaking of the betrothed.

The Ilyushin on the delayed Flight SU-318 from Washington to Moscow touched down at Sheremetyevo Airport just before midnight.

Massey and the rest of the tour group were driven by minibus through dark, snow-patched streets to their hotels. His companions chattered excitedly, but Massey was silent.

It was beginning to snow. The flakes charged the bus like moths, before veering away. Woods of silver-birch flitted past, skeletons on the march.

Massey noticed the blurred outline of looming wooden crosses, tilted to look like battlefield fortifications. "Where the glorious armies of the Union of Soviet Socialist Republics defeated the forces of German Fascism in the Great Patriotic War," their female guide recited into a microphone.

"Is where they stopped the Krauts in World War II is what she means," a man in the party translated.

Could anything defeat the Russians? Massey wondered as the minibus crossed a bridge and dived into a brightly lit tunnel.

Their hotel, the Ukraina, reminded Massey of Grand Central Station. It took the party an hour to register.

In his room at last, Massey undressed and climbed into bed. The sheets were cold. He closed his eyes and wondered whether, if he talked in his sleep, his words would be recorded on a hidden microphone.

When he awoke in the morning, the room was filled with bright snow-light and his fears had fled. Today, he thought, the battle for the soul of Nicolay Talin begins.

PART TWO

TREATMENT

5

"IT'S arrived," Talin said, standing at the window in his dressing gown, gazing at the falling snow.

"What's arrived, Nicolay?" Sonya's voice, buried in the pillow, was muffled and sleepy.

"Winter. The first snow was a warning. This is the real thing. Moscow will be locked up for seven months now."

She turned lazily on the bed. "Don't sound so cheerful about it," she said. "And, before you start telling me about winters in Siberia, go and make some tea."

Smiling, he bent down and kissed her. "Did I ever tell you . . ."

"Yes," she said. "Tea."

In the tiny kitchen he boiled water and sliced a lemon. Faintly he could hear the scrape of the *babushkas'* shovels on the sidewalks. That meant the snow had stopped for a moment. During each pause the old women pounced, then retired fatalistically to watch the next fall cover their handiwork.

He brought the tea into the bedroom. The snow had stopped, but the sky was still full of it. Sonya's apartment was on the top floor of an old, four-story building. From the window he could see the white envelope roofs of the few antique wood houses still standing in the Arbat; beyond, a series of anonymous high-rises towered up; through a gap he could see the gold dome of a disused church.

Sonya sat up in bed and took the cup of tea. "We should buy a samovar," she said. She was wearing a filmy white nightgown with flowers embroidered at the neck. Through the material he could see her breasts and was instantly aroused.

Carrying his cup of tea, he left the blue and white bedroom and went into the living room. It contained the usual dark furniture, fumed oaks and mahoganies, but Sonya had lightened the atmosphere with touches of grace and comfort. A small chandelier hung with cut-glass tears was suspended from the ceiling; one wall was crowded with photographs of ballet dancers—Pavlova was there, frozen in a pirouette—a low-slung, modern couch imported from Finland was scattered with red and orange cushions; a philodendron with shiny green leaves was climbing around two icons that glowed with the colors of winter fires.

Talin sipped his tea. He glanced at his watch. 8:20. In one hour and ten minutes he had to meet Sedov to fly to the factory where they were building the fusilages of the fleet of Doves.

In the bedroom he heard the chink of cup on saucer, the rustle of sheets. He was still aroused—this almost-married state acted like an aphrodisiac. What would their honeymoon be like?

He went back to the bedroom. She was sitting on the edge of the bed searching with her feet for her slippers. He returned to the window and said: "Come here and look at the snow," and thought: *Sly dog.*

He put his arm around her. He could feel her warmth and the curve of her hip. Her body wasn't as soft as those of other women he had known: it was fit and disciplined and supple.

He slipped a hand inside her nightgown, cupping one firm breast.

"Nicolay," she protested, without removing his hand.

He turned her toward him and pressed her to him so that she could feel his hardness.

"Nicolay!"

He removed his hand from her breast and, with both hands, lifted the nightgown from her body and threw it on the bed. She stood naked, nipples hard. Every time they made love they made progress. This was the first time she had stood like this, previously she had always slipped swiftly between the sheets, like a shy schoolgirl in a dormitory—although she had soon discarded her inhibitions. The snow, now pouring from the sky, probably helped, made her feel that she was veiled from outside. He undid the belt of his dressing gown and they were both naked and his penis ached to be inside her.

He was a little ashamed of the directness of his need. It was too much part of the old image of the selfish Russian male. Impatient thrusts, duration decided by the intake of vodka, climax followed by snores as crude as belches. Selfish? Well, those old goats missed a lot.

Talin remembered the intense pleasures of the previous night, pleasures derived both from arousing and being aroused. From kissing her lips and kissing her breasts and kissing her lingeringly between the golden curls between her thighs while she . . .

He pulled her toward the bed. She lay down, thighs open, and, despite his slavering lust, he started to make love the selfless, enlightened way. Huskily she said, "No, not now," and pulled him down onto her and, as he slid easily into her, he realized that they had both wanted it this way.

There was a time, he mused afterward, for sophistication and there was a time to be an old goat. He smiled and she asked him what was so amusing him and he told her. That, too, was progress.

"But no children yet," she said. "You understand, don't you, Nicolay? I have to dance . . . for a few years, anyway." She snuggled up to him. "And now I'll let you into a secret."

He stroked her cheek. Outside the snow fell steadily. "Well?"

"They're writing a ballet especially for me. Do you know what it's about?" He shook his head.

"It will be performed next year. It's a choreographer's dream. It's all about the future, about space. It's called *The Red Dove*," she whispered into his ear.

On the way to Domodyedove, Moscow's domestic airport, in the back of a black Volga provided by the ministry, Talin considered the tailend of his conversation with Sonya.

She had remarked how simple it was for Soviet women to avoid pregnancy by taking contraceptive pills, apparently unaware that more than half of them still relied on the abortion service provided by the State.

That was typical of Sonya, typical of her class.

Beside him sat Sedov. His eyes looked as though they hurt and he barely spoke. Too much vodka, Talin guessed. And probably drunk alone.

The Volga swung through the gates of Domodyedove. They climbed out of the car and ducked through the snow into the departure lounge.

It was very different from the antiseptic smartness of Sheremetyevo, the international airport. Soldiers and peasants lounged on worn seats as though they had been left over from summer; lines stood becalmed in front of Aeroflot check-in desks; passing stewardesses looked like the ugly sisters of the svelte girls on the foreign routes.

Every one of the 350 seats on the elephantine Il-86 was taken. Sedov closed his eyes and instantly fell asleep. Ten minutes before they were due to land at Voronezh, 360 miles south of Moscow, Talin woke him.

As Sedov opened his eyes he said, "It's a boy, my love," and transiently, there was pain in his eyes that owed nothing to vodka before he asked, "How much longer?"

The car waiting to take them to the Tupolev factory was a new Lada, pale blue and snappy. A wind from Siberia was driving misty rain across the city. The driver, overcome by the presence of his passengers who were actually going to fly the Doves, answered questions in monosyllables.

Yes, the shuttles were almost finished. No, the ordinary citizens of Voronezh weren't supposed to know what was being made at the factory. But, yes, they did.

"Amazing, isn't it?" Sedov said. "The Americans have got satellites and spy planes that can pinpoint a single missile silo on the Chinese border, but they can't find out where we're building a dozen shuttles."

"It can't be that easy," Talin said.

"Why not? Their embassy in Moscow is crawling with CIA. It doesn't take a superhuman intelligence to work out that if Tupolev abandons building the TU-144, the Concordsky as the Americans called it, then they must be building something exceptionally important instead."

"You'd think they'd make the connection," Talin agreed. "After all we stole the TU-144 from them. Much good it did us," referring to the disaster at the Paris Airshow in 1973 and the two subsequent crashes in Soviet territory.

"One Minuteman missile here," Sedov said as the Lada stopped at the heavily guarded gates of the factory, "and we've lost the heavens to the Americans."

"You make it sound like a war," Talin said, showing a militiaman his red passbook.

Sedov didn't reply.

The chairman of the Works Committee was much like any other factory manager whose mind buzzes with quotas. He was worried, fussy, pompous, and intimidated by anyone who could fly his products. Talin decided that the manager himself had been conceived as part of a five-year plan. But he displayed his merchandise with commendable pride.

The line of Doves looked awesome, but only when you knew their capabilities. Otherwise they didn't look all that different from conventional jets. The set of the main engines in the rear with a sea-level thrust of 400,000 pounds was frightening, the set of the nose endearing.

Talin smelled oil and paint and power.

"Which is *Dove II*?" he asked the committee chairman.

"You're standing in front of it."

Talin stared curiously at the bird. It stared back—impudently, he thought. "I should have known," he said.

Could you form an attachment to an inanimate object? More fancifully, could it form an attachment to you? The former certainly, the latter well . . .

no harm in believing it as long as you didn't communicate your feelings to humans and get carted off to a clinic. He restrained an impulse to wink at *Dove II*.

Instead he appraised her with a professional eye. Within the next few months he would be flying her, and the Russian people would be following "another giant step forward into space"—Talin could hear the commentator's words.

They would be told that *Dove II* was more revolutionary than any American shuttle; that it was more maneuverable and could return to orbit if anything went wrong on reentry to the earth's atmosphere; that the flight was the final rehearsal for actual construction of a station 150 miles above the earth.

What wouldn't be labored was the fact that the great asset of a shuttle, its reusability, hadn't yet been implemented, because, in addition to the fault in its glide controls, three other potentially disastrous flaws had been discovered in *Dove I*, and she had been scrapped.

Talin frowned. There was something different about *Dove II*. Different, that was, apart from obvious modifications such as the emergency engines designed to take her back into orbit if there was a failure in the Earth's atmosphere.

He asked the committee chairman if there were any other differences.

An infinitesimal pause. A moment's understanding between the chairman and Sedov. Or is it my imagination?

"Apart from the engines, it's virtually the same," the chairman told him. "There have, of course, been some refinements. I don't believe your landing," clearing his throat, "was quite all it should have been."

Irritably, Talin said, "I know all about the modifications to the manual controls. Is that all?"

"As far as I know. Major differences, that is."

"Well you would know, wouldn't you."

Sedov clumped an arm around Talin's shoulders and said, "Come on, Nicolay, just because you're getting married there's no need to sound like a nagging wife."

Talin shrugged. There could be a thousand minute differences that would never concern him. A bolt here, a hinge there. . . And yet.

The chairman said, "Now perhaps you would like to meet the men who are building the fleet."

"Of course."

Talin and Sedov shook a hundred hands. The regimentation of the exercise depressed Talin. This wasn't what space was all about.

What had been achieved? Talin wondered on the way back to the airport. A boost for the factory workers to meet the men who were going to take

Dove II into space? Work plans were full of incentives like that. A fillip to the cosmonauts who had been languishing since the flight of *Dove I?*

The rain had hardened to sleet. The tires of the Lada threw up wings of slush.

"Impressive, wasn't it?" Sedov remarked. "But I thought you were a little hard on the chairman."

"He was a pompous little tzar."

"A word of warning," Sedov said quietly. "Don't let the Cult of Personality go to your head. Not everyone can look down on the frailties of Mankind from up there," jabbing a thumb toward the leaking heavens.

But that wasn't it. There had been an understanding between Sedov and the committee chairman to which he hadn't been admitted.

At the same time that Talin and Sedov were shaking aching hands with the men building the Doves, Nicolay Vlasov, chairman of the KGB, was studying the daily reports from his deputies.

They were the key pages in his survival manual.

The reports were digests of intelligence from scores of KGB departments employing a secret army 500,000 strong. (*Divide and Rule* was the subtitle of the chairman's manual.)

Within a few minutes, Vlasov had digested pro- and antiSoviet intent throughout the world on information supplied by embassies, consulates, trade missions, spies, traitors—and satellites.

All this intelligence was supplied by the First Chief Directorate. Vlasov studied it dutifully, but, because treachery as well as charity begins at home, it was the reports from the Second and Fifth Chief Directorates dealing with domestic matters that most interested Vlasov, the survivor. The activities of dissidents in the Ukraine, the activities of Jews everywhere, suspicions of espionage at Saryshagan where scientists had developed CPB weapons, anti-State rumblings in cultural circles—even the Bolshoi was troublesome these days—protests smuggled out from camps housing Prisoners of Conscience . . .

At the domestic level, Vlasov also had his priorities. First he absorbed any significant items about the behavior of members of the Party hierarchy. The Politburo had tried to safeguard itself from its own secret police by establishing a watchdog, the Administrative Organs Department of the Central Committee. The KGB had retaliated by penetrating the private lives of Party VIPs through high-class *stukachi*, informers.

Watchdog watched watchdog and Vlasov survived. But only just. What he desperately needed was an intelligence coup that would reassert his power. With his instructions to find a way to negate America's aspirations in space, the President had given him a direction. What he still lacked was a vehicle.

Externally, Vlasov's gray-stone headquarters at 2 Dzerzhinsky Square, did not flaunt power. They were dingy, in fact. Long ago, before the Revolution, they had belonged to the All-Russian Insurance Company. Today, below ground, they also housed Lubyanka Prison. Lavrenti Beria, Vlasov's most infamous predecessor, had been "processed" in Lubyanka before being shot, a salutory lesson to all his successors.

Vlasov's third-floor office, however, did look like a seat of power. It had a lofty ceiling, long windows overlooking Marx Prospect, and a king-sized desk with a battery of phones linking him to the Kremlin, the home of the President of the Soviet Union, his six KGB deputies, and various lackeys.

Today, Vlasov took the time to examine some of the more detailed reports that accompanied the daily digests. You never knew, there might be a vehicle of salvation among them.

He picked up a report from the Seventh Chief (itself comprising six sections) of the Second Chief Directorate that monitored the movements of foreign tourists in the Soviet Union, and perused some earnest prose from a girl named Natasha Uskova, Intourist guide to a tour group from the United States. She had singled out one man as being worthy of consideration: Robert Massey.

The next paragraph would elaborate. Frowning, Vlasov lit a cardboard-tipped cigarette and tried to anticipate it. The name Massey rang bells. An American movie star? No, that was Raymond. Irritated with himself, Vlasov paced the spacious office. He prided himself that his memory was as keen as it had been in his youth, but Robert Massey was testing him. Severely.

Space.

An astronaut.

A report from the KGB coordinator in the Soviet embassy in Washington, supplemented by information supplied by a paid informant at the Johnson Space Center at Houston.

Robert Massey had flown to the moon!

And come back crazy. Which was why the KGB coordinator in Washington had advised Moscow against pursuing rumors that Massey wanted to collaborate. He had been barking in the night, by all accounts.

Pleased with himself, Vlasov returned to his desk and read the paragraph that corroborated his memory.

But men who were still barking in the night didn't get places on tours.

Old zests—and new hopes—stirred inside Vlasov. The thrill of the chase when, as a young man employed by the MGB, forerunner of the KGB, he had been actively engaged in espionage in the West.

Why had Massey suddenly materialized in Moscow? He was apparently sane—according to Natasha Uskova. Had the Intourist operatives in Washington reported his booking to their superiors at the Embassy? If so, had the Embassy informed Dzerzhinsky Square? And, if they had, why hadn't the information been promoted to the daily digest?

What so many agents lacked was instinct. They lost it in the labyrinths of bureaucracy. Well, he hadn't lost his. He picked up a blue telephone and summoned Yuri Peslyak, head of the Second Chief Directorate.

It was five minutes before Peslyak put in an appearance. He had probably been speed-reading his underlings' reports in case he was going to be put on the spot.

Peslyak, a bulky man with raggedly cut black hair, a fleshy nose, and quick dark eyes, sat in front of Vlasov's desk and waited. He was a Georgian, like Stalin, and therefore a schemer.

Vlasov offered him a cigarette, lit it with a table lighter shaped like the first sputnik, and said, "So, what about Massey?"

"An interesting case," Peslyak said smoothly, exhaling smoke.

So, he had managed to read the report. But had he given himself time to make further inquiries? It must have been an agonizing decision—everyone knew that Nicolay Vlasov was fanatical about punctuality.

Vlasov attacked. "Did Intourist report the booking immediately?"

"That, Comrade Chairman, is surely the responsibility of the First Chief Directorate."

"A joint responsibility, comrade. The booking was made abroad, but as Massey was flying into the Soviet Union, he was entering your territory."

"Well," Peslyak said, composure unruffled, "you can see that we have it under control."

"A chance reference in a routine report by some chit of a girl. Is that what you call having it under control?"

"We are following it up. Surely you don't want to be bothered in the digests with every lead we encounter?"

True. If he did the digests would become tomes. But *he* had picked up this lead and he was a young man again scenting a quarry. Big game?

"What I do want," Vlasov snapped, "is selectivity in the digests. See to it in future."

Peslyak's eyes flickered, his bulky body straightened a little. "Very well, but . . ."

"I want Grade 1 surveillance mounted on Massey."

"If I may ask . . ."

"I want the surveillance taken away from your Seventh Department and handed over to Department V of the First Chief Directorate."

Peslyak's eyes slitted. "Is that really necessary? My men are perfectly capable."

"Department V," Vlasov repeated. He had once worked for Department V, formerly known as Line F; its true title was the Executive Action Department and it was responsible for foreign sabotage and assassinations, *mokrie dela,* wet jobs. Not that Massey was necessarily a *mokrie dela,* it was merely that Department V possessed the most competent agents, with the bonus that Peslyak, who had been gunning for him since the 1980 fiasco, was being humiliated. "I'll make the necessary arrangements with Moroz, the head of the First Chief Directorate."

"This Massey," Peslyak said thoughtfully, "must be very important."

Vlasov ignored him. "This girl Natasha Uskova—do her duties extend beyond routine observation?"

"You mean is she a swallow?" Peslyak rubbed his fleshy nose as though trying to reshape it. "She has slept with visitors from the West, yes. The photographs were excellent . . ."

"Then tell her to make an approach to Massey. He might be weak in such matters. Most men are vulnerable in some area of sexuality."

Peslyak said abruptly, "I don't understand."

Vlasov picked up a red telephone and said, "Get me Moroz." Within seconds Moroz was on the line, a lesson in response to Peslyak. He told Moroz to find the best agent in Department V and alert him to stand by for a home-based operation.

Moroz agreed without question. Another lesson.

Vlasov hung up and said to Peslyak, "Thank you for coming, that will be all."

"I think I have a right to know what this is all about," Peslyak said stiffly, "as it comes within my jurisdiction."

"It's all about instinct," Vlasov said softly.

Massey's morning was interesting but he was preoccupied with what he had to do later.

After breakfast the tour group wandered around the lobby of the Ukraina. A tour in itself, Massey thought. The lines of guests were still there, like refugees waiting for a last boat. Crowds swarmed around the kiosks buying foreign Communist newspapers, such as the British *Morning Star,* and picture postcards. Children played among groups of tourists. From time to time the main door opened, admitting a shaft of white light.

At 10 A.M. Natasha Uskova rounded them up and announced brightly, "And now we're going to see Moscow's wonderful subway system."

"Whoopee," said the man who had translated Great Patriotic War the previous night. He was balding, with a creased face, and he smoked cigars. He had been to Moscow before, and he wasn't going to let anyone forget it.

Ignoring him. Natasha Uskova said, "I hope you are all dressed warmly. Not that we shall be in the cold very much. You will find that, in winter, Moscow is the warmest place on earth—indoors."

"I know what she means," the man with the cigar said.

She led them outside. The minibus was waiting, pumping out clouds of white exhaust. The snow was ankle deep, still falling. They drove over the Moskva River in the direction of the Kremlin.

The man with the cigar pointed at Tchaikovsky Street. "Get in any trouble," he said, "and that's where you go, the little old United States Embassy."

Natasha Uskova said, "You speak from experience, Mr. Belton?"

The rest of the party laughed. Massey warmed to the girl. She was black haired, wearing sensible clothes, and a fur hat that, with the collar of her coat, framed her face and softened it. You could only guess at her figure beneath the clothes. Massey guessed it was generous, like Rosa's.

The memory of Rosa saddened him. Her quiet acceptance when he had departed had been more of a recrimination than tears.

"Will you be back?" she had asked. Not "When will you be back?" As if she knew.

He had kissed her and left for Corpus Christi where he boarded the airplane. When he had arrived at Washington he told Reynolds to make available to her $100,000, but to invest it and pay it to her in monthly checks because Rosa would have been frightened by such a sum of money.

Reynolds had agreed without question.

"Your Mr. Belton is a pain in the ass." Natasha Uskova sat down beside him.

"That's a very American expression."

"I worked in the Aeroflot offices on Fifth Avenue in New York before joining Intourist."

"You mustn't be too hard on Mr. Belton. He's had a hard life making a few bucks. This is probably the first time he's felt important."

"Now you make me feel ashamed."

"Control him," Massey said, "for all our sakes, but don't ride him." He nodded across the gangway. "Who's the new guy?"

"Herr Brasack from East Berlin. He's a journalist writing a series of articles for the East German press."

Brasack was staring through the falling snow. He was a man of medium height, with sandy hair and a dab of a moustache to match. He wore a brown leather overcoat and brown gloves. In the hotel he had been eagerly affable and Massey suspected that he was a bore.

The minibus stopped outside a subway station near another building that, like the Ukraina, looked like a wedding cake. "Stalinesque Gothic," Natasha Uskova whispered to Massey. "There are seven of them. Even now we don't know whether to admire them or ridicule them."

As they hurried into the warmth of the subway Massey wondered why he was being singled out for such confidences.

The station was beautiful, like an underground church except that, instead of a crucifix, the centerpiece was a bronze sculpture of muscular Soviet workers. It was as clean as a hospital ward. When Belton tossed his cigar butt on the floor, Natsha Uskova pointed accusingly at it. Grinning awkwardly, he picked it up and deposited it in a trashcan.

Remembering the New York subways, Massey was impressed. In this area, at least, Communism had a lot going for it.

A train pulled into the station. Natasha Uskova took his arm to jerk him from his daydream. A small shock passed between them. She smiled. "That often happens in the winter. It's static electricity."

In the train he sat beside Brasack, who was full of the marvels of the Metro. So much so that Massey began to tire of the mosaics and sculptures sliding past the windows.

"Such beautiful architecture," Brasack breathed. "Such heroic achievement."

"Then why are they ashamed of it?"

"What do you mean?" Brasack fingered his sandy moustache nervously.

"Why do they keep it all underground?"

Brasack smiled. "I see we're going to have a lot of interesting ideological conversations," he said.

They left the train at Byelorusskaya station. For a few moments they stood huddled on the edge of the platform. In the distance they heard the rumble of another train approaching. The platform trembled; the nose of the train emerged from its burrow just as Brasack stumbled against Massey. For a moment Massey teetered on the edge of the platform. Fleetingly he thought: *So this is how it is going to end. How mundane.* Hands reached for him. He stepped to safety as, with a hiss of brakes, the train stopped. Brasak apologized profusely.

For lunch, they went to the revolving restaurant halfway up the Ostankino TV tower. Below them, Moscow, draped in white wraps, circled slowly.

From Natasha Uskova, Massey learned that the tower was the tallest structure of its kind in the world. Moscow apparently had many superlatives. The biggest cinema, the largest hotel in Europe, the Rossiya—"Twenty cafeterias and ten miles of corridors," she breathed.

"So you're not so different from us Americans," Massey said.

He, Natasha, and Brasack were led to a table for three. Could it have been prearranged? Massey glanced at the toy blocks of Moscow, 1,090 feet below. He said to Brasack, "How about you sitting next to the window?"

In the afternoon the group visited the treasure chambers of the Kremlin. Stood dazzled by the array of thrones, crowns, carriages, jewel-encrusted robes, vestments, and mitres—gold, silver, and precious stones as plentiful as pebbles on a beach.

Quoting from her script, Natasha told them that, when he saw these riches, the first Soviet Minister of Education had commented, "Workers in the museum ate only brown bread but preserved diamonds."

Back in the lobby of the Ukraina, Brasack suggested a drink. Massey said, "Later maybe." Brasack looked disappointed.

In his room, No. 2604, overlooking both Kutuzovsky Prospect and the river, he checked to find out if it had been searched. It was one of the lessons he had learned in a crash-course at the CIA training establishment at Camp Peary, between Williamsburg and Richmond, Virginia. That and communications, cooperation with other agencies (in particular Britain's MI6, Britain being less suspect in Russia than the U.S.), penetration of hostile agencies such as the KGB, encoding and decoding, paramilitary and psychological (PP) operations, flaps and seals, i.e., secretly opening mail, diplomatic pouches, etc.

Even more importantly, he had been beckoned into the Soviet Mind through Russians who had turned. Mind? An enigma. But one thing he had learned from an old Russian who had fled the Stalin purges after World War II:

"Never doubt their patriotism. That is their strength. Never mind Communism, they joke about it too. But never criticize Mother Russia. Westerners wonder why Russians put up with Communism. They don't understand—everything, but everything, is endured for Country. All they have ever known is oppression. They expect it and they've got it. They're masochistic patriots. Knock Party as hard as you like, but never country."

When he had finished speaking, the old Russian, who had been a major in the Red Army, had turned away. With his new knowledge, Massey guessed why. Country.

In between lessons, Massey had been reconditioned. Three months of calisthenics and jogging, swimming and unarmed combat. He felt ten years younger.

He had also been interrogated via a polygraph to see if he had any tendencies that could abort the operations, apart from disorientation in space. They had attached a cuff to his arm to measure blood pressure and pulse variations, a band around his chest to register changes in respiration, and electrodes to his hands to measure his sweat output, and asked him questions. Scores of them. Then they had taught him how to beat the polygraph.

He decided that his room *had* been searched. Objects such as his attaché case in the wardrobe, that the maid needn't have touched, had been marginally moved—he had checked their alignment with scratches on the walls. The pen in the inside of his jacket that had covered the first B of Brooks Brothers on the tab now covered an O. There were tiny, fingertip whorls in the dust above the cupboard drawers where he had put his shirts and underclothes. The search hadn't been particularly professional, but they hadn't expected a professional to check on them. At least that was reassuring.

Massey wondered where they had placed the bugs. He surveyed the room. The furnishings were an incongruous clash of heavy wood and cheap plastic. The plastic lampshade was printed with pink roses; probably a microphone up there somewhere. Another possibly in the headboard of the bed. Almost certainly one in the bedside telephone. According to the agent who had trained him at Camp Peary, a whole floor of the Ukraina was set aside for surveillance equipment. All the eavesdroppers had to do was activate the connection to a particular room and listen. "Don't make the mistake businessmen make," the agent had warned. "They wait till they get in their car to mouth their indiscretions. But, of course, the car's bugged, too."

Massey didn't bother to try and locate the microphones. It would only arouse suspicion, and, in any case, he wouldn't be in the room much longer. He glanced at his watch: 8 P.M. He planned to leave at nine, although Natasha Uskova wouldn't like it—dinner was scheduled for tonight at the National.

A knock at the door.

"Who is it?" Massey called out.

"It's me, Natasha."

Which wasn't scheduled.

Massey opened the door.

"May I come in?"

"I was just going out," Massey said.

But she was in the room, smiling, closing the door behind her. She wore a dark blue skirt and a white blouse. "I like to visit all the members of my party," she said, sitting down on the only chair in the room and crossing her legs, "to see if there's anything they want."

Massey looked at her legs, good legs, wondering if he had just been propositioned.

"Is there anything you want, *Gaspadeen* Massey?" She hitched her skirt up her thighs. If this was seduction Soviet-style it was pretty basic.

The words of another of his Camp Peary advisers came back to him: "Don't kid yourself that you'll be above that sort of thing, Bob. We had a saying at college—a standing prick knows no conscience."

"Everything's just fine," he told Natasha Uskova.

"I think *Gaspadeen* Brasack would like to be friends with you."

"And me with him. Only not too friendly."

Scintillating stuff for the eavesdroppers. Massey sat on the edge of the bed. From there he could just see the tops of her stockings. The most traumatic day of his new life and he was looking up a girl's skirt . . . *knows no conscience.*

"Are you enjoying Moscow?" she asked.

"What I've seen so far is beautiful," he said truthfully.

"Not how you imagined it? Nor was New York how I imagined it. It's bad PR on both sides of the Atlantic. Western photographers always take pictures of Russians with their heads bowed into a blizzard to show what a miserable existence they lead. How would the photographers look, bowed into a blizzard? And Soviet cameramen search the sidewalks for fat Americans smoking cigars." Had she forgotten the eavesdroppers? "Would you like a drink, Mr. Massey?" dropping the *Gaspadeen*. "On Intourist, of course."

"Not just now, thanks."

"We have nearly an hour till dinner . . ."

Three-quarters of an hour till I make my move. "Just a mineral water," he said.

"Before I went to New York I thought all Americans liked hard liquor."

"And afterward?"

"I found out I was right." She picked up the phone and called room service. Miraculously she was put through immediately. She ordered a bottle of Narzan mineral water and tea for herself.

He offered her his pack of Marlboros. She took a cigarette and, when he had lit it for her, puffed out small jets of smoke without inhaling them. She should have been languorously smoking a Balkan Sobrani in a holder!

She sat down again. The legs again. He concentrated on Rosa. The saying from the Camp Peary agent's college was wrong.

A waiter brought the tea and mineral water and departed.

She poured herself tea, and said, "Having lived in both American and Russian environments gives me an advantage. I know what's good and what's bad about both. Here we have bureaucracy gone crazy, shortages, five-year plans that never materialize, a certain uniformity." Perhaps the room wasn't bugged. Then again, perhaps she was permitted indiscretions to elicit indiscretions. "In the West you have riots, violence, unemployment, and smog."

He wanted to say, "And freedom," but, if the room *was* bugged, that wouldn't help his cause. Instead he said, "An interesting equation."

"What do you do for a living, Mr. Massey?"

"You mean you don't know?"

She smiled conspiratorially. "Well, I have you down as pilot, retired. But you look too young to be retired."

He made a performance of looking at his watch. "Well, if we're not going to be late for dinner . . ."

"We still have half an hour."

"I have to change."

She shrugged. Put down her cup and saucer. At the door her breasts brushed against his chest. He smelled her perfume. Rosa. The college axiom *was* wrong.

She said, "Perhaps after dinner . . ."

"Perhaps," closing the door behind her.

Twenty minutes later he put on his sheepskin jacket, with microfilms sewn into the lapels, and made his way to the elevator doors. His step was springy, a man with a cause.

In the cavernous lobby a swarm of tourists from Cuba had just arrived. "You always know where to find them," his political adviser had told him. "At the end of the line in the worst restaurants in town. Ivan doesn't have much respect for Cubans, much better to be an American in Moscow."

Massey thought he spotted Natasha Uskova across the lobby, but he couldn't be sure. He pushed his way through the Cubans, past tottering piles of luggage. As more Cubans came through the doors, he squeezed between them. Outside it was snowing lightly. The snow in front of the doors had been trampled into cobblestones of white ice, beyond, it was thick and soft.

Massey glanced behind him. More Cubans. He climbed into a battered black taxi and told the driver to take him to the Metropole Hotel. There were certain destinations, he had been advised, that taxi drivers didn't question or report.

As the cab swung away from the hotel a white Lada 2105 parked at the curb took off. It was still behind the cab at Arbatskaya Square.

As they drove along Kalinina Prospect, Massey caught a glimpse through the falling snow of the illuminated red star on the spire of St. Saviour's Tower overlooking Red Square. He suddenly told the driver to stop. Startled, the driver braked, and the cab skidded to a halt. The white Lada sailed past, stopping farther along the avenue of high-rise buildings.

Massey stuffed some ruble notes in the driver's hand and ran toward the Lada. The taxi began to follow, then accelerated away, throwing up slush.

Massey yanked open the door of the Lada. "Good evening, Bob," said Herr Brasack, "I have a message for you from Mr. Reynolds."

After the first pulse of shock, Massey thought, "Anyone could get hold of Reynold's name." He began, "Who . . ." but Brasack interrupted. "No time for questions, Bob. How about 512 937-2621?"

It was the Padre Island National Seashore phone number, agreed in Washington as identification.

Massey asked, "What do you want?" peering inside the car.

"Just making contact. We wanted you to know that you weren't alone."

"Protected by an East German?"

"That's the way it's done, Bob." Brasack's voice was still friendly, but now it had a cutting edge to it. "The Company can't rely on embassy operatives. Too obvious. So they farm out the work to foreigners like me. East German journalist. What could be better?"

"What was the message from Reynolds?"

"A quotation. 'All this and heaven too.' Mean anything to you?"

Massey nodded. For heaven read space.

Brasack leaned across and grasped the door handle. "I've got to be going now, Bob. It doesn't pay to hang around in Moscow. Are you making your move now?" he asked abruptly.

"On schedule," Massey said. He shut the door and walked briskly away. On schedule but with a change in plan. He saw no point in telling Brasack that, instead of defecting at the Soviet Foreign Ministry, he had decided to go straight to the altar of intrigue—No. 2 Dzerzhinsky Square.

6

THE spool of tape was labeled ROBERT MASSEY: POLYGRAPH
INTERROGATION BY YAROSLAV DRABKIN.

Vlasov pressed the white ON button on the console recorder built into the
wall and, elbows on his desk, fingertips to his fragile-looking temples,
listened.

At first trivialties.

Then, "When did you decide to defect?"

A pause. "A long time ago, I guess."

Q: How long?

A: When I was ill.

Q: When you were crazy?

A: No, ill.

A splice of fresh tape had been inserted at this point for a comment by
Yaroslav Drabkin. "The question was deliberately brutal to discover whether
subject had been trained to deceive the polygraph. Such brutality would have
produced extreme pulse, blood pressure, and sweat reaction in a genuine
subject, minimal reaction in a subject coached to control emotions."

A pause. Drabkin clearing his throat.

"Well?" Yuri Peslyak, sitting opposite Vlasov, addressed the recorder.

"The subject's reactions were extreme."

Q: Why did it take you so long to implement your decision?

A: Because I was sick. At least I thought I was.

Q: Please explain.

A: The Central Intelligence Agency shot me full of drugs to make every-one think I was crazy. Me included.

Q: Why did they do that, Mr. Massey?

A: So that no one would take me seriously.

Q: Are you sane?

A: As sane as that machine of yours.

Q: Why have you defected?

A: Think about it, Mr. Polygraph. Think what they did to me.

Q: They?

A: America.

Q: So your motives changed?

A: I guess so. The first time I was . . . disorientated. Space can do that to you. I wanted to share. . . . Now I hate.

Q: How did you discover you had been drugged?

A: A psychiatrist at the Company clinic in Washington suddenly felt guilty. He was dying of cancer. Said he didn't want to meet his Maker with me on his conscience.

Q: You realize we can check this out?

A: Not him, you can't—he's dead.

Q: Who did you speak to in the white car?

A pause.

Vlasov said, "This Drabkin, he's good."

"The best," Peslyak agreed. "Married to his lie detector. I sometimes wonder how *he* would react under interrogation. If he lied to his machine it would be like lying to himself."

"We all do that from time to time," Vlasov said.

A: What white car?

Q: The white car that stopped in front of your taxi two nights ago.

A: I think the driver was an intelligence officer from the United States embassy.

Q: Think?

A: Know.

Q: Why did you meet him?

A: I didn't. I realized a car was following me so I told the cab driver to stop.

Q: What did he want?

A: He wanted to know what the hell I was playing at. The CIA has kept tabs on me ever since I got sick, I guess. Suddenly I book a passage to Moscow. They want to know why.

Q: Did they question you in the United States?

A: Sure they did. I told them I was taking a vacation. They seem to think that was okay. As far as they knew I was no longer a threat to security—any information I might have had was years out of date.

Q: So they didn't know that you had gained access to secret material?

A: I figure the fact that I'm here speaks for itself.

Another splice in the tape. Drabkin's voice: "The question about the white car was vital. If Massey had been trained to deceive a polygraph then he would have been able to control his reactions to such a question, because he would have been taught to anticipate shock tactics. Again his reactions were extreme."

Vlasov leaned across his desk and pressed the STOP button. "What about that white Lada, Peslyak?"

Peslyak consulted a blue notebook. "According to the operative from the Executive Action Department who was working a two-man surveillance, they traced the number to the Lada export outlet, Avtoexport, at 14 Volkhonka. It was a demonstration model on loan to a Dutchman whose company was said to be considering a big order."

"And he hasn't been seen or heard of since?"

"Correct. The Lada was abandoned outside Avtoexport that night."

"The surveillance team did well to get the registration," Vlasov said, realizing that he was defending Department V and, indirectly, his own judgment.

"It wasn't difficult," Peslyak replied. "The second half of the team was driving Massey's taxi."

Vlasov grunted and pushed the ON button.

In a dimly lit but comfortably furnished room in the same building, close to the interior entrance to Lubyanka Prison, Robert Massey listened to a duplicate of the same tape. With him was his interrogator, Yaroslav Drabkin, a small bespectacled man with a fringe of black hair across his studious brow. They sat on leather armchairs, their manner appreciative as though, Massey thought, they were listening to a ball game. But he guessed that he was participating in an extension of the interrogation; that even now Drabkin was observing him.

Thank God for the instruction in defeating the lie detector at Langley. His tutor had looked a little like Drabkin. He, too, had conducted a long love affair with his polygraph and didn't enjoy teaching anyone how to deceive it.

First priority: anticipation. If you had anticipated the questions and prepared the answers, got them word perfect, then the needles on the dials wouldn't flicker LIES. If the interrogator was worth his salt, the tutor had said, he would try to shock—"throw a couple of hand grenades into the Q and A." That was fine, because Massey's reaction would make him appear all the more genuine. Massey might even find himself indulging in some low-key lying; that too would be fine . . . (The white Lada!) The other trick was to concentrate on some inanimate object during the questioning, a picture maybe. Massey had concentrated on a painting of Lenin.

Q: How did you get access to classified material?

A: Through a contact at Vandenberg Air Force Base, the headquarters for the U.S. military shuttle operations.

Q: Did he contact you?

A: I contacted him when I found out about the drugs.

Q: Where?

A: At Shelter Island, San Diego. He was on vacation.

Q: What does he do at Vandenberg?

A: Computers. He's into computers like you're into polygraphs . . .

Drabkin's dark eyes regarded Massey across the room. Unsmiling. He lit a parchment-colored cigarette and blew a jet of smoke into a shaft of sunlight.

Q: What is this man's name?

A: Gordon.

Q: Why did you choose Gordon?

A: Because I knew him when I was an astronaut. I knew his strengths . . . which some people might interpret as weaknesses. As far as I know, he only confided in me.

Q: What were those strengths . . . or weaknesses?

A: Like Fuchs, Nunn-May, and Pontecarvo before him, he believed that weapons of mass destruction should be shared. That the balance of power would save the world. They were concerned with atomic weapons. Gordon was concerned with military aggression from space—the logical progression from the nuclear weaponry that those idealists—or traitors, according to one's view—sought to spread evenly among the superpowers.

Q: He believed all this when you were still a cosmonaut?

A: Sure he believed it. But he was more of an idealist than a man of action. In any case, in those days the United States wasn't that much ahead of the Soviet Union in military application in space.

A long pause.

Q: And they are now?

A: Light years ahead.

Peslyak pulled at his fleshy nose. Vlasov pressed the REWIND button. The tape gave a clattering whine.

Q: He believed all this . . .

Vlasov speeded up the tape.

Q: . . . are now?

A: Light years ahead.

Vlasov switched off the recorder and asked Peslyak, "Do you believe that?"

"That's up to the First Chief Directorate."

"I asked you."

Peslyak shrugged. "Of course not." He smoothed his crumpled suit. "What has Massey got to offer?"

"A lot," Vlasov said, "if he's telling the truth." He restarted the recorder.

Q: You seem very sure of this.

A: Gordon is.

Q: What exactly is Gordon's job?

A: Director of communications at Vandenberg.

Q: The microfilm that you gave us, did that originate from him?

A: It did. It contains details of the latest Elint satellites.

Q: Elint?

A: Electronic Intelligence, known as ferrets in the States. Your people at Tyuratam, or wherever, know all about them. They orbit 400 miles up and photograph other satellites.

Q: And is that all you have to offer?

A: *All?*

Q: We understood you had something a little more ambitious in mind.

A: Ambitious—the understatement of the decade.

Q: Could you elaborate, Comrade Massey?

A: Okay. I brought the microfilm as an act of good faith. I also brought you the means to control space and therefore the globe.

Peslyak spread his hands incredulously. "He *is* crazy."

Vlasov held up a hand. "Listen."

Q: (an uncharacteristic note of excitement in the interrogator's voice) Explain yourself, Comrade Massey.

A: It's quite simple. Computers are the most sophisticated pieces of machinery man has invented. They are also the most vulnerable. If you know the codes it's relatively easy to penetrate their brains.

Q: *If* you know the codes . . . and all the other security checks. The terminal identification number, for instance—that must change every day.

A: So you're into computers as well as polygraphs.

Q: (another uncharacteristic note, irritation) Even a street sweeper would appreciate such difficulties.

A: Like I said, not so difficult. Staggeringly easy, in fact. If you know the codes.

Q: You do?
A: I don't. Gordon does.

Drabkin said, "I think we've listened to ourselves long enough, don't you?"

"Yes, I think so." Massey said.

Drabkin stopped the tape. He switched on the electric light and offered his pack of cigarettes. Massey refused. Drabkin took off his steel-rimmed glasses and went to a cupboard in the corner of the room. "Drink?" taking bottles of Stolichnaya vodka and mineral water from a shelf piled with polygraph spares.

"If you're having one," Massey said.

"A word of warning," Drabkin said, pouring vodka into two none-too-clean glasses and mineral water into two others. "Whenever you drink firewater stoke the fires. In other words eat, Comrade Massey." From a tin box he took a handful of small salted crackers and put them in a saucer on the table between the two armchairs. "*Nasdarovya.*" He raised his glass.

"Mud in your eye."

They each drank half the measures of vodka, washed them down with mineral water, and bit into their crackers.

"What you are suggesting is quite incredible," Drabkin remarked.

Massey assumed that the conversation was still being recorded. Friendship was not being tentatively proffered. It was the hot-cold technique, as old as interrogation itself.

Drabkin ran one finger through his fringe of black hair. "I'm not really 'into computers' as you put it. But could we really penetrate a computer system as sophisticated as Vandenberg's?"

Massey said, "Look, I'm not 'into computers' either. I can only interpret Gordon. According to him, all you need is a communication terminal, i.e., a distant terminal from which you can make contact with a central computer system, i.e., Vandenberg."

Drabkin refilled Massey's glass; not his own, Massey noted. "Come now, Comrade Massey, there must be more to it than that."

"Not, as I understand it, if you have (1) a terminal identification number; (2) a key code; and (3) a data code."

"You say Gordon has access to such codes?"

"Sure he does, but they're changing all the time."

"How would he convey these codes to us?"

Massey smiled at Drabkin. "He wouldn't." He sipped his vodka, crunched up another cracker.

"I don't understand."

"If your computer experts and Gordon set up a two-way communications system, then I could become . . . dispensable. I wouldn't want that, Comrade

Drabkin, so I've taken precautions to make sure that Gordon will only communicate with me. That also puts me in a strong bargaining position."

"Bargaining?" Drabkin lunged again with the vodka bottle but Massey pushed his hand away. "You are seeking asylum, yes?"

"More."

Drabkin frowned. The splash of vodka into his own glass disturbed the gathering silence. Finally Drabkin broke it. "What more could you possibly want. Money?"

"A very bourgeois observation. I was thinking on a much higher plane."

Patches of red had appeared on Drabkin's pale cheeks. Vodka or anger or both. "Please be more precise, Mr. Massey."

"Very well. I want to return to space. I'm giving you access to the United States military program for space. In return, I want to be taken to Tyuratam and retrained as a cosmonaut."

Massey returned to the room provided for him in an annex in Dzerzhinsky Square at 5:14 P.M. By 5:20, Vlasov and Peslyak were listening to a tape of his final exchanges with Drabkin.

After he had expressed his wish to return to space, Drabkin said, "So, if you are to be believed, the Soviet Union could ultimately obtain details of all the United States' classified military material in space."

Massey replied, "I think you've missed the point, but I doubt whether the others listening to the tape have."

Peslyak glanced at Vlasov; Vlasov stared back impassively.

"It's not a question of extracting information," Massey continued, "it's a question of inserting it. Input not output. By feeding Vandenberg's computers incorrect information, you could totally wreck the American space program. You would then command space—and thus the world."

Drabkin and Massey parted company. A door closed. The tape ran out.

Vlasov stood up and walked to the window. The sky was dark, with a few clear, black pools among the clouds. "Crazy, Comrade Peslyak?"

"Still highly suspect."

"There will be other interrogations. Narcoanalysis, hypnosis. Meanwhile I'm going to try something more practical."

Peslyak looked at him inquiringly.

"I'm going to see if Massey's scheme works."

To see if he really is the vehicle to follow the direction indicated by the President.

My salvation!

Vlasov stared into the sky. From one of the black pools a star glittered back at him.

7

IN a small house located in the coastal desert of southern California, forty-two miles southwest of Santa Barbara, Daniel Gordon, director of communications at Vandenberg Air Force Base, lay in bed fighting the temptation to take his temperature.

Like many men and women who seek perfection in their calling—in Gordon's case, computers—he had allowed a personal weakness to run riot.

That weakness was hypochondria. "I've got it so bad," he once told a friend, "that I'm hypochondriac about hypochondria."

It was at its worse when he was worried. And this morning he was very worried. Often his wife could dispel the fears about his health, but not this morning. With the new day only a green rim on the horizon, it wouldn't be fair to wake her.

His mouth felt dry, his eyes tired despite eight hours' sleep. Had he got a fever? Only the cool, mercury-filled bulb of a thermometer beneath his tongue could answer the question. And the pulse, of course. He didn't have to take that—he could hear it against the pillow. As he listened, it began to gallop.

Don't give in to the temptation. Lying on his back so that he couldn't hear his heartbeat, Gordon forced his thoughts away from the symptoms of fever, away from the crisis that lay ahead of him later that day, and guided them toward his vision, his refuge.

It was Gordon's ambition to be alive when the UIM was perfected—UIM representing Ultra-Intelligent Machine.

The UIM, he figured, would be a reality within the next twenty years. That would put him at around seventy, well within the average life expectancy if, that is, his health held out.

But there were many obstacles ahead. Not the least of them the speed of light that limited electronic signals within a machine to around 300,000 kilometers a second, thus making computerized brains slower than their human counterparts, which could process thousands of impulses simultaneously. And mankind's own resistance to producing a phenomenon that could be as intelligent as himself, and, one day, more intelligent.

Gordon, however, believed there was a more immediate and much more dangerous obstacle: Communism. The future was computers, of this there was no doubt. But, because its system stifled enterprise, Russia was at least a decade behind the West in electronics.

Gordon feared that, appreciating this fatal flaw in its scheme of things, the Soviet Union might launch a limited nuclear attack on the United States to redress the balance. Thereby aborting the birth of the UIM within his lifetime and retarding, perhaps annihilating, a computerized future or, for that matter, any future at all.

Therefore Gordon had offered his brain, and his machines's brains, to the United States government, which had accepted gratefully, because Daniel Gordon was acknowledged to be the best in his field. He was sent to Vandenberg Air Force Base, also known as the Western Test Range, on the Californian coast.

Ten thousand service personnel and their families live at Vandenberg. It is not only a launch site for shuttles, spy satellites, and other items of esoteric hardware, it is a storehouse for intercontinental ballistic missiles housed in underground silos. As such, it is not the most popular base in the United States Air Force.

But it was not the pressure of the IBMs or the threat of an attack by Soviet missiles that bothered Daniel Gordon this fine, late November morning. What concerned him so acutely was the first phase in an exercise in computerized disinformation that was to be launched later in the day. An exercise on a scale never attempted or envisaged before. An exercise that scared the shit out of Daniel Gordon.

He looked hopefully at his wife, but her freckled, still-pretty face was in deep repose. Outside the dawn had flushed red.

Gordon swung his legs out of bed and made for the bathroom. He contemplated opening the window and breathing deeply of the salty air blowing in from the Pacific but decided that, if he had a fever, it wouldn't be a good idea. He opened the cabinet, picked up the thermometer, but replaced it abruptly in the tumbler of diluted disinfectant.

What upset Gordon most about his weakness was that he knew damn well it was just that, a weakness, because he was a strong, ruddy-faced man of fifty who still scuba dived and played a mean round of golf.

Firmly closing the door of the cabinet, Gordon, wearing old-fashioned striped pajamas and floppy slippers, walked along the corridor to a door marked PRIVATE—NO ADMITTANCE. Not that the notice would put off a determined intruder, but the two Secret Service guards outside the house would. Gordon unlocked the door and went into his private brain center.

By Vandenberg standards the equipment in the room wasn't extensive or sophisticated. It consisted of a single-user operating system of the Digital PDP-11 family. But it was sufficient for Gordon's needs before he went to the big, humming nerve center of the Air Force base where he was king.

It was also sufficient to make contact with Massey in Moscow.

But that wasn't for another six hours.

He activated the equipment. Next to his wife, he liked best to have intercourse with his private computer, to tap the resources of the data banks. The room was lit with soft green light, the screen glowed.

He sat in a chair with a back specially molded to offset lumbar complications. He would have liked to smoke a cigarette, but he had long ago heeded the health warnings.

Into the computer, he fed basic details of the planned deception. Finally, he asked the question that had been bothering him all night. Back came the answer: IT IS POSSIBLE.

Gordon sighed. It wasn't the answer he had hoped for. He switched off the current and, locking the door behind him, returned to the bathroom.

Resistance shattered, he opened the door of the cabinet, took out the thermometer and placed it beneath his tongue. He gave it two minutes in case it was slow in reacting. Fatalistically, he read the level of the mercury. 98.6° F. Normal.

Reynolds's Boeing YC-14 touched down at Vandenberg airfield to the north of the base at 10:38 A.M., one hour and twenty-two minutes before the Moscow connection was to be made.

Standing on the tarmac, the breeze ruffling his soft silver hair, he gazed around with satisfaction. Not so long ago the coastal scrub had been the habitat of a few farmers and their stock, sea birds, Californian valley quail, and rabbits. Today it was the launch pad to dominance of space. From Space Launch Complex 6, on a plateau above the ocean, military shuttles would soon be launched as regularly as the phases of the moon.

Gordon was waiting for him in his '79 silver Mercedes. With him was his deputy, Chuck Raskin, who had been brought into the deception in case anything happened to Gordon. Raskin was in his early thirties, studious, crew cut and quiet. The few friends that he possessed reported that he released all his inhibitions watching ball games. He became a man possessed, they said, and figured that he was an athlete born without muscles.

Gordon's wife was leaving the house as they arrived. Gordon, wearing a tartan jacket and gray slacks, led them into the living room and poured the coffee his wife had made. Reynolds thought how fit he looked.

"Well," Reynolds said, sipping his coffee, "is it going to work?"

"No reason why it shouldn't work this end. The other end? Well, that's up to Massey."

"What do you think?" Reynolds turned to Raskin who was glancing at a sports magazine lying open at an article about Jack Quinn, who had pitched for twenty-three years at the beginning of the century.

"I reckon it'll work," Raskin said.

According to Gordon, Raskin was a genius, young enough to take full advantage of the exploding age of the computer. Gordon was right— Raskin's CIA assessment confirmed that—but, Reynolds thought, he didn't inspire confidence.

Reynolds glanced at his watch. "We've got an hour, let's run through it."

Gordon led them into his private brain center. "Okay," he said, "so we know that Massey has got access to a terminal. As a matter of fact, all he needs is a telephone and a portable digitronics audioverter and a typewriter. But let's assume that he—and the guy sending the message for him, my counterpart—are working from some sort of conventional terminal. So they connect with my terminal identification number. This is a private thing between me and Massey, remember."

"I remember," Reynolds said. "It was my idea."

"Provided they identify themselves correctly—and Massey will be using a different identification each time he makes contact so that he doesn't become expendable—this box of tricks," patting the equipment, "will come up with the answers to his questions."

"Which will be the terminal identification, key code, and minimum access code to the central processor at Vandenberg," Raskin said.

"Or what we want them to think are the codes and identification," Gordon corrected him. "Okay, so Massey gets his codes for the day. Now, let's move to where the action's going to take place."

Gordon drove to the NASA complex in the center of the base. There was considerable activity on the roads. "An ICBM test launch down there," Raskin explained, pointing toward the launch area at Point Arguello to the south.

"I know," Reynolds said.

Gordon drew up outside a small, white-painted building sprouting aerials. It was guarded by Air Force police. Gordon, Reynolds, and Raskin identified themselves and went into the building.

The interior was stacked with computer hardware. Consoles, flickering screens, data files, spools of magnetic tape as big as automobile wheels gently on the move.

Gordon was proud of the complex. He was also very apprehensive about it. Because it was fraudulent. "The most elaborate fraud ever conceived by an intelligence organization," was how Reynolds described it. With the infinite permutations of facts at its electronic fingertips, it had to be.

Under Gordon and Raskin there was a staff of six. Controller, programmers, engineers. Reynolds went behind the programmers and glanced at the flickering digits on their screens. Gordon, he conceded, had performed a miracle in the three months allocated to him.

Into the main store, *facts* about Vandenberg's role in space, specially tailored for the operation, had been fed. The leeches in Russia bleeding the system would receive a plausible blend of truth (information already known to have been obtained by the KGB), half truths, quarter truths, and downright lies.

Reynolds returned to Gordon who was pacing the floor nervously and said, "I don't profess to know too much about the intricacies of your profession. Am I right in assuming that you're using the FORTRAN language?"

Gordon said, "You know more than most laymen. And you're right, FORTRAN. Formulatranslation. Input and output implemented through statements recognizing the peripheral unit . . ."

"The Russians, of course, are familiar with FORTRAN?"

"They've got to be. They rely on American systems and imitations. So they've got to be into all the high level programming languages. FORTRAN, COBOL, ALGOL, and a few others besides."

It wasn't until they had returned to his private control center, ten minutes before Moscow was due to make contact, that Gordon voiced his fears.

He activated the computer and asked, "Have you ever wondered, Mr. Reynolds, what might happen if there *was* a traitor with access to Vandenberg's central processor?"

Reynolds nodded. "Or the processor at Fort Knox for that matter. Or the FBI or CIA headquarters. Or the Pentagon."

"Because now we've given the Russians the idea . . ." Gordon sat down in front of the green-glowing screen. "I asked the computer this morning if what the Soviets are about to try could ever succeed."

"And?"

"It said it was possible."

"I entirely agree," Reynolds said, sitting down beside Gordon.

Gordon felt tension building up inside him. His heart seemed to flutter. He decided that, as soon as Reynolds had left, he would take his blood pressure.

In a modern block, situated in the northeast suburbs of Moscow on the route to Kaliningrad, Gordon's innocent partner in deception crouched over a computer terminal. He, too, was consumed with worry.

Like Gordon, his worry also had a physical manifestation: it made him hungry. As he was frequently worried, Sergey Yashin, who was thirty-two, was almost always famished, but as skinny as many a French chef.

At that moment, with five minutes left before the California Connection, he could have put away a huge bowl of borsch thick with cream, followed by Chicken Kiev washed down with a liter of tea.

Yashin's worry had been seeded early in his career when he had discovered that Russia's domestic computers were at least eight years out of date. In America they had already perfected memories with a million switching units etched on a micro chip: In the Soviet Union, they couldn't manage more than 100,000.

Why? Because the whole Soviet effort was channelled toward military might, that was why. Without any thought for the benefits that computers could bring to society. Benefits that would give people time to enjoy their world. That sort of thing.

Yashin's exceptional appetite took a gluttonous turn on his twenty-fifth birthday. Standing in Red Square on November 7, watching the elephantine missiles trundle across the cobblestones, he suddenly thought: *Most people in this city are lucky if they've got a car.*

He worried and he ate and he got thinner.

Within the past few days his anxiety had been complicated by guilt. By taking part in this plot to rob the American computers of their space secrets, he was furthering Russia's militarism. At the expense of the micro chips of peace.

In fact, the only difference between the immediate worries of Daniel Gordon and Sergey Yashin was that, whereas Gordon feared that one day the Russians might truly penetrate Vandenberg, Yashin feared that day was today.

As he crouched, fingers touching the keyboard of the out-of-date terminal, poised to make contact with an extremely up-to-date system, Yashin was a very confused young man.

And his confusion wasn't helped by the presence in the KGB communications HQ of Nicolay Vlasov, chairman of the KGB, and Yuri Peslyak, head of its Second Chief Directorate. Vlasov had always seemed as remote as the President of the USSR to Yashin; Peslyak a little less so because Department 8, which employed Yashin, was part of his Directorate.

The American named Massey who seemed to be the key to the whole thing, said in passable Russian, "Three minutes. Are you ready?"

"Ready," Yashin said, rubbing his fingertips together like a cardsharp.

Peslyak brushed cigarette ash from his jacket. "You look worried," he said.

Worried? He was weighted to his seat with guilt and apprehension. "I'm fine, Comrade Director."

Vlasov said to Massey, "I hope this works, Mr. Massey." His voice had a threatening softness, a mildness more severe than bluster.

"Now!" Massey snapped. He dictated Gordon's terminal identification number, XR 58437219, to Yashin. Yashin's thin fingers danced across the keys.

A pause. Then the screen responded. Massey handed Yashin a scrap of paper bearing the figures 97639914. "Send that," he said and explained to the other two, "That's the personal identification between Gordon and myself. It's untraceable. It will also be different every time you want to make contact. A personal safeguard," he said to Vlasov.

Another pause, longer this time.

"I've also taken another precaution," Massey said pleasantly as they waited. "It only takes effect if you should one day decide that my presence is an embarrassment, i.e., the day you figure you've penetrated Vandenberg completely."

"We shall never consider you an embarrassment, Comrade Massey." Vlasov's greenish eyes appraised Massey. "But, out of interest, what is this precaution?"

"I've arranged to make contact with Gordon every six days. If he doesn't hear from me for a period of longer than seven days, then he blows the whole operation—without incriminating himself, of course. In fact he'll come out smelling of roses."

"Interesting," Vlasov said, "but an academic exercise because we shall never cease penetrating Vandenberg. Why should we? American scientists will continue to make progress. We shall continue to keep up with it."

Peslyak said, "What I don't understand is how Gordon thinks he's going to get away with it. American security must have contingency plans for such a theft."

The pause continued. Yashin's belly ached with hunger. He stared at the screen and saw a bowl of stew, smelled the spicy fragrance from its bubbles. His mouth watered and his stomach whined.

Massey said to Peslyak, "What you don't understand is how vulnerable

95

these highly sophisticated pieces of hardware are. And what you're forgetting is that Gordon's in charge. He *is* security. As soon as he's given us the codes he'll erase the entire communication from the computer's memory."

Figures appeared on the screen. The first sequence, Massey told them as they recorded them, was the terminal identification for the day for Vandenberg's central processor; the second was the key code; the third the minimum access code.

"Cut the connection," Massey ordered crisply.

Yashin looked inquiringly at Peslyak and Vlasov. Vlasov nodded. "Cut it. And now," he said, "we come to the interesting part." He handed Yashin a photostat of a report received by Soviet Military Intelligence (GRU) from which the source had been erased. "We *know* this about *Columbia's* activities is true. So we're going to ask the computers at Vandenberg about it. If they come up with the same information then your idea will begin to assume some credibility. I have to admit," he added, "that the information is far from new." He touched Yashin on the shoulder. "Start transmitting."

Yashin tapped out the first number.

A moment's hesitation. Then they were through.

The second number. Through again.

The third. And they had access.

Yashin immediately requested information on the project described in the GRU report. The reply came back in a snowstorm of letters and algebraic formulae. "FORTRAN," Yashin explained, glancing over his shoulder.

He disconnected the line, stood up, and removed the print-out from the adjacent machine that had simultaneously translated the FORTRAN. He handed it, with the original report, to Vlasov.

Vlasov began to read aloud, pausing to compare the print-out with the GRU report: "Deposited by Columbia OV-103 . . . deuterium fluoride . . . lasers of five megawatts directing 500 joules of energy . . ."

He folded the print-out and report together and slipped them into the inside pocket of his jacket. He smiled thinly at Massey. "So far, so good. Vandenberg has confirmed what the GRU report said. That your compatriots are planning to use a shuttle to deposit a satellite armed with lasers in space. The object of those lasers, Mr. Massey, is to destroy our satellites—and to think we signed an agreement with the United States to do no such thing. However," he shrugged, "we're not here to discuss the politics of space. The point is that it would appear—and I put it no higher—that we have gained access to Vandenberg."

"*It would appear,*" Massey repeated. "What sort of proof do you need?"

"The object of the exercise is to feed information *into* those computers. I'll only be convinced when I've seen the results of such misinformation. In other words, Mr. Massey, I want to see something go wrong with the United States program. Something for which the Americans blame themselves while we know we are responsible."

Yashin said, "Will that be all, Comrade Chairman?" looking at Vlasov. His stomach made a noise like a violin string being plucked.

Peslyak said, "Get out of here and fill that miserable gut of yours."

As Yashin departed, Massey turned to Vlasov and said, "The next connection is scheduled for Thursday, in six days time."

Vlasov shrugged. "Very well. We won't attempt anything sensational. Not just yet."

"There is something pretty sensational as far as I'm concerned," Massey told him. "The connection will be made from Tyuratam. By that time I want to be enrolled as an advanced student in a cosmonaut training program."

Nine thousand five hundred miles away, in California, Chuck Raskin handed Reynolds a print-out confirming the Russians's electronic heist. As Reynolds had predicted, they had tested the leak by extracting information they could check, information that the CIA already knew had been lifted through routine espionage channels.

"It was what I would have done in their place," Reynolds remarked as Gordon drove them to the airfield in the silver Mercedes. He snapped his fingers. "Which gives me an idea."

Gordon glanced at him nervously. "Involving us?"

"Oh, yes," Reynolds said. "It sure as hell involves you."

When he got home, Gordon took his blood pressure. 150. Good for his age! Obviously there was something wrong with the apparatus.

PART THREE

SCRIPT

8

ROCKET City, according to Novosti Press Agency, "cannot boast a mild climate."

Cynics have suggested that the author of this observation must have got wind of some award for understatement, because in summer, Leninsk, to give it its real name, is as hot as a sauna and in winter the cold can take your ears off.

It is situated in Kazahkstan, one of the Soviet Union's fifteen republics, some 1,500 miles southeast of Moscow. It has a population of 60,000, most of whom are connected directly or indirectly with the Tyuratam space center whose launch pads are located twenty-one miles away.

The Soviet authorities have always been coy about the very existence of Leninsk. It isn't marked on any Russian maps designed for public consumption—and the charitable suggest that this is because it is so brash, square and ugly, built in haste as the dormitory for the space center.

It stands on the banks of the Syr Darya river on the desolate steppe, once the crossroads of tribes from China and Mongolia seeking plunder in the West. Today it boasts a university, three theaters, a couple of hotels, and a sports stadium. It is saved from uniform drabness by its shops, which are stocked with relative luxuries for the *nachalstvo* from the space center.

But if the Russians are coy about Leninsk, they are positively paranoiac about Tyuratam, which they still insist on calling Baykonur even though the railway station of that name is 230 miles to the northwest. To compound this deception, they have stated categorically that the map reading for the space center is 47.3 degrees N and 65.5 E, the reading, that is, for Baykonur and not Tyuratam.

Thanks to photographs from Landsat, no one takes these figures seriously any more. And, when American observers visited the space center for the *Apollo-Soyuz* docking in 1975, the Russians bashfully admitted that the highway leading to it passed "near the Tyuratam railway station."

Tyuratam itself looks not unlike Kennedy with its hulking, great assembling buildings, towering gantries, launch pads, skeletal crawler transports, and featureless roads. Like Lubyanka Prison, a lot of its vitals are underground, and, with their periscopes, the command cellars have been likened to submarines.

Few employees from the space center like living in Leninsk and most of the cosmonauts prefer staying in the pre-launch hotel, complete with swimming pool, to the small houses provided for them by the state. But there are exceptions, among them Nicolay Talin. The city, with its geometric high rises, reminded him of Khabarovsk, minus the old wooden houses with their fretted eaves, and in the bleak surrounding countryside he observed stark beauties not apparent to others.

But, thrusting his way along the sidewalk through a blizzard, he wondered if Sonya Bragina would observe them. Or for that matter if she would like anything at all about Rocket City. For her a city had to possess a soul. In Leninsk you had to bring your own.

At least she wouldn't be short of home comforts. He had even bought a washing machine with a spin-dryer for her. And now, although he loathed shopping, he was intent on stocking the freezer.

He pushed his way into one of the stores and surveyed sausages, cheeses, polished fruits, peppers and tomatoes, cold meats, jars of black and red caviar, dishes of gherkins and black olives and pickled herring, lying on long counters beneath neon lights. His face began to ache, his heavy, fur-lined topcoat to steam.

He remembered shopping with his mother. Keeping her place in a line in Khabarovsk for scrag-ends of meat while she jumped the line to a faster lane for bread. Standing red-faced while brawny women harangued her for making a small boy her partner in crime, reaching the head of the line as the last scrag-end was sold. Well, it wasn't so different in many parts of Russia today; but at least his mother, whose son had become one of the élite, could now shop at her leisure.

He took off his mittens and fur *shapka* and began to shop.

He was examining a bag of apples from Alma Ata when a man wearing a green parka jostled him. The apples fell and the bag burst. Together they knelt to pick them up. While they rescued the apples from passing feet, the man apologized. He spoke Russian with an American accent.

"Forget it," Talin told him, picking up the last apple. "An accident."

"Beautiful apples," the stranger remarked as they straightened up. "Quite a store this. I didn't realize you had shops like this over here."

Talin resisted the temptation to tell him it was exceptional. That would have seemed disloyal to the women all over Russia doing battle in their food stores. He contented himself with, "And we don't have violence in the streets either."

"Sorry," said the stranger. "*Gaspadeen . . .*"

"Talin." He regarded the stranger curiously. "May I ask what an American is doing in Leninsk?"

"I wish I could tell you."

Like everyone else in Rocket City, Talin lived with secrecy and he accepted what the American said. "Your name?" he asked.

The American smiled, one of those smiles that can transform a face. "No harm in divulging that, I guess. It's Massey. Robert Massey."

He shook Talin's hand and walked away.

The man who had been examining the box of chocolates from Hungary at a counter near the exit, followed Massey into the blizzard, walking almost immediately behind him. That was the trouble with snow: you had to stick close to your man. You ran the risk of blowing your surveillance, the alternative was to lose him.

Massey appeared to be heading for the small black Zhiguli loaned to him by the Ministry of Defense. Good. That meant that, with luck, the rest of the day's work could be conducted from the warmth of his own Volga M-124.

Normally he liked to work out of doors, but not when the snow sweeping into the city from Siberia was so hard that it stung your face.

The man following Robert Massey was known to his colleagues in Department V of the first Chief Directorate of the KGB as the Hunter. Off duty he hunted moose and wild boar on the *taiga*: on duty he hunted men, sometimes women.

Few—animals or humans—ever realized they were being pursued because, although he was a stocky man with an outdoor face and powerful, hair-tufted hands, the Hunter was capable of great stealth. He was also a chameleon: On a river beach on the Volga in summer he looked like a truck driver on vacation; at a diplomatic cocktail party, wearing a blue mohair suit and white shirt, black hair slicked back, he looked like a military attaché and his company was much coveted by women.

When, as now, he was part of the outdoors, he always carried a knife. A special knife that he had designed. Like some bayonets, it was grooved to facilitate withdrawal from a dead or dying body. It was also slightly curved so that if, for instance, it entered the back close to the spine, its long blade would slice through the heart horizontally. But its great assets were the cutting edges of the blade: one was razor sharp, the other delicately saw-toothed so that, if the kill wasn't clean, it could rip through tendon and bone and finish the job. He also carried a small Tula-Korovin 6.35 mm automatic, favored by the KGB because it was easy to conceal, but he much preferred to kill at close range with his knife.

A killing was for the Hunter the climax that rightfully lay at the end of any pursuit. He saw no moral objections to killing—death was ordained and he was merely its executioner—and he usually had an orgasm as the knife sunk home.

He was disappointed, therefore, that word had come from the top that this was not to be a *mokrie dela,* a wet affair. It was like sex without penetration. If, however, he discovered that an operative from a foreign intelligence agency was also keeping Massey under surveillance, then he had authority to kill the operative.

Massey reached the Zhiguli, a Fiat made in Russia under license, and settled behind the wheel. The Hunter slid into the driving seat of his gray Volga. Both cars took off immediately because their engines had been left running to prevent them from seizing up in the cold. (The Hunter had poured vodka into his radiator because it was more efficient than Soviet anti-freeze.)

Massey drove in the direction of the large building in which he had been allotted an apartment. The Hunter followed fifty yards behind. It was like pursuing a phantom. Snow pellets bounced off the windshield. Above the whirr of the heater he could hear the tires crunching the frozen slush.

When they stopped at a red light suspended in the snow, the Hunter checked the TK in the shoulder holster beneath his jacket and the knife, sheathed and docile, strapped to his thigh.

The light changed to a blur of green. Massey's rear wheels spun, gripped. Two minutes later he turned into the parking lot behind the apartment building; he left the Zhiguli beside an area hosed with water to make a skating rink. The Hunter drew up beside the wall of the building and showed his identification to a fur-hatted militiaman who practically knelt when he saw it. "Just get the fuck away from me," the Hunter said, and the militiaman slunk back to his sentry box.

Head bowed, Massey ran across the lot to the entrance. As soon as he had disappeared, the Hunter moved his Volga forward and switched on the receiver tuned to the bugs in Massey's apartment. He heard a door open and slam. Simultaneously a light came on in Massey's apartment on the fourth floor.

As the light cut a square in the wall of the building, the Hunter became aware that a fawn Moskvich had pulled into the lot. He waited for the driver to get out; the driver stayed put. The Hunter became interested. The snow had thinned, but the late afternoon light was poor and he could only make out a silhouette. The silhouette removed its *shapka* and the features became sharper. Male. The Hunter assessed the tilt of the man's head: it seemed to be aimed at Massey's apartment, but that could be imagination, wishful thinking.

Over the radio from Massey's apartment came the sonorous voice of a Voice of America newscaster. Something about a shuttle launching in Florida.

The Hunter climbed out of his Volga on the passenger side, out of the vision of the Moskvich driver, and made his way to the sentry box. The guard sprang to attention, relaxed a little when the Hunter said, "I'm not a general, you stupid prick." Although he *was* a major.

"What can I do for you, comrade?" the sentry asked.

"The Moskvich that just came in. Who was the driver?"

The sentry began to shiver. "I don't . . ."

"You must know. It's your duty to identify any stranger who comes here."

"I don't remember his name. But I did see from his identification papers that he was from East Germany."

The Hunter made his way back to his Volga, blending with the dusk. He would be able to trace the Moskvich from its license plate. An operative from a foreign intelligence agency? It was just possible that he was going to get lucky. The realization made him sexually aroused.

Two days later Nicolay Talin gave a lecture at Tyuratam to a class of cadet cosmonauts in the last year of their training. His subject: First Impressions in Space. The idea was to teach the trainees to adapt to infinity. Disorientation was still a problem, despite all the attention psychologists had given it.

As he talked, he was vaguely bothered by a face in the fifth row. It was familiar, but he couldn't place it.

"As you probably know, considerable changes take place in your body in space due to the lack of gravity. Your face becomes larger due to the flow of blood from the lower extremities of your body. If you've got any wrinkles you'll lose 'em. I know a few ladies who would like to have a journey in space" (laughter).

The man in the fifth row was older than the other cadets. "Your waistline will shrink, your posture will change—you'll crouch a little—and you'll grow taller by anything up to two inches because, without the pull of gravity, the discs between your vertebrae won't exert any restricting influence."

And he had the air of a man who had heard it all before.

"Why's he telling us all this old stuff? you're asking yourselves. I'll tell you—so you'll ask yourselves, *If this can happen to our bodies what can happen to our minds?*"

Apples! The man who had bumped into him in the food store.

"I don't mind telling you that the first time you gaze down on the earth and see how minute it is in relation to the rest of the firmament, your brain seems to expand."

Massey. Robert Massey. After the lecture, Talin asked him to stay behind.

"So," said Talin, "your work *is* secret. Do you mind telling me why you, an American, are being trained as a cosmonaut in the Soviet Union?"

"It's a bit complicated. Do you have half an hour?"

Talin consulted his wristwatch. "I was going for lunch . . ."

The help-yourself canteen was clinically clean, with stainless steel chairs and white plastic tables. The food was wholesome, stuffed with vitamins. They chose tumblers of natural orange juice tinkling with ice, steaks, salad, and yogurt.

"All right," Talin said, slicing a tomato, "explain."

"I defected," Massey said.

"Mmmm." Talin drank some orange juice. "No one likes a traitor. *Gaspadeen* Massey." He frowned. "But I remember you now. You piloted the command module on a lunar flight. Why . . ."

". . . did I defect? Have you ever felt you were going crazy?"

"Frequently."

"I mean really crazy. I went really crazy. At least I was *persuaded* to think I was . . ."

Blow by blow, pill by pill, shot by shot, Massey told Talin what the CIA had done to him. "All because I was disorientated. A vestibular complication. It could have been put right just like that." Massey snapped his fingers. "But the CIA weren't going to take the chance."

"And when you found out what they had done you decided to defect?"

"Wouldn't you?"

"I doubt it." Talin stared through the window misted with condensation. Outside he could see a 100-foot high gantry built years ago to test a G-1-e rocket. "I doubt it," with unnecessary emphasis, hearing again the voice from Mission Control announcing the invasion, albeit short-lived, of Poland.

"I don't think you understand," Massey said. He put down his knife and fork. "You don't understand my reasons. I'm not a traitor."

"What are you then, a patriot?"

"I believe in mankind. We are participants, you and I, in the greatest revolution man has ever known: he is stepping off the planet Earth and establishing himself in space, in eternity. And he has a chance, this one chance, to share eternity in peace. To leave tribal warfare behind him on earth."

106

Talin listened, fascinated to be hearing his own thoughts from the lips of another man, but all he said was, "I still don't understand what any of this has got to do with your defection."

"To share space, the superpowers have got to have access to each other's information. They've got to know if one or the other is planning a criminal act. I've brought that access."

When he had explained about the computers Talin said, "But that's one way traffic."

"At the moment," Massey replied. He picked up his knife and fork and tackled his steak. It was the tenderest he had ever eaten.

Talin, who always ate fast, a legacy of Siberia where, in the outdoors, you gobbled your food before your lips froze, started on his yogurt. He was disturbed by the visions that Massey was conjuring up. An engineer whom Talin vaguely knew came to the table, but Talin waved him away. He said, "Where did you first have these ideas?"

"You know where. In space." And when Talin looked puzzled, "Don't forget I was listening to your lecture. You were talking about disorientation. Right, well I know all about that. A vestibular condition. I've got no reason to disbelieve the diagnosis. But there *is* something else up there, isn't there, Nicolay? A vision?"

To disguise his confusion Talin asked Massey if he wanted tea. He went to the counter and turned the tap on a stainless steel urn. Scalding water hissed into two mugs containing tea bags. Talin took the cups to the table and returned for slices of lemon.

The canteen was filling up. They wouldn't be able to keep the table to themselves much longer. Squeezing lemon into his tea, Talin said, "I got the impression to start with that your motives in defecting were far more commonplace."

"Revenge? You're right. That was the detonator. The fuse had been lit a long time before."

Talin finished his tea. He stood up. "I have to go. Three Doves are being brought in today." He didn't say from where. As they collected their coats and fur hats from the cloakroom attendant, he asked Massey about his cosmonaut training.

"It's a refresher course. Private tuition. Nothing too daunting because I'll only be orbiting as an observer. Your lecture wasn't part of my curriculum. I went because I wanted to."

Which, at the time, didn't strike Talin as odd.

Driving back to Leninsk later that day, Massey brooded on the success of the first phase of the campaign, drawn up in five stages by an expert in psychological warfare at Camp Peary.

Phase 1: Contact, common ground to be established.

Phase 2: Relationship development, sow seeds of doubt.

Phase 3: First hit, with devastating revelation, preferably personal.

Phase 4: Second hit. The clincher.

Phase 5: Exit.

The CIA psychologist had been one of the first to interrogate Lt. Viktor Belenko who, on September 6, 1976, had defected to Japan at the controls of a top-secret MiG-25. He had based a lot of Massey's campaign on that interrogation.

What disturbed Massey was the ease with which Phase 1 had been accomplished. The blandishments had flowed too freely. Why? Because I believed in them. *I believed.*

Worse, he knew that Talin also believed. They had both looked down! That was the "common ground" of Phase 1—idealism. And I'm using it to betray.

The only mitigation that Massey could summon was the genuine argument that what he proposed to do would curb Russia's hostile intentions in space. He discovered that he was a hard man to convince.

He stopped the Zhiguli at the gates to the apartment house, identified himself to the militiaman, and drove into the parking lot.

It was dark now. Snow was no longer falling and teenagers and children were skating on the hosed area lit by the headlights of parked cars. A bonfire sent sparks spiralling into the night; skates flashed like yellow flames in its glow.

Massey drove the Zhiguli to a corner of the lot outside the penumbra of light. As he locked the door, a figure approached through the parked cars. Massey tensed himself to fight or run.

"Good evening, Mr. Massey," Herr Brasack said. "Washington wants to know if you've made contact."

9

ON November 29, the President of the United States and the President of the Soviet Union both held private meetings to discuss Robert Massey.

The 72-year-old American President was sitting at the breakfast table in the residential quarters of the White House buttering a muffin, when George Reynolds was ushered in.

On the table beside him were copies of *The New York Times, Washington Post,* and *Wall Street Journal.* In front of him a tiny, dead-eyed TV set and a bowl of freesias and anenomes, his wife's favorite flowers.

The President wore a silk paisley dressing gown over slacks and crisp white shirt, a very different man from the ax-wielding champion of the Great Outdoors on the West Coast, Reynolds thought. Thank God.

The President waved the muffin and said, "Help yourself to coffee, George." When Reynolds had sat down at the table, "So, how's the spectacular progressing?"

"Massey's made contact. Phase One is complete."

"Phase Two?"

"That should follow naturally from Phase One."

The President drank some orange juice, tapped a black desk diary embossed with gold. "Less than one year of my term left. We need the spectacular pretty damn soon so that the smart-asses can't say it was engineered as an election stunt."

"You can't rush this one, Mr. President."

"We both know that in a way it *is* an election stunt. But it's more than that. The West needs our type of diplomacy, George. If a President who advocates appeasement is elected then we've lost the world. One of the saddest phenomena I've witnessed during this term is the manipulation of ideals. Kids demonstrating for disarmament, encouraged indirectly by a regime hellbent on building enough weapons to destroy the world."

Reynolds said, "A defection of this scale would knock hell out of their prestige. And, if Massey deals his cards skillfully, then Talin should bring back with him enough information to win the war in space."

"When do you figure we can expect our spectacular?"

Reynolds sipped his coffee and shrugged. "It depends on Massey and the Soviet authorities. Hopefully they might put *Dove II* into orbit in about ten weeks. Their problem has always been over-eagerness. Our problem is to maintain Massey's credibility for as long as that."

That day the President of the Soviet Union held two audiences in his sprawling apartment at 26 Kutuzovsky Prospect, near the Ukraina Hotel. One with a soldier, one with a spy.

To the soldier, Grigory Tarkovsky, his winter-faced Minister of Defense, the President advised caution.

The President sat in his study at his desk, on which stood photographs of his wife, a gray-haired, homely woman rarely seen in public, his three children, and his two grandchildren. All were on vacation by the Black Sea.

Tarkovsky sat opposite him in a deep brocade armchair in which he tried, without success, to maintain an upright, military posture. Like the armchair, the rest of the furniture in the apartment was dark and solid, more comfortable and reassuring, the President felt, than the Finnish rubbish that Vlasov imported into his home two floors below.

Tarkovsky had brought with him a red dossier containing his proposals relating to the fleet of Dove shuttles and their role in containing (Tarkovsky's own euphemism) American expansionism in space.

The President flipped through the pages, twenty-five of them; at least Tarkovsky's impetuosity had been retarded to that extent. He tapped the dossier and said, "This is roughly as you explained it to me over the chessboard?"

Tarkovsky nodded. "Only in more detail."

"And you haven't discussed it with anyone?"

"No one, Comrade President."

"Did you make a rough copy?"

"And I destroyed it."

The President stood up and walked to the silver samovar in the corner of the room. His movements felt clumsy; tomorrow he was due for a check-up at the Kremlin Clinic. He poured tea, sharpened it with lemon, and looked inquiringly at Tarkovsky who waved away the invitation. "Once upon a time, we would have argued over a carafe of vodka," thought the President as he went back to his desk and sat down.

"So you think the old nuclear age is over, Grigory?"

"Completely. If there are battles they'll be fought in space."

"And will there be?"

"Battles?"

"Yes."

"Let there be one soon, when the preponderant power is ours, and we would most certainly win it. I might actually be the earth's last soldier. Armies will not be necessary when the whole world has one party."

"No armies!" the President said, shaking his bearlike head, an amused note creeping, in spite of everything, into his voice. "Wouldn't that make you sad, Grigory?"

"It would, Comrade President. Still I'd rather that than die without knowing what lies ahead."

"What would cause the Americans to surrender?"

"They have only five flight centers—Houston, Kennedy, Vandenberg, Wallops off the Virginia coast, and White Sands, New Mexico—from which they could send up the troops, the gunships, and the satellites to wage a war in space. Destroy all five in one limited nuclear attack and they are no longer a space power. If, at that time, we have satellites and shuttles in space armed with particle beams, then we could shoot down their land and submarine based missiles as they fired them—if they were mad enough to try. They, on the other hand, could do nothing to stop us from devastating their cities with as many nuclear weapons as we wished. Under the circumstances, I do not think they would fight."

The President said nothing. He found the impetuosity of this old man terrifying. Although Tarkovsky knew more of the technical aspects of the matter than he, he felt that *he* knew more of human nature. The whole scheme smelled of the Apocalypse. He put his cup and saucer down on the desk and, looking up at the general, said, "What you say may be right, Grigory, but first I intend to try other alternatives."

"Of what sort?"

"That needn't concern you, but, until I give you the authority, you are to take no further steps."

"I would not consider doing so, but the other alternatives you speak of intrigue me."

"If they develop then you will hear of them, and if they do not then I will see to it that the Politburo, in secret session, gives a respectful hearing to your proposal."

He felt the old warlord's iron disatisfaction radiating across the room from the depths of the brocade armchair.

"Will you promise me that . . ."

"Nothing. I take what you say seriously, Grigory. I do not have to promise you anything at all."

To his urbane secret service chief, Nikolay Vlasov, the President urged speed.

In Vlasov's opinion, nothing had happened to indicate that Robert Massey's coup might not be feasible, and this gave the President hope. The information extracted from the computer at Vandenberg was definitely genuine, but that proved nothing if the Americans were planning an elaborate deception. The next exercise would be to feed destructive information *into* the computer.

"If we carry out a trial run and an accident directly traceable to what we've inserted occurs then I think we can be reasonably sure that Massey is genuine," Vlasov said, standing near the President who was at the window gazing into the thick veil of snow.

"And when is your trial run?"

Vlasov took a gold watch, complete with calendar, from his vest pocket. "In five days time," he said, "when Massey next makes contact with Gordon. Then we'll extract information about a forthcoming American mission. Six days later we'll inject instructions that should wreck that mission."

"And after the trial run?"

"Then we begin to consider the possibilities very seriously."

"The sooner the better," the President said.

"Is there a time limit?"

"Please believe me, Nicolay, the sooner the better."

"With respect, Comrade President, is there something else I should know?"

"Not at this stage," the President said. He turned from the window and sank into the armchair recently vacated by Tarkovsky. "But be quick, Nicolay."

So, he thought as Vlasov left the room, I have two options. And neither Tarkovsky nor Vlasov knows about the other's intentions. If you are a Kremlin chess master, that is the way it has to be.

But to the God his creed didn't acknowledge, the President prayed, "Let Vlasov succeed before Tarkovsky."

His heavy lids closed over his eyes. He slept. Outside the snow continued to fall relentlessly.

In the elevator returning him to his apartment beneath the President's, Nicolay Vlasov considered the set of circumstances that had been offered to him.

Coincidence? Well, that wasn't a word that Vlasov readily accommodated in his vocabulary. In his book, coincidence was merely a facile expression for events that had a logical explanation.

The President had now urgently consulted him twice about measures to confound American ambitions in space. Both consultations had been immediately preceded by discussions between the President and Grigory Tarkovsky.

That wasn't coincidence. Tarkovsky had proposed a plan so extreme that the President had felt obliged to seek an alternative.

Vlasov had found an alternative. But to what? That was what he now had to discover.

10

COLD must be confounded. You mustn't cower before it, head tucked into its bitter presence. That way it shows its contempt by biting the flesh, creeping into the bones. Instead you must thrust out your chest, tame it. That way it becomes an ally, provided good sense also prevails—*shapka,* felt boots, wool mittens. . . . In parts of Siberia you have to cover every part of the body because the wind chill factor can kill flesh within seconds.

The ultimate defiance of the cold is swimming in the open air. Not as suicidal as it sounds. In Moscow there is an open-air pool with water so warm that steam rises to a height of 100 feet to meet the falling snow. In Leninsk, where nothing is too much trouble to keep the space employees happy, a similar pool has been constructed.

To maintain his new fitness, Robert Massey liked to swim there every morning. Sometimes he walked to the pool, sometimes, when it was snowing heavily, he drove.

This morning, the first day of December, he walked. It was warmer than it had been, the snow was falling lightly in Christmas flakes and there was a blue sheen to the sky. Ahead of him, as he walked through the ravines of high-rise buildings, a snowplow spewed fountains of snow into the gutters.

Behind him, at a distance of a hundred yards, walked Brasack. Massey sensed his presence but he didn't bother to look around. He did not sense the presence of the man known as the Hunter and, even if he had, it was doubtful whether he would have spotted him walking fifty yards behind Brasack, because he was such a chameleon.

A *babushka* scraping the snow from the sidewalk with a shovel grabbed Massey's arm. She pointed to his cheek. "The teeth of winter," she said. "Take care."

Massey felt his cheek. The skin was numb, the first sign of frostbite. He should have tied the flaps of his *shapka* beneath his chin: they deflected the cold. But the warm water in the pool should do the trick; he had been warned never to rub frostbite, that destroyed the tissues.

When he stopped to talk to the *babushka,* Brasack also stopped. So, too, did the Hunter, pausing at a kiosk to buy a copy of *Pravda.*

At the next set of traffic lights Massey turned right. Ahead he could see the mushroom of steam above the pool. He paid his entrance fee to the cashier, a big woman in white, and went into the changing rooms, followed at spaced intervals by Brasack and the Hunter.

The Hunter and Brasack both had to hire trunks. Brasack glanced at the Hunter without interest. They both began to undress, hidden from Massey by a row of dark green lockers.

The changing room smelled of ozone and carbolic. At one end naked men, goose-pimpled and winter-white, washed themselves with bars of red soap, watched by another implacable woman in white.

Brasack stripped down to his underpants. The Hunter noted that, beneath the friendly face with the ridiculous dab of a moustache, his body was packed with hard muscle. He presumed that he carried his gun in his coat pocket.

The Hunter had left his gun behind. He had not left his knife behind.

Just as Brasack was about to make his way to the washbasins, the woman cashier came running into the room shouting hysterically and pointing at the ceiling. A sparrow, seeking warmth, had flown in from the street. When the woman overseeing the ablutions saw it she, too, began to scream.

Peasants, thought the Hunter. Betraying their origins by their superstitions. The sort of stock that wouldn't shake hands across the threshold because it was a prelude to a quarrel. The sort that clamped a hand across your mouth if you whistled indoors because it brought bad luck. Such people believed that a wild bird flying inside a building was accompanied by death. Some of the Hunter's contempt for superstition evaporated because this sparrow, fluttering terrified against a window, *was* accompanied by death.

After the two women had dispatched the sparrow into the street with brooms, Brasack went to the washbasins and began to lather himself. Crotch and armpits, these were the suspect areas. The Hunter watched him from a distance, his excitement mounting but controlled. He waited until Brasack had slipped into the tunnel, waist-high in warm water, leading to the pool, then returned, still wearing trousers and shirt, to the cashier at the entrance.

He explained what he wanted. When she protested he showed her his identification. She stopped protesting. When he told her that a murderer was believed to be loose in the pool area she began to tremble. The bird! She took him to a room where the soap, towels, and swimming trunks were stored. He removed the rest of his clothes, glancing at his hirsute body in the mirror, noting that his penis was semi-erect. He took a light blue bath robe from the grip he was carrying and put it on to cover the knife strapped to his thigh. The woman unlocked a door for him and he walked into the pool area.

Steam rose thickly from the warm water. Like the fog in those old movies about London, the Hunter thought. Heads wearing bathing caps bobbed like corks in its swirling depths. High above he could see snow falling and melting at the frontiers of the steam.

He removed his robe and dived immediately so that no one would notice the knife. Surfacing, he began to search for his prey.

He passed Massey, who looked at him without recognition. A pretty girl and a muscular young man were flirting boisterously, the girl's shrieks and laughter muffled by the steam. He swam with a slow, steady crawl, head turning from side to side.

He finally spotted Brasack treading water in the deep end. He must have lost sight of Massey but he obviously knew that the American always spent exactly ten minutes in the pool.

The Hunter, peering across the surface of the water, changed to the breaststroke so that he could approach Brasack more silently. Two youths splashed past, racing each other on their backs. A fat man belly-flopped from the side, flesh smacking water.

Now Brasack was alone.

The Hunter approached to within five yards. Brasack spotted him, frowned, then smiled his recognition. The smile said, "We shared that stupidity about the bird."

The Hunter lowered one hand beneath the water and slipped the knife from the black rubber sheath, feeling both its razored and saw-toothed edges with the ball of his thumb.

He raised the other hand in a gesture of recognition, at the same time propelling himself forward with his legs.

When he was within striking distance the expression on Brasack's face changed. This is no friendly approach, the new expression said. Excellent. The Hunter liked to see fear on a victim's face before he killed.

He was gorged with excitement.

He struck to the far left of Brasack's rib cage, knowing that the curve of the blade would slice it into the heart.

Brasack's face registered surprise, then, as he saw his blood staining the water, primeval terror. His scream lost itself in the steam.

The Hunter pulled the knife across Brasack's chest with a sawing motion. The shark's teeth on the blade cut through the sternum.

Brasack opened his mouth once more to scream but died with the sound drowned in his throat. As he died, the Hunter reached the climax of his hunt.

When Brasack's friendly face submerged beneath the bloodstained water, he swam rapidly to the side of the pool.

On his way to the storeroom he heard a woman scream.

Within minutes he was dried and changed. Outside the pool he took up a position beside an ice cream vendor—ice cream in this weather!—and tried to anticipate how long it would be before Massey emerged. Half an hour? Longer, he decided as a police car skidded to a halt outside the pool. Everyone would be questioned, many detained. A foreigner, an American at that, would attract more than his share of suspicion. But he could always call his KGB contacts. Vlasov's name would make the homicide detectives twitch a bit, the Hunter thought with a smile. He had been told Massey was an intelligent man. . . . Yes, he would call the KGB. Half an hour hadn't been such a bad estimate. Then he would be able to resume surveillance. Meanwhile all I can do is wait. When my time comes, the Hunter mused, it will be while I'm waiting. He bought an ice cream.

It was Oleg Sedov who told Talin about the murder. As usual, nothing had been reported in the press. You only read about crime when Party or State were publicizing an offender's punishment as a deterrent. Usually the crime was black-marketeering. Rarely, if ever, murder. According to Sedov this was defensible: Violence was contagious and in the West it was spread by publicity. Talin believed that it could also be encouraged by suppression.

"Do you know why he was killed?" Talin asked.

He increased his pace across a field of snow. They had been cross-country skiing for two hours. He felt tired but exhilarated. The sky was blue, jewels glittered in the white expanse stretching unbroken to the horizon.

Sedov caught up with him. "The police haven't the slightest idea. Brasack was a journalist from East Berlin. Brilliant apparently. He was writing an article about Tyuratam and Leninsk—restricted, of course—for circulation in all the Warsaw Pact countries."

"Perhaps," Talin ventured, watching an eagle swoop across the sky, "he discovered something that he wasn't supposed to know about." From where the eagle was flying he and Sedov in their crimson parkas would look like drops of blood on the snow.

"Then he wouldn't have written about it. In any case the article would have been censored."

"Wasn't he accompanied by a guide? Someone from Intourist or Novosti or the Ministry?"

"Only at Tyuratam. He was an experienced man." Sedov pointed at a cluster of pine trees isolated in the snow. "Let's stop there." He accelerated, leaving Talin behind.

Beneath the trees he unbuckled the ungainly cross-country skis. From the pocket of his parka he took a leather-covered flask. He handed it to Talin who tipped it into his mouth. The vodka slid down his throat. He shivered pleasurably, handed the flask back to Sedov.

"So," he said, "when do we fly *Dove II*?"

"In the New Year. And I have news for you, hence the vodka." He held up the flask. "We're celebrating, Nicolay, you and I."

Talin looked at him questioningly.

"You have been appointed commander of the whole shuttle fleet. You take over after *Dove II*'s inaugural flight. Which, incidentally, will be my last excursion into space."

Stunned, Talin reached for the flask. Started to speak but choked on the firewater. Finally he said, "I'm very honored," conscious of the triteness of the words. He cleared his throat. "But what about you, Oleg?"

"Don't worry, I'll still be there on the ground. There are a lot of new cosmonauts in the shuttle program. I have my own particular responsibilities."

Reminders that Sedov was jointly employed by the Ministry of Defense and the KGB, always came as a slight shock to Talin.

"But," said Sedov, "they haven't thought up a new title for me yet. The Grandfather of Space, perhaps." Sedov was forty-eight. "I am very happy for you, Nicolay."

If Sedov's son had been born alive he would now be twenty, thirteen years younger than me, Talin thought.

"And I'm very grateful to you, Oleg. You must have had a lot to do with this."

"Very little." Sedov's voice was gruff. "Now, one last drop of rocket fuel and then we must get back to Leninsk. When is the wedding?" he asked as they took to the snow once more.

"We haven't fixed a date yet. But Sonya's flying here tomorrow with a Bolshoi company for a trial performance of this new space opera of theirs. I'll let you know," he said. "And the First Deputy Commander in Chief of the Soviet Air Force," he added.

It was the first sour note of the day.

The second came as they neared the stark outlines of Leninsk, silhouetted against the late afternoon sky. The hollows in the snow were filled with shadows, the cold had acquired a brooding quality.

Sedov said, "There was one thing I forgot to tell you about Brasack's murder. Your friend Robert Massey was in the pool at the time."

Friend?

The following morning, Oleg Sedov flew back to Moscow. The flight took three hours. By 11 A.M. he was in a taxi taking him to the belt of forest twenty miles to the west of the city where the *crème de la crème* of Muscovite *nachalstvo,* the élite, have their weekend homes—the President and other Kremlin leaders, academicians, poets, authors (for a while Solzhenitsyn lived in a cottage here), KGB generals, Party theorists. Here, among the cathedral-quiet pine trees overlooking the Moscva River, these exalted personages enjoy their rewards—magnificent dachas built in anything from clapboard to Stalinist yellow brick—for their contributions to a Marxist-Leninist society.

The forest is divided into hamlets, each an island of rank or calling. Writers live at Peredelkino, once the home of Boris Pasternak who wrote the unwelcome epic *Dr. Zhivago,* Politburo members reign near Usova, while Zhukovka, perhaps the loveliest of the hamlets is itself divided into two rustic ghettos, one for high-flying politicians, the other for pioneers of space, nuclear physicists, and luminaries of the arts. It is possible in this part of Zhukovka, to meet a man who may have given the world a weather satellite, a concerto, or a refinement of the hydrogen bomb.

It was to Zhukovka that Sedov told the taxi driver to take him. To a clinic. Not the Sanitorium for the Central Committee on the Podushkino Highway but to a more humble establishment on a side road half a mile away.

The driver handled the taxi badly. His face was gray, his eyes bloodshot, vodka eyes.

Sitting in the back, clutching the strap as the taxi skidded around bends, Sedov considered the killing at the pool at Leninsk. No way was it his concern but, since the KGB had taken over the investigation, he had heard details. Taken over? Killed stone-dead was a better way of putting it.

As far as Sedov could make out, Brasack had been a CIA spy who had tried to make contact with the American defector Robert Massey. Probably to threaten him—maltreatment of relatives back in the U.S. perhaps – possibly to kill him. Whatever the plans were, they had been terminated by Department V.

What worried Sedov was Talin's acquaintanceship—not friendship, that had been an exaggeration—with Massey. The more he worried the more the worries multiplied.

Ostensibly the reason for his anxiety was plain. Massey was a traitor. No one wanted to pass the time of day with a traitor—look how Philby and his ilk in Moscow were boycotted—unless he had come armed with some gentle persuasion.

Persuasion of which I know nothing! This led to a worry about the state of Talin's mind. Long ago he had taught the brash and handsome young Siberian to stifle his rebellion. Stifle—not necessarily exterminate. God knows what protests pounded away inside his skull. His heartbeat, for instance, when Mission Control had announced the incursion into Poland.

This led to a worry about his own motives. Exhaustively, he cross-examined himself to see if he could identify jealousy. He found himself Not Guilty. All that he uncovered during the examination was intuition. A policeman's intuition, which was a far more positive force than the dictionary definition. If the dead CIA agent had been making contact with Massey, then Massey was tainted. And he would taint Talin.

The taxi skidded on hard-packed snow and majestically sailed along broadside. The driver spun the wheel. The cab skidded right around, straightened up. Sedov swore at him.

But how can I warn Talin? He won't believe me. He will believe that I . . . Sedov's mind baulked at what Talin might believe.

Fur-hatted militia appeared in the road. One, hand on pistol, gestured to the driver to open the window. "*Zdrastvuite*," he said, but Sedov already had his ID in his hand, and after a quick look the militiaman stepped back smartly, waving the driver on.

At this display of Sedov's authority the driver became even more nervous. Sedov tapped him on the shoulder, "Take the next left." They took it on two wheels.

The clinic, an old dacha from tzarist times, was a rambling wood mansion with fretted eaves and ochre-washed annexes added more recently. It was besieged on all sides by regiments of pine trees; it was suspended in time; it was a home for incurables. Sedov left the cab at the entrance to the drive.

When he rang the bell, a finger of snow fell from the porch. He heard the bell peal in the depths of the dacha.

The door was opened by a girl in a starched white uniform. Her youth looked out of place, an anachronism. But not to Sedov who had been there many times before.

She smiled at him and led him down a long corridor. On either side the doors were shut. Luxurious condemned cells, where life and death could hover entwined for decades.

She opened the door of No. 23 and left him with the woman inside. She lay on a couch, staring at the snow-covered lawns outside. She wore an eggshell blue dressing gown patterned with roses. Her hair was gray and wild, the skin on her face was parchment. She had once been beautiful.

He sat beside her. She smiled at him vaguely. At least she wasn't unhappy, better off than many in the clinic. She looked seventy: It was her thirty-ninth birthday.

"Happy birthday," he said. He took a small packet from the inside pocket of his jacket. She took it from him and placed it on the table beside her. "It's perfume," he said. "The one you like." The one she had worn on their honeymoon.

Her eyes focused on him, a flicker of interest in them. "And how is our son today?" she asked.

He took her hand. "We should be very proud of him," he said. "He has been promoted to take command of a whole fleet of spaceships."

11

THE Bolshoi touring company arrived complete with costumes, sets, and discord.

Talin heard about the latter when he took Sonya on a tour of Leninsk, stage-managed so that she could appreciate its merits, which, he had to admit, were few and far between.

He started off with his own small house down the street from the cottage where Yury Gagarin had lived. Gagarin had died in a conventional air crash, of all things, and the cottage was now a shrine.

If Gagarin's house was a shrine, then Talin's home had become a show-piece. The kitchen was packed with gadgetry, even a dishwasher from Helsinki, and in the living room stood a television. A color one at that.

The freezer was stuffed with good food, the furniture dusted, parquet floors polished. The place was an invitation—to Sonya to live there when-ever the Bolshoi gave her leave from Moscow.

But first they went to the bedroom where Talin had installed a double bed. They had been apart for several weeks and they made love eagerly, without bothering to undress completely.

Half an hour later, Sonya inspected the house. She approved but, Talin noted, took it as her birthright, as an annex of Bolshoi *nachalstvo*. She switched on the television. For a couple of minutes they watched Yuri Senkevich plugging his Sunday evening program, *Film Travel Club*; briefly the Himlayas beckoned them.

"In color," Talin pointed out.

She smiled. "So it is."

Talin switched it off.

Just before they left to tour the city, the phone rang. It was Massey. "I've got a favor to ask," he said. "You remember how we talked about space?"

Of course he did.

"Well, the Bolshoi has sent a touring company to Leninsk. They're performing a ballet about space. Giving it a trial run. I've been told that you are engaged to be married to one of the dancers."

Talin glanced at Sonya, who was staring through the window at the other small, detached houses. "*One* of the dancers?"

"Sorry, *the* dancer." Sonya had turned around, interested. "I wondered if you could . . ."

"Get you a ticket? I'll see what I can do."

Sonya crossed the room and kissed Talin. "Who was that?"

"A man called Massey."

"English?"

"American."

"What's he doing in your secret city?"

"Advising," Talin said. "Can you get an extra ticket?"

She looked doubtful. "An American? Well, I'll try." shrugging away the request. "Anyway, we won't be dancing the whole ballet here, just the highlights. The director doesn't think that Leninsk is quite ready for the extended version!"

It was while they were walking through the center of the city, a route intricately plotted by Talin to embrace the theater, cinemas, and best shops, that Sonya mentioned discord at the Bolshoi. The trouble, he gathered, was divided into two categories: the first he vaguely appreciated with the indulgence of the layman peering into the artistic temperament; the second he understood utterly.

Many of the dancers, apparently, were disenchanted with the artistic director, Boris Pudovkin. He was pigheaded and he had favorites.

When Talin pointed out that she was one of the favorites, she replied with spirit, "That's not the point. Favoritism has no part in either our society or its artistic expression."

The pigheadedness, she told him, was evident in his choice of new ballets. Surely not in the space ballet, *The Red Dove*? No, that was acceptable. But some of his ideas were, well, degenerate. Not only that but he seemed unable to distinguish between traditional and modern ballet. "He has done dreadful things to *Romeo and Juliet*," Sonya said, tucking her arm into Talin's.

124

He stopped and kissed her cold cheek. Her face framed in mink looked lovely. They walked past a cinema showing Mikhalkov-Konchalovsky's *Siberiada*. He would like to see it, Talin decided: It was the story of a village in Siberia.

The complaint about the Bolshoi that interested him was the clamp-down on foreign tours and the increased KGB surveillance.

Hurrying her past two particularly ugly barrack-block apartments, Talin asked, "Why have they done that?"

She looked at him in surprise. "Don't you know? Because of the defections on the last tours of Britain and the United States, of course."

Talin's interest quickened. "How would I know? Such things aren't reported in our newspapers."

"Why should they be? We aren't proud of them."

Today he didn't want argument so he contented himself with, "Why did they defect?"

"The usual pathetic reasons. The freedom of life in the West. Artistic liberty, all that hypocritical nonsense."

"But I thought . . ." Talin stopped himself.

"Thought that *I* was complaining about loss of liberty in the Bolshoi? You misunderstood, Nicolay. I was merely telling you how others felt." She withdrew her hand from his arm.

"Wouldn't it be wonderful," he said, hailing a taxi, "if we could solve this equation in our lifetime." They climbed into it. "The rival merits of Communism and Capitalism, that is."

"Impossible," she said, as the taxi accelerated in the direction of Talin's house, "because there is no such equation."

The equation, or lack of it, made several more appearances during the day, in between lovemaking, eating, planning, and dancing. It augured well for their marriage, they agreed, that they could argue without rancor.

When they made love for the second time that day it was more leisurely— to begin with at any rate—and experimental. Every time there was something new, every time Sonya shed a veil of reserve. He, too, amazed himself. He found that lying beneath her was just as pleasurable as dominating on top: It was more comfortable, he could fondle her breasts, and, more importantly, they could see each other. Tell an old Russian goat that and he would assume you were a cripple.

He tried to make their orgasms synchronize. But, biting him, she said it didn't matter a damn when it happened as long as it happened, crying out and digging her fingernails into his back.

Later, while she was searching for a needle and thread to sew a button on her blouse, she introduced *defitsitny,* shortages, into the day's debates. You couldn't buy a needle or thread in Leninsk for love nor money, Talin told her.

Defensively, she said, "So, you can't buy a needle and thread, but you can buy food, and for that we should be grateful."

Such an illogical response startled Talin. Until he realized that, without comprehending it, she was embarking on the stock defense of *defitsitny* drilled into her since childhood. The defense had one great merit: it was true. Until the Revolution the peasants had lived on their wits, during the last war too. Even Talin could remember existing on potatoes, buckwheat, and fish plucked silver-bright from holes in the ice. The flaw in the defense was that it didn't attempt to explain why *defitsitny* existed at all, nearly forty years after the war.

"And an apartment costs only a fraction of the rent in the United States," she said, taking the next step in the defense and, by doing so, brandishing aloft Russia's inferiority complex about the West.

Wishing fervently that Sonya had found a needle and thread, Talin said, "True. But a Russian worker only earns a fraction of his American counterpart."

So there it was, the equation. A vacation could cost an American a fortune: A Russian could have a month by the sea for a song. A tiny Soviet car was twice the price of an American compact. A visit to the dentist could cost a New Yorker an arm and a leg, whereas a Muscovite had his teeth fixed for nothing.

What we lack is freedom. He didn't voice the thought. Sedov had taught him well. Perhaps when he and Sonya were married . . .

When she began, "Sometimes you seem to admire the West more than . . ." he took her arm and said, "Come on, let's go and buy you another blouse."

They had dinner in a hot little restaurant with misted windows and lots of shiny-leaved plants that gave it the feel of an aquarium. There, over coffee, it was the American boycott of the Moscow Olympic games back in 1980 that surfaced.

Followed by Afghanistan and then, of course, Hungary, Czechoslovakia, and Poland.

And space? Again the thought passed unspoken.

Overjoyed at their capacity for friendly debate, they strode gaily from the restaurant and crossed the street to the city's only disco, a dark concrete cave thumping with bold music. Light-spots spun around the walls, and the floor was crowded with young people dancing. The records were three or four years old, but who cared? It was rock 'n' roll and the skirts swirled and the blue jeans swayed.

Sonya danced with uninhibited inspiration, he with strength and agility. They were given the floor. When they returned to their table they were applauded.

They drank beer. Briefly, following up a remark that a few years ago such exhibitionism would never have been allowed, they touched on decadence and hooliganism. All right, Sonya agreed, the crime rate, especially among young people, was alarming but it was nothing compared with crime in the States.

Always the comparison. The ever-brooding complex that had so much to do with Soviet aggression.

"Let's just blame vodka," he said, smiling. "It's the scapegoat for most of our evils." He took her hand. "I thought we should get married soon."

"Mmm."

"Two weeks?"

She leaned across the table and kissed him. "Two weeks. Did you discuss this with Sedov?"

"No," he lied.

"This man Massey?"

He looked at her in astonishment. "Why should I discuss it with him?"

"No reason. I just wondered. It just struck me as odd that he should ask you to get him a ticket to the ballet."

"I've only discussed space with him," Talin said.

"Sometimes," she said, tracing the outline of his cheek with her fingers, "I think of you in space when I'm dancing."

"And how does it affect your performance?"

"I feel as though I'm going to fall. You can't know what it feels like—to know that the man you love is . . . severed from the earth." She looked into his eyes. "How many more times, Nicolay?"

"I don't know. The shuttle, it's a different concept. Soon we will be flying up and down into space just like jet pilots."

"But when will you stop?"

"When you stop dancing," he said. "Come on, let's jive again and give them a treat."

When they went to bed, Sonya immediately fell asleep in his arms. After a few moments he, too, slept and dreamed about shooting stars burning themselves out in the darkness of infinity wherein lay the answer to all things, even equations.

At first she was a dove fluttering around a village square but chained, figuratively, to a cote. When she beat her wings in protest at her captivity she was also beating them against the mockery of the other doves. Then into the square came a young man, the Prince of Light. He and the dove danced a *pas de deux* in which he enticed her toward freedom, toward space. Her wing-beats grew more frantic until with a ringing chord of music, he severed her invisible ties. Pink spotlights bathed the spinning figure of Sonya Bragina as she was lifted on a trapeze toward the heavens.

"The second act is our act," said Massey consulting the program as the lights came on. "Let's hope they get the flight path right."

Sonya hadn't been able to get him a ticket; hadn't tried, Talin suspected. But Sedov was still in Moscow so Talin had given his ticket to Massey.

"The audience doesn't look as if they care one way or the other," replied Talin. One man at the end of their row was asleep. This wasn't Moscow.

But the audience became more attentive in the second act. The stage was space: stars glittered, beams of light swept the heavens, shivering and deflecting when they touched. The Red Dove was now more incisively graceful in her solo, circling the stage in *adagio* movements, in orbit. Then from the wings sprang the Prince of Darkness.

"He's got to be an American," Massey whispered to Talin.

The Prince of Darkness gave chase. The beams of light became sharper, slicing through the star-shimmering darkness above the dancers. Lasers, thought Talin.

But the Red Dove was saved by the Prince of Light. In a crescendo of music he bore down on the Prince of Darkness, who was hurled from orbit to drift eternally in space.

In the last act, the dove returned to the village square to be welcomed by the other doves. She no longer minded being a prisoner. She knew what lay beyond the earth's horizons. As she danced her last solo, she gazed upward and there in the firmament was a spaceship.

Massey and Talin were deeply moved. They, too, had been where the dove had been, looking down.

The audience responded cheerfully. But there was none of the feverish applause that the company might have expected in Moscow.

Talin went backstage because he knew Sonya would be despondent. He took Massey with him.

Sonya, sitting in front of a mirror removing her makeup, was certainly despondent, but also angry. "Peasants," she said, the familiar dismissal of the unappreciative. An unfortunate expression, Talin always thought, because it dismissed half the citizens of the Soviet Union.

Sonya barely acknowledged Massey.

Talin put his hands on her bare shoulders. "Don't worry," he said, "it was fantastic. Wait till you dance it in Moscow. And London and Paris and New York."

She was mollified because she valued his opinion. "You really think it was good?"

Massey, answering for Talin, said, "It was the best thing the Bolshoi has done since *Spartacus*."

For a moment the remark hung incongruously. Talin wasn't sure why, but it contained a flawed note. The remark of a man who had done hurried homework?

Sonya said. "You've seen Grigorovich's work, *Gaspadeen* Massey?"

A tiny pause? Or is it my imagination? In any event Massey answered convincingly enough, "Sure, I saw it in New York in 1979 when the Bolshoi toured the States," and Talin forgot his doubts.

In the foyer of the theater, emptied now of "peasants," Massey hesitated before leaving Talin. Almost shyly, he said, "We have a lot in common, you and I, Nicolay. Did you know that I learned quite a lot about you in the States?"

Intrigued, Talin said, "What sort of things?"

"Perhaps," Massey said quickly as Sonya approached, "you'd like to drop around to my apartment one day this week for a drink? Say Tuesday?"

"I look forward to it," Talin said. Why not? After all, the ballet had been all about freedom.

Depressed, Nicolay Vlasov examined the photographs of his children, two boys and a girl, on the wall of his study on Kutuzovsky. They seemed to be appealing to him to try to understand them. But their appeals had gone unheeded.

At least, Vlasov thought, I am not so hypocritical that I ask myself, Where did I go wrong? I know where I went wrong and, given my time again, I should probably do so again.

Because it had been written. He had been born a schemer and he would die one. A curse, a blessing, he knew not which. But his scheming had lost him his children and the respect of the stranger in his home, his wife.

Wherever he went, suspicion accompanied him. It was with him now in the pink dossier on his desk marked ROBERT MASSEY. Only the faintest breath of it, true, and quite possibly unfounded. Just the same it had to be laid to rest.

What bothered Vlasov was not the arrival—and abrupt departure—of Brasack in Leninsk. The arrival of a CIA agent either to turn or kill Massey had always been in the cards. When Department V had put out a trace on the East German journalist before the killing, the SSD, the East German political police, had gained access to his home. He was CIA all right, and the SSD director in East Berlin had subsequently been summoned to Moscow to explain his lapse.

No, what bothered Vlasov was Massey's burgeoning relationship with Talin. The chance meeting in the food store observed by the man known as the Hunter, the lunch in the canteen, the adjacent seats at the ballet . . . these were the sort of incidents that, by not assigning a minder to Massey, Vlasov had expected to hear about. If Massey was double-dealing, then, unrestricted, he might give himself away.

But all the incidents had been perfectly logical. Massey and Talin obviously had a lot in common. Which was why, when Vlasov had acceded to Massey's demand to return to space, he had decided to put him up there with Talin. Not next time, of course, but soon.

Perhaps tht was what had ignited the flame of suspicion: Massey and Talin had anticipated his plans for them.

From the dossier Vlasov extracted Talin's latest computer assessment.

> YOUTHFUL SIGNS OF REBELLION COMPLETELY SUBORDINATED. SUBJECT HAS DEVELOPED AS ADVENTUROUS BUT OBEDIENT SERVANT OF THE PARTY . . .

So he would let the relationship develop naturally. But, at the same time, keep it under scrutiny.

He stared at the photographs on the wall. They stared back at him, through him.

If I bring off the Vandenberg coup, Vlasov decided, then I shall go and see the owners of those faces on the wall and explain. If I fail, then the likes of Peslyak will be baying at my heels.

Phase 2. Relationship development, sow seeds of doubt.

Well, I have developed the relationship, Massey thought as he lay on the bed in his apartment. I haven't yet sowed doubt but I have intrigued Talin. Time to make a progress report.

And it was only then that Massey realized that he no longer had anyone to whom he could report. His only contact was dead.

In Leninsk he was a satellite thrust out of orbit to drift in a void. Like the Prince of Darkness.

12

THE second Russian connection with Vandenberg was OUTPUT
FROM THE AMERICANS.

Vlasov wanted details of an imminent U.S. rocket launch that could subsequently be sabotaged through the computers. Again Sergey Yashin was chosen to steal the information. He was transferred from Moscow to Leninsk and allocated a small apartment, which he stocked with enough food to withstand a six-month siege.

Vlasov didn't fly to Leninsk for the second operation. Instead he dispatched Yuri Peslyak and Viktor Moroz, Director of the First Chief Directorate. Broadly speaking, Moroz was responsible for clandestine operations overseas, Peslyak for domestic surveillance. As Massey's scheme was open-ended, both had responsibilities.

The link-up was timed for midday. Both Peslyak and Moroz took the 7 A.M. jet from Domodyedove. They sat near the flight deck, screened from the other passengers by curtains. Behind the curtains, on the passenger side, sat two KGB guards.

Moroz, small, plump, and fastidious, was in an ebullient mood. News had been coming in all night of further mass demonstrations in the West in favor of disarmament. The mood, dormant for several years, had been reactivated by Moroz's agents in 1981 and encouraged to erupt at carefully calculated intervals ever since.

The operation hadn't presented too many difficulties: idealism and fear were soft targets for manipulation. In fact, Moroz had nothing but admiration for the dreams of youth on the march and felt that it was sad that the young crusaders had no idea that they had been manipulated, having no conception of the subtleties of deception.

Sad it might be, but the collective human condition was even sadder. Naiveté was cynicism's chopping block, and if one alliance decided to give the lead in disarmament, then the other would be sorely tempted to take advantage of such trust. Far better in the ground plan of things to let the West take the initiative.

Moroz ordered coffee and Georgian brandy from the stewardess assigned to the two of them and pointed at the headlines in *Red Star*. WESTERN YOUTH ORDERS CAPITALIST MASTERS "LAY DOWN YOUR ARMS." "A satisfactory exercise. Even you must concede that, Yuri."

Peslyak grunted. "Satisfactory until some idiot destroys it all. Like that submarine commander who surfaced in Swedish waters in 1981 with nuclear warheads on board."

"Come now, don't let your jealousy show." Moroz poured the brandy into his coffee. "You look after your dissidents and your Jews and your ethnic minorities while I take care of the globe. Speaking of minorities, I read the other day that soon we true Russians will be a minority in the Soviet Union. If you don't watch out, Yuri, they'll be calling the Muslims to prayer in the Kremlin by the end of the century."

Moroz thought Peslyak was vulgar. Peslyak, he knew, derided his small stature. This bothered Moroz not at all; Stalin had been a small man.

Peslyak said, "If we bring off this computer penetration, neither of us need worry. Unless there are more foul-ups."

"Such as?"

"Brasack. He should never have been allowed to enter the Soviet Union. The SSD is under your control, isn't it, Viktor?"

Moroz said calmly, "And once inside the Soviet Union he should have been detected immediately and liquidated. Instead he was permitted to get into a swimming pool with Massey. A swimming pool! The killing was a little . . . melodramatic, wasn't it, Yuri?"

Peslyak stared at the pastures of cloud below. He rubbed his fleshy nose and smiled faintly. "It must have scared the shit out of Massey," he said.

The Il-86 began to descend toward the clouds. Mist swarmed past the windows. Then below them were the pygmy hangars, launch-pads, gantries, and access roads of Tyuratam and the toy blocks of Leninsk.

Sergy Yashin was ravenous. It was 11:55 A.M., five minutes before he was due to make contact with Vandenberg, and his stomach was whining, groveling, for food.

It had been bad enough when he was transmitting from Moscow. But here at Tyuratam his appetite was razored by the knowledge that he was at the core of Soviet expansionism. When micro chips could have been put to so many wonderful uses . . .

True this terminal wasn't quite as old as the antique in Moscow. But that was only because it was being used for the colonization of space.

Onion soup followed by Chicken Kiev as tender as butter.

Yashin's stomach rumbled. His taste buds popped.

The other three men gathered around the terminal stared at him coldly. Peslyak as roughly brutal as an old-style commissar; Moroz even more forbidding; Massey, a man whose features had settled into contradictions.

Massey said, "One minute to go."

Yashin's fingers went to the keys.

Massey handed him a number and said, "Go," and Yashin fed in Gordon's terminal identification and, when this was acknowledged, the pass number handed to him by Massey.

While they waited, Moroz observed, "If this works, then anything's possible. We could rob Fort Knox."

Massey said, "You can be sure devious minds are already working on it. But so's Fort Knox."

"Is it really that simple?"

Massey shook his head. "Far from it, there are a whole lot of safeguards. The active file for one. That alerts the people at the other end to the fact that a record, a unit of data, has been referred to. Our trump card is that the guy in charge is on our side."

Figures materialized on the screen. Yashin looked up. "We've got the terminal identification for the day, the key code, and the data code."

Moroz handed Yashin two computer print-outs. Old-fashioned ones, Yashin noted. "This is what we want to know," Moroz told him.

Yashin glanced at the print-outs, then began to feed the questions into the terminal.

Ten minutes later they had the answers. In seven days the Americans were going to test-fire a modified Minuteman ICBM over the Western Test Range, which stretched 4,900 miles across the Pacific from Vandenberg.

Massey said, "It couldn't be better—one day after the next contact."

As they left the control Yashin heard Peslyak say to Moroz, "Has it occured to you that we could divert that rocket to fall on Washington?"

Trembling, Yashin switched off the current and hurried toward the canteen, accompanied by the guards who, these days, never left his side.

Nine thousand five hundred miles away Daniel Gordon turned to Chuck Raskin and said, "So far so good."

Six days later, Sergey Yashin, watched by Massey, Moroz, Peslyak, and, this time, Vlasov, began his INPUT.

They had raided Vandenberg's "smart machine," now they were going to hoodwink it.

If the connection was made satisfactorily, counterfeit data would be fed into Vandenberg's central processor and relayed to the computer in the Minuteman's launch-control center in a blast-proof capsule fifty feet below ground.

According to Soviet Intelligence, the underground silo housing the sixty-foot long, 70,000 pound Minutemen would be covered by electronically operated sliding closures four feet thick. And the control room, serving ten launchers, would be guarded by officers of the Strategic Air Command.

All as ineffectual as gossamer floating in the breeze if you could penetrate the silo through a micro chip as small as a baby's thumbnail.

"Maybe," said Peslyak reflectively, "we could even launch the Minuteman prematurely."

Moroz said crisply, "If this works, we could probably launch every damn missile in America—and contaminate the world."

Vlasov interrupted. Addressing Peslyak, he said, "Viktor has relayed to me your remark about diverting the missile to Washington. The object of this exercise, my dear Yuri, is to control space, not to destroy the globe. I have assumed your remark was flippant, although in the worst possible taste. The President," he added smoothly, "has assumed the same."

Peslyak glared at Moroz and Yashin thought, "I am listening to a nightmare. If this power I have at my fingertips got into the wrong hands—"

Massey said, "Hit it."

Yashin made contact.

A fragment of a pause.

He was through.

He began to inject his poison.

As he transmitted, he resurrected his own vision of the future. A world in which health, energy, and food problems were all solved by micro chips. In America, the Cyber 205 could perform 800 million functions in a second, probably more by now. They had smart machines that could both speak *and* understand spoken words, albeit slowly. One day they'd have machines that talked to each other.

And here I am, sabotaging the inertial guidance system and solid propellent ignition of a missile designed to carry a thermonuclear warhead across continents.

134

"That's it," he told the four men gathered around him as he completed the INPUT.

Vlasov said, "Until tomorrow."

They left the room.

It was done.

At 9:23 the following morning, when the night cloud and fog that frequently blankets the area had lifted, the United States Air Force embarked on its 483rd launch from Vandenberg.

They needn't have bothered about the cloud base. The rocket had ascended to only a few thousand feet when its thrusting flames suddenly died.

The rocket faltered and plunged into the Pacific two miles from the shore.

Associated Press and Reuters had the story within an hour, enabling the afternoon newspapers to plaster it across their front pages. True, the missile hadn't been armed with a warhead but what, they speculated, would have happened if it had been? Vandenberg, the Pentagon, and the White House were inundated with press calls but no one pursued the story as zealously as the Washington bureau of Tass, the Soviet news agency.

When the story landed in the head office of Tass on Moscow's Boulevard Ring, the top teletype and three photocopies were rushed to Dzerhinsky Square.

Vlasov read and reread the report sitting at his desk. So it had worked. They had penetrated the United States's military space program: while Russia dispatched an armory into orbit, America would be crippled.

Eventually, of course, the penetration would be traced. But by that time it would be too late. The military shuttles primed to distribute spy and killer satellites equipped with beam weapons, interceptors, and possibly orbital nuclear bombs, would be incapacitated.

Unless this was an elaborate CIA set-up. But for what possible reason? Vlasov frowned, then, remembering the photographs on the wall of his study, thrust aside the suspicion—for the time being at least. If his luck held, he would soon be able to visit his middle-aged children and explain.

He picked up a telephone and called Moroz. "It worked," he said.

"It worked," Reynolds told the President on a scrambled line.

"Glad to hear it, George. Bring me the details at six o'clock this evening." The line went dead.

The details were simple enough, Reynolds reflected, sipping a plastic cup of coffee in his office at Langley. And relatively cheap.

All they had done was to launch an obsolete Minuteman denuded of most of its equipment and with only enough propellant to take it a few thousand feet into the air.

135

The danger, as always, was the human factor. Technicians involved in the deception had been kept to a minimum. Each had been exhaustively screened and sworn to secrecy. None knew the motive behind the exercise. Two known KGB informants normally used to pass on misinformation had been deployed elsewhere.

However, there was always a risk. If the Minuteman deception was blown, then the spectacular would be blown. And Massey would be dead.

Reynolds finished his coffee and paced his office in a modern building on the highway ringing Washington. It was a spartan place, furnished with a government-issue desk, chairs, and filing cabinets, but at least, unlike the office of his Russian counterpart, Nicolay Vlasov, it overlooked trees.

Reynolds respected Vlasov. If the spectacular was aborted, it would be his doing. *And I will be the sacrificial lamb of the congressional inquiry.* Vlasov versus Reynolds . . . President versus President . . . Sedov versus Massey . . . Department V surveillance versus . . . Who?

Brasack was dead, and, now that the shell of the ancient Minuteman had been fired, the first priority was to find a replacement. Otherwise Massey had no way of communicating any developments.

Suppose the Russians decided to launch their shuttle prematurely, suppose Talin agreed to defect, suppose we knew nothing about it . . .

Reynolds buzzed his intercom and told his secretary to summon a cypher expert from the Office of Communications to encode a Telex message to the United States Embassy in Moscow.

The American Embassy in Moscow is located on Tchaikovsky Street and looks like a large, bankrupt hotel. It stands flush with the pavement, and there is an arch in the center of the façade, guarded by two militiamen, which leads into a courtyard. At one corner of the building stands a KGB post manned by four operatives. The edifice owes nothing to the spirit of Tchaikovsky.

The brain center of the CIA and other intelligence agencies is often assumed to be the offices of the military attachés. Wrong. Intelligence is indeed collated in these sections but it is superficial stuff. Attachés are far too obvious—accredited spies who at ceremonial occasions are more the stuff of Gilbert and Sullivan than John Le Carré. The real heart of the CIA operation is contained in other departments and, as with the KGB—intelligence agencies are great plagiarists—seniority bears no relation to diplomatic status. A lowly third secretary in the commercial section could, in his clandestine way, wield more power than the ambassador himself.

The CIA head of operations in Moscow was, ironically, a First Secretary in the Information Department. His name was Palmer, he was forty years old, with slightly oriental features and mild manners and he was, on this December morning, a very worried man.

A few weeks previously he had been summoned to Langley and briefed on Massey's mission. The brief: to maintain contact but not to interfere. The operation, Reynolds had said, could produce the biggest coup ever achieved by Western intelligence. And almost immediately Palmer had lost Brasack.

Next to China, Russia was the most difficult country in the world in which to establish agents. The restrictions on movements for one thing. Any American traveling anywhere was automatically under surveillance. He might just as well carry an ID in his hat-band spelling out SPY.

So Palmer had to enlist other nationalities. Soviet satellite states (Brasack) and Russian citizens who didn't consider that they owed any allegiance to the Kremlin. Georgia, where corruption was a way of life, was a fertile field, as was the Ukraine, particularly its western reaches, which, culturally and historically, have always been at odds with Moscow. In World War II, the Ukrainian Division fought with the Germans against the Soviet Union in the hope of winning their freedom. Most of them were subsequently butchered by the Russians for their pains.

Being half Japanese, the ethnic tensions inside the Soviet Union intrigued Palmer. He had no doubt that, like all empires before it, the Union would one day collapse. And he believed that the cracks were widening by the day inside its borders.

The phone on his desk rang. The *Boston Globe*. A visiting correspondent wanting an interview with the ambassador. Palmer said he would see what he could do. He logged the inquiry.

Where the Kremlin made its mistake was in regarding the inhabitants of the fifteenth and largest republic as the only true Soviets and suppressing nationalist feeling elsewhere. Well, pretty soon the Russian Republic would no longer have an overall majority, and pressing hard behind it would be all the other factions of the USSR led by the forty-five million Ukrainians. True, the Kremlin had tried to appease the Ukrainians by giving them some central powers but, in Palmer's opinion, these were quite inadequate.

The OUN, the Organization of Ukrainian Nationalists, was still active despite KGB attempts to exterminate it, and it was to their ranks that Palmer's mind turned as he searched for a replacement for Brasack.

Next to Plesetsk, Russia's military space center, Kapustin Yar, the test launching site for ABMs, and Saryshagan, the missile base on the Chinese border where they were testing charged particle beam weapons, Tyuratam and Leninsk were the most difficult places in the Soviet Union into which to infiltrate an agent.

In the file in his mind Palmer ran through the list of OUN agents who also worked for the CIA. It was a formality. Already he knew there was only one man for the job, but he hesitated to nominate him.

His real name was Rybak. Years ago he had assumed another identity and he had once been Olympic middle-heavyweight weightlifting champion and was therefore *nachalstvo,* privileged. This meant that he could travel far more freely than most of his fellow countrymen, an inestimable asset if you were engaged in espionage.

By profession, Ryabak was an electrical aeronautical engineer specializing in Yakovlek jets. Yak-42s had begun to fly into Leninsk. So, with his *nachalstvo,* there was a chance that Rybak could get himself assigned to Rocket City.

Rybak, Palmer reflected, had a lot going for him. He also had a lot running against him. Although he was grossly fat, he was still immensely strong, and whenever he was engaged on a clandestine operation a body seemed to surface, ribcage crushed as though it had been embraced by a bear.

Palmer needn't have worried about the immediate transfer of Rybak to Leninsk: On December 12, Talin, Massey, and ten other cosmonauts and mission specialists were transferred to Moscow for medical examinations at the Institute of Aviation Medicine.

Before he left, Talin inspected the three Doves that had arrived by train from the Tupolev factory at Voronezh. One squatted wingless in an annex; the second was stretched out on a ramp in the processing facility, the third was suspended inside the shell of the fifteen-story vehicle assembly building, ready to be joined to the giant external tank and solid rocket boosters, which would be shed as she escaped from the pull of the earth.

The Dove suspended in the assembly building was the shuttle Talin would shortly fly—rumor had it on February 23, Armed Forces Day. The bird on the ramp was the one in which Massey, as an observer, would later accompany him; it was scheduled to fly in the summer.

Talin showed his ID, waited while he was checked out electronically, then climbed into the flight deck of the hanging Dove.

He sat in the pilot seat, scanned the dials, and touched the hand controller. Then he moved to the other controls that would concern Sedov and himself while they were in orbit. As before, the cargo bay would be Sedov's responsibility.

Indisputably, this mission was more important than the previous maiden flight. They would, for instance, be testing a space arm that could flex its metal muscles and reach out from the cargo bay to deliver the components of stations being constructed in space. To do this, Sedov would have to turn the Dove upside down so that the instruments in the bay faced earth; but that was no problem because when you were weightless in space it didn't matter which way up you sat or stood.

The Americans had already successfully tested a similar arm. The Soviet version was far more sophisticated, designed to build in space.

It must have been the fitting for the arm that had struck Talin as out of place at Voronezh. He climbed out of the flight deck and examined the cargo bay. There was no arm there! Only fittings. Odd. Frowning, he walked out into the daylight.

Far away, on the other side of the space center, a conventional rocket screamed, bloody-tailed, into the air.

13

THEY were married at the Palace of Weddings in Moscow's Leningrad Prospect.

Sonya wore a white taffeta gown made by the Bolshoi costumiers. Her parents flew from their dacha on Lake Ladoga near the Finnish border. Talin's mother sent a cable from Khabarovsk—she was sixty-nine and 4,000 miles was a long way to travel.

The sun shone, fresh snow sparkled.

Theirs was the thirty-second wedding that day. They were married by the director of the Palace, a matronly woman wearing a purple dress. With them at the ceremony were the best man, Oleg Sedov—accepted without complaint by Sonya—and the bridesmaid, a member of the Bolshoi *Corps de Ballet,* a girl with flirtatious eyes named Anna.

As they entered the lofty wedding chamber, a tape of Tchaikovsky's Symphony No. 4 poured from two loudspeakers. On the director's desk stood a bust of Lenin and a vase of pink and white carnations flown in from Georgia. When they stopped in front of her desk the music stopped, and the director told them that the State had empowered her to marry them. Talin didn't care who had empowered her. Nor did he care that they were being married on an assembly line. Sonya looked beautiful, a dusty shaft of sunlight found the fragility and not the strength in her face, her fine blonde hair loose on her shoulders. She was his and he was hers and these moments were theirs, outside the thrall of the State.

Sedov nudged him. The director had finished her homily, there were papers to be signed.

Then the director handed them two gold rings. He and Sonya exchanged them and he looked into her eyes and saw love.

The director smiled for the first time. She talked to them about sharing. The sunshine felt warm. He could smell the carnations. She pronounced them man and wife. They kissed. As they walked out of the chamber, taped music flowed again, "When the Saints Go Marching In"—very popular at Soviet weddings.

Then more Tchaikovsky as another couple prepared to enter.

In the foyer, they drank champagne and Talin kissed the bridesmaid and Sedov kissed Sonya. Sedov, Talin thought, looked touchingly proud.

A Zil limousine festooned with streamers, a plastic bear on its hood, took them to the Aragvi for the reception. There were two hundred guests from the arts and aerospace present. Among them Robert Massey, who congratulated them. Sonya received him coolly and, fleetingly; it occurred to Talin that she had transferred her hostility from Sedov to the American.

The press was there in strength. The interviews went on too long. Finally, when a reporter from *Komsomolskaya Pravda* asked Talin whether he thought he and Sonya had been united by "ideological concord," Talin snapped, "No, by sex," and was led firmly away by Sedov.

As they cut the cake, surmounted by a ballerina doll and a tiny cosmonaut, the restaurant was lit with electronic camera flashes.

Then, as though a starter's pistol had been fired, the guests turned to the food and drink. Sweet champagne, vodka and brandy, and a larder of *zakuski*—smoked salmon, black and red caviar, salted herring, salami, chicken, gherkins, black bread, bowls of sliced pickled beets. It disappeared at astonishing speed. "Locusts," Sedov remarked.

Replacements were brought by waitresses in black and white uniforms.

As the vodka took hold, moods changed and the chatter rose a few decibels. A weeping poet toasted Love; two Uzbeks retired outside to fight over Anna, the bridesmaid; glasses smashed; a man who looked like a prizefighter found his baritone voice deep in his barrel chest and aired it, singing of tragedy with unfettered relish. As one, the guests mourned and celebrated their lot.

Talin and Sonya left at 1 P.M. to catch a plane to Sochi. No one, except Sedov and Massey, seemed to be aware of their departure. They looked for Anna, but she had locked herself in a bathroom with the baritone while her other two suitors slugged it out on the sidewalk.

In Sochi, Talin and Sonya found another Russia. In the late afternoon, they
142

strolled in the warm sunshine along the esplanade with its pergolas and flights of white steps, gazed over the cypress-speared forest sweeping down to the shore from the snow-capped peak of Mount Elbrus, Europe's highest mountain, watched the hydrofoils skimming the green waters of the Black Sea, smelled blossoms on the air. In the evening, the streets were alive with guitar music.

That night they went to bed exhausted and didn't make love.

On successive nights they made up for the lapse.

Daily they grew happier and more relaxed among Sochi's spas, solariums, clinics, sanatoriums, and rest homes. Every year 500,000 tourists visit Sochi to take the air, the waters, the tonics. In the cafés the topic is health, good or bad.

They strolled along the beaches, climbed the mountain road to Dagomys, capital of Russian tea, took a bus to a grove fifteen miles from the center of Sochi to look at yew and box trees reputedly 800 years old; ate trout from a hatchery filled with clear green water.

Occasionally Talin became aware that a thin man wearing a fawn suit seemed to be haunting them. Following them? Smiling, Talin derided himself. Leninsk security had got to him. There must be a thousand men wearing fawn suits in Sochi.

On Friday, December 20, they flew back to Moscow.

On the same Friday, Boris Rybak got drunk on the Ukrainian circuit in Moscow.

He was not alone in his drinking, Friday being Moscow's prime night for boozing, closely followed by Saturday and Sunday. Monday was the prime day for absenteeism.

Rybak was always puzzled by the reasons put forward by sociologists for Soviet drinking. Failure to complete their work output, escape from responsibility, the cold, etcetera.

Rybak drank to get drunk.

And, like most Russians, he drank vodka, the libation, liberation, and hard currency of the people. If you wanted a job done properly, pay the carpenter or plumber with a liter of firewater.

Rybak drank mostly in the homes of Ukrainians where, as the vodka unleashed their tongues, the toasts grew louder and the language of their land, banished by Stalin, lived again.

By and large Rybak was an amiable drunk, disciplined enough, even when carrying half a liter of vodka in his belly, not to be indiscreet about his OUN activities. His one weakness was, paradoxically, his strength. When, after recalling his Olympic endeavors, he demonstrated that strength, a cord of restraint sometimes snapped inside him, particularly if, because of his girth and blubber, his power was questioned. Once at a party a lithe, olive-skinned

143

Armenian who taught judo at night classes remarked, "What is the good of muscles if they've melted," and, with a shrug, accepted Rybak's challenge to fight. The Armenian swayed at Rybak, trying to use his weight and strength to his own advantage, but whatever he did Rybak just came at him until he was trapped in the corner of the room. Rybak encircled him with his arms. To the onlookers it looked like a friendly embrace, until they heard the Armenian's ribs crack.

Tonight Rybak resolved not to get Friday-night drunk because the following day he had to make contact with an American named Massey.

But vodka is a sly drink. Down the throat it slides to ignite small fires, which the drinker believes he has extinguished with mineral water and *sakuski*. What, in fact, he has done is induce internal combustion and it only needs a few breaths of fresh air to set the flames roaring.

Rybak visited four homes, using his sophisticated electrician's skills at each to detect any bugs before the anti-Soviet toasts became too explicit. On the first three occasions he navigated his exit into the sharp-toothed night reasonably well. It was the fourth visit, to a wooden *izba* in the Arbat, that was his undoing.

The old cottage with its incandescent stove brought the past back and reminded them of the outrages of history. After the first two liters of vodka, the hosts and guests, all Kievans, stormed down their city's Kreshchatik Street beneath the chestnut trees, resurrecting their heritage prior to the October Revolution. After half an hour they stumbled back to the cottage.

Glasses were hurled at the glowing stove.

Then Rybak demonstrated the latent strength of the Ukraine by lifting above his head a huge table. He issued a spate of challenges but, remembering the fate of the Armenian who even now breathed with pain, no one took him up.

Out into the street he finally strode, all 280 pounds of him. He sucked down the crackling air, and, whoosh, the fires inside him were rekindled. Their ferocity spun him around, and, to escape them, he took cover in the gutter, where, five minutes later, the militia's vodka patrol shovelled him up and, with considerable effort, piled him into the back of a van and carted him off with the other drunks to a sobering-up station.

He came to gazing at Christ.

The sobering-up station was part of a derelict monastery. Recently the Soviet authorities had been renovating it to prove their respect for religion. Fifty years of dirt, rust, and pigeon droppings had been scraped away, blue cupolas had been polished, crosses burnished.

Above the entrance, the face of Christ was reemerging in mosaic pebbles and some of the staff of the sobering-up station asserted that its effect on the drunks was more potent than the usual jets of ice-cold water. To an extent this was true, because the boozers believed the Day of Judgment had arrived and immediately began to dry out.

Not so Rybak. Seeing Christ peering down at him, he decided he was reproaching him about his gross appearance and challenged him to a bout of wrestling.

Two attendants turned the water hose on him, then tried to strap him naked on an iron bed, but he resisted. A needle slid into his buttock. He continued to struggle for a few seconds before collapsing on the bed, a great mattress of flesh. They strapped him down and threw two gray blankets over him.

Punctiliously they entered him in their records. "The eighth time this year," one of them noted, "I wish he'd piss off back to Kiev and get drunk there."

The following morning, Rybak departed with the considerable dignity of the very fat and caught a bus to his rendezvous with Massey in one of the establishments where Russians, like the British in their pubs, debate the human condition—the *banya*, the bathhouse.

Phase 3: First hit, with devastating revelation, preferably personal.

Massey awoke from a nightmare: When he had made his *devastating revelation*, Talin had produced a razor, slit his own throat and smiling, said, "Pray continue."

Massey felt the sheets. They were wringing wet. Blood? No, sweat. He glanced at the illuminated dial of his wristwatch. 6 A.M. Six hours before he was due to make contact with a Ukrainian named Rybak.

He switched on the bedside lamp. There hadn't been a vacancy in the military billets in Moscow, and he had been put back in his old room, 2604, in the Ukraina Hotel.

He swung himself out of bed and padded around the room. On the glass-topped table lay a magazine published in English for visitors. He flicked the pages. And there were Nicolay Talin and Sonya Bragina staring at him, Talin with his fair hair swept back from his bold features, Sonya smiling up at him.

If everything went according to plan he was going to destroy their happiness.

Massey began to read.

> Soul mates joined by a common ideology ... he spreading the cause of Socialism in the heavens, she in the arts ... both the physical and mental embodiment of the glorious spirit that has prevailed since the October Revolution ...

145

Massey put down the magazine. Rubbish like that helped his reaffirmation.

Nevertheless, I am betraying Talin. *Nonsense, he is an intelligent man capable of making up his own mind.* I'm taking over where Reynolds left off, Massey thought.

He is a happy man. He has a wife whom he loves and his joy is traveling in space. *He knows that space must not be violated, he knows there is a greater scheme of things.*

How do I know that what I'm supposed to tell him is true? *You don't, but in this case the end indisputably justifies the means.*

And my motives? *Idealism. At least give yourself that.* But compounded by selfishness, the desire to return to space. *Well, of course, you could accept the Russian offer—and have your throat cut when they discover they've been deceived.*

To summarize, Massey thought, I have no choice. He parted the curtains. The windows were covered on the outside with frost patterns; it was still dark.

He lay down on the bed again and closed his eyes, and the nightmares returned.

The *banya* was a relic of Tzarist indulgence. From the outside it was nondescript, a doorway in a row of leaning tenements painted in flaking yellow. Inside, the foyer was fashioned in marble the color of old teeth but grand just the same. A flight of stairs covered in worn red carpet led down to the changing rooms.

Massey paid his entrance money, one rouble, to the woman at the cashier's desk and received in return a white towel and a bunch of birch twigs with which to beat the dirt from his own and others' skins.

He changed and, draped in the towel, made his way into the bathhouse proper. The heat hit him a fierce blow as he entered. He closed the door and peered around. Steam scented with eucalyptus billowed around the chamber. Blinking the moisture from his eyelids, he saw that it was generated by firebricks in an oven. Every so often a masochist threw a bucket of water on the bricks and more steam was discharged out of pipes snouting from the walls. The room was shaped like a small amphitheater with benches rising on all sides. Massey assumed that it was hottest at the top.

He sat half way up. The wet heat seared his eyeballs, scalded his lungs. Around him other bathers were beating the dirt out of each other with their twigs. Massey sat and waited and endured.

The slip of paper making the appointment had been thrust in his hand beside the bookstall in the Ukraina. Just a time, midday, and the location of the *banya.* He had spun around but he was surrounded by the usual throng, indistinguishable from the crowd that had been there the night he arrived. Any one of them could have passed on the message.

"A barbaric custom." The voice issued from the steam on Massey's left. "But part of our character."

Massey wiped moisture from his eyes with his towel. The voice belonged to an elephant.

"I can see from your expression that you would not want to beat me with birch twigs. I must admit there is a lot of me." A chuckle.

Could this great hulk of blubber be the contact?

Massey said, "I'll beat you if you want but I've got a strong arm."

"Strength is everything," the fat man said inconsequentially. "But don't worry, I don't want to be beaten." Grappler's hands gestured at the steam. "This is enough for me." He pointed at the other bathers. "Let them beat each other to death. But don't misunderstand them . . ." *Had he said* Massey *or had it been a hiss of steam?* ". . . it is not just the pain that they enjoy."

"What *do* they enjoy?"

"You will see," wiping the sweat pouring from his face. "Are you English?"

"American."

"I went to America once."

"What part?"

"Texas."

"What part of Texas?"

"An offshore island."

"Name?"

"Padre Island. Even now I can remember the telephone number of the Padre Island National Seashore—512 937-2621."

The contact. Enough flesh there for two contacts. Despite everything Massey grinned.

Rybak said, "Come, the heat is getting to you. We must go." They stood up. Rybak gripped Massey's arm, fingers like steel hooks. Bodies parted before him. Near the entrance he picked up a bucket and tossed water onto the firebricks. As steam hissed around them he said, "Do you have a message?"

"Just tell them Phase Three starts tomorrow."

"Very well. We'll meet in seven days at the same time at the chessboards in Gorky Park. Is this your first visit to a *banya*?" as they made their way into the changing room.

"First and last."

"It's not so bad. Look." Rybak pointed to an area at one end of the changing room that Massey hadn't noticed.

Men, young and old, fat and thin, were lounging in their towels playing chess and dominoes, laughing, talking, eating, and drinking.

"The *banya* is the great equalizer," Rybak said. "Even more so than Communism," he whispered. "Here you might meet a general literally rubbing shoulders with a peasant. And now you see what I meant about our enjoyment. It isn't just the suffering in there," pointing toward the bathhouse, "it's the blessed relief after it. A beer?" he asked.

Massey nodded.

"And something to eat. Some salted fish I think." He spoke to a male attendant who departed, returning with tankards of beer and a plate of fish as tough as shoeleather.

As they drank and chewed, Rybak observed, "You look strong to me. Do you like to arm wrestle?"

"No," Massey said.

"Not even against a barrel of lard like me?"

"Not particularly."

"I haven't paid for the beer and fish yet. Shall we arm wrestle to see who pays?"

"If you must."

Elbow to elbow, forearm to forearm, hands clasped, they strained against each other on the floor. Three times Massey almost forced Rybak's arm flat; three times it sprang back as though a spring had suddenly been released. Finally it was Massey who broke.

Rybak wobbled with merriment. "You pay," he said, popping the remains of the salted fish into his mouth and washing it down with the last of Massey's beer.

Observing them from across the room where he was reading the latest spy thriller by Julian Semyonov, the Hunter thought, "If I ever tangle with that fat slob I shall have to watch my step."

Nicolay Vlasov read the Hunter's latest report in the back of the black Zil taking him from the Kremlin, where he had attended a Politburo meeting, to his apartment on Kutuzovsky.

The Zil occupied the center of the darkened street, a Kremlin privilege. Occasionally the driver glanced in the rearview mirror at the elegant passenger with the expensively barbered hair and fragile-looking skull. One crack with a blunt instrument and the bone would shatter like china. Greenish eyes glittered from the mirror as though Vlasov had heard his thoughts. The driver shivered.

Vlasov's eyes refocused on the report.

0555 hours. Subject heard through microphones in his room in Ukraina Hotel to shout "Phase Three!" then lapse into gibberish.

0600. Heard to rise from bed. Spent fifteen minutes walking around room.

0615. Returned to bed.

0648. Another shout, words incomprehensible.

Phase Three? Vlasov frowned. Probably a reference to the flight of the shuttle. He would have to find out if such a term was in common usage in shuttle parlance. Perhaps it was an American expression. Or it could have been a generalization; he would have to listen to the tape to see what the tone was.

0800. Woken by early call from switchboard. Breakfast.

0900. Called at Passport Office, Room 20, on first floor of Ukraina. Took stairs to groundfloor. Bought newspaper, *Pravda,* and crossed river across Kalininsky Bridge, strolled along riverbank. Returned to hotel.

1030. Coffee in room.

1104. Traveled by bus to Pushkin Place. Visited Museum of the Revolution.

So far a model morning, Vlasov thought with relief as the Zil pulled up outside his apartment building.

Militiamen snapped to attention. Plainclothes guards hovered. Vlasov entered the lobby, slid a magnetized card into the elevator control.

He continued to read as the elevator glided upward.

1145. Emerged from museum and made way by foot to *banya* off Petrovka Street.

Noon, entered *banya.*

1210, approx. (Perhaps the Hunter had left his watch in the changing room to avoid the steam.) Approached by fat man who struck up conversation.

1220. Moved to recreation room with fat man. Stayed with him until—

1245. Left *banya* and returned by taxi to hotel.

The rest of Massey's day until the Hunter handed over surveillance to another agent at 1800 hours was innocuous. Come to think of it, so was the first part. The footnote to the report was the most interesting part of it.

The elevator stopped. Vlasov emerged into a carpeted corridor. A plainclothes guard stood back as Vlasov opened the door of his apartment with three keys. He went through the hallway to his study and poured himself a Chivas Regal on ice.

The footnote to the Hunter's report read: "At the end of my duty I returned to the *banya* to check out the identity of the fat man. Luckily he is a regular. His name is Rybak and he is a Ukrainian. That was all they knew."

A Ukrainian. Our Achilles Heel. Well, one of them.

Rybak. If he was a suspected member of the OUN then he would be logged in a computer program. Vlasov picked up the telephone and called Peslyak. It took Peslyak eight minutes to find out. No Rybak in the OUN data.

So they would have to check out every Rybak living in Moscow. Not such a gargantuan task: All the inhabitants of the Soviet Union were somewhere in the computers.

Vlasov called Peslyak again. "Think yourself lucky his name isn't Ivanov," he said. While Peslyak launched into a catalogue of the precautions he had taken to suppress the OUN, Vlasov thought, "Phase Three . . . fat Ukrainian . . . We must take other safeguards."

He interrupted Peslyak. "I want you and Moroz to cooperate on an Indirect Interrogation."

"On whom, Comrade Chairman?"

"On Robert Massey," Vlasov said.

A snatched intake of breath. "When?"

"Now. And Yuri . . ."

"Nicolay?"

"Make good use of that swallow of yours. Let her spread her wings."

She was preceded by a waitress carrying a chromium-plated tray on which stood a bottle of champagne and two long-stemmed glasses.

Here it comes, thought Robert Massey. He began to muster the defensive tactics he had learned at Camp Peary. He wished he was wearing more than slacks and an open-neck shirt, but it was insufferably hot in the room.

"Good evening," said Natasha Uskova smiling at him. "I decided to celebrate."

The waitress shut the door behind her.

"Celebrate what?"

"Your return to space."

"How did you know about that?"

"There was an item about it in *Pravda Ukrainy*." From her purse she took a brief cutting. "There." She handed it to him. "Perhaps you have connections in the Ukraine?"

"None." He glanced at the clipping. It could have been printed specially for this evening.

"Well, the Ukrainians know all about you." She pointed at the bottle. "Will you open it, please?"

150

While he unscrewed the wire and began to prize off the cork, she sat down and crossed her breathtaking legs. She wore a red, knitted dress, buttoned from breast to hem, and black, ankle-strapped shoes. Her glossy black hair was parted in the middle, the bow of her lips was exaggerated with wet-look lipstick, and her eyeliner was extravagantly applied. In the West her appearance would have been considered old-fashioned but in Russia style was dateless. Indisputably she was dressed for seduction. Effectively for a man who hadn't had sex for months. Not that he would succumb: He had been trained not to.

The cork hit the ceiling. Champagne fizzed. He poured it frothing into the two glasses. "*Nasdarovya,* here's to you." She stood up. They touched glasses. They were so close that he could feel her body heat. She sat down again.

Massey sat on a green sofa opposite her. "Did you ever hear again from Herr Brasack?" he asked conversationally.

"No, he went to Rocket City to write an article. I expect he'll contact me when he returns." Changing the subject from the very boring (and very dead) Herr Brasack, she asked, "So, what do you think of Soviet women, Robert?"

The *Robert* sounded incongruous.

"You see a lot of them but you don't see a lot of them."

She frowned.

"They're all wrapped up for winter."

She understood, carried the feeble joke a step further. "And underneath, I'm afraid, a lot of them are still all wrapped up. Too much bread, too many potatoes. But we're changing," she said, leaning forward. Somehow the top button of her dress had come undone and he could see her breasts. "We're finding ourselves, becoming more feminine."

"Women's Lib?"

"Up to a point. But we've always had a sort of equality. Lenin was all for it. You know, we do the same work as the men. The trouble is that married women have to come home and become housewives as well. Do two jobs while the man only does one."

"While he sits with his feet up watching television?"

"Or tilting the vodka bottle."

"You should visit parts of Brooklyn."

"But we are beginning to assert ourselves. No help in the house, no . . ." She hesitated.

"Sex?"

"Affection." She smiled demurely, a contradiction of the undone button. "Could I have some more champagne, Robert?"

As he refilled the glasses, she said, "Russian men are becoming much more sophisticated in their attitude to women. At least the *nachalstvo* are," she corrected herself. "A peasant will always be a peasant. The *nachalstvo,* well,

151

they have learned from the West how to treat women. Are you married, Robert?" she asked abruptly.

"Was."

"You didn't leave anyone behind?"

"Sure I left someone behind."

"But it doesn't matter all that much?"

He drank champagne, shaking his head at the same time. They had taught him to renounce all ties.

"You must get very lonely."

A delightful euphemism. "Not too much." By now she must suspect that he was either gay or a eunuch.

"You're a very attractive man."

When he didn't reply she followed that up with, "I find you so, anyway. You exude—is that the right word?—virility."

"It's the moustache," he said.

"You look as if you've suffered. Your face has contradictions."

She finished her champagne. "Here, let me," she said as he stretched out a hand to pour them both more. "Equality." She smiled at him, stood up and, with her back to him, poured the champagne.

His mistake, he realized a few minutes later, had been to let her pour the champagne while shielding the glasses with her body.

Stupid!

The words of an instructor at Camp Peary, a willowy young pharmacologist, came back to him: "Don't get totally sold on modern techniques. A few of the old tricks still work. So don't let the bastards slug your drink."

Well, he had let the bitch slug it. And it was too late to take evasive action—"Stick your fingers down your throat and throw up"—but, because he had realized what had happened, it wasn't too late to resist.

"Even if you are dumb enough to take a slugged drink you've still got a lot going for you," the instructor had told him. "You've got the truth going for you. Force yourself to concentrate on what we did to you. The CIA, the Company, those fucks."

Those fucks, he thought as she led him on folding legs to the bed. The ceiling wavered and he was so cold. Drugs. CIA or KGB, it was always drugs.

Closing his eyes, he saw the rim of the moon that was the earth. The stars chimed. If you had been up there you were different.

Drugs were dragging him to the threshold of madness again. *If I topple over this time I shall never return.*

The almost naked figure on the bed moaned. With practiced hands she removed his shirt and underpants. Then began to take off her own clothes.

He opened his eyes. The stars withdrew. Her breasts were full, swinging as she undressed. Garter belt, panties, stockings. . . . She touched her breasts, smoothed her flat belly.

With her naked body pressed against him she said, "Robert"—not *Roberto*—"why did you come to the Soviet Union?"

Those fucks! "Because of what they did to me."

"Who?"

"The Company, the CIA."

"What did they do to you, Robert?"

He told her.

Closed his eyes. The nose of the spaceship was pointing at the moon that was the earth and it was rushing toward them. The earth was out of control. *When it fills the screen in front of me I will be mad.*

Her breasts filled the screen. A hand was stroking his belly, inching downward, bringing warmth. "Who is the Ukrainian, Robert?"

"They shot me full of drugs, the bastards."

"The Ukrainian."

"And told me I was crazy. Do you think I'm crazy?"

"Do you want to make love, Robert?"

"I'm as sane as . . ."

"If you tell me about the Ukrainian we can . . ."

". . . you are."

The earth had almost filled the screen. It was spinning. Oceans and continents melted. A spinning top. One color. Green.

"Open your eyes, Robert."

Fingers opening them. Returning to his crotch. "You like me doing this? Ah, I can see you do. And this?" The warm wetness of her mouth.

Those fucks! But not much longer . . .

A door opened. *In my mind? The door to insanity? No, a real door.*

A man's voice, a lascivious whisper. "Down again, that's fine." An intake of breath. A flash.

"He's a spy, isn't he?"

"A spy? Who's a spy?"

"The Ukrainian."

Hatred dispersing. He reached out for its last tattered fragments.

"That's why I came to Russia."

"The truth, Robert. You want to be inside me, don't you?"

"Ah the truth." *You've got the truth going for you.* "You want the truth?"

"That's all. Then I want you inside me. I want you so much."

Another voice. "Give me his jacket."

"Then you shall have the truth."

"Oh, Robert."

Another flash.

The spinning globe was obliterating the screen, only a perimeter of light left.

"The truth is that I wanted to share."

"To share what, Robert? Quickly, I'm so excited."

"The stars."

Her breasts were above him. She was kneeling astride him.

"The real truth. Tell me now while I . . . ah, there . . . filling me . . . so big and strong . . ."

Hatred, where is the hatred?

Only a rim of light on the screen.

The globe a spinning blur.

Madness.

"Tell me. I'm going to stop now if you don't tell me. Now, just before you . . ."

He shuddered.

The spinning globe receded.

He smiled up at her. "Rosa," he said.

Later that night another fragment from Camp Peary surfaced. "After drugs look for bugs."

He found the tiny microphone sewn into the lapel of his jacket. He decided not to remove it; instead he crushed it with his foot. An accident.

But why did they still suspect him?

14

FRAMED between the Presidential flag and the Stars and Stripes, the President gazed through the bow windows of the White House's Oval Office at the Rose Garden.

"Good morning, George," he said without turning around. "Where do you think we should talk. Out there?" pointing at the lawns sugared with frost.

Wearing topcoats and scarves, observed at a respectful distance by two Secret Service men, they strolled across the lawn, shoes crushing the frost glittering in the sunshine.

"An appropriate setting," the President remarked. "This is where the first team of American astronauts was received. Well, how's it going?" voice as crisp as the frost.

Reynolds was wearing spectacles. The lenses were plain glass, a defensive disguise. "Tight," he said. "I looked at the latest satellite pictures of Tyuratam this morning, and the Dove isn't even on the pad yet."

They turned at the end of the lawn on which, in recent years, everyone from a Chinese table tennis delegation to Queen Elizabeth II had been received.

The awkward question from the President came as they began to walk beside a boxwood hedge toward the colonnade. "How much longer can we stall?"

"Maybe a month. You see we always figured that they'd launch *Dove Mark II* in mid-January. Now it's beginning to look as though we might have been premature."

"So?"

"We'll have to box pretty damn clever."

"Elaborate, George."

"Well, we've fooled them twice so far. The next time they'll want something more convincing than a rocket abort immediately after a launch. They'll want"—Reynolds smiled thinly—"a spectacular."

"Can we give them one?"

"That depends on our budget, Mr. President."

"How much?"

"Ten million, give or take."

The President was silent. Budget, Reynolds thought, was the key word to silencing presidents. A jet crayoned a white line across the sky. Above the pulse of the city, Reynolds fancied he could hear carols being played. There were two more shopping days to Christmas.

The President said, "A spectacular always costs a lot. But think of the returns."

"If it's a smash," Reynolds said.

"We'll have to write off the cost against NASA military contingency funds."

"In that case," Reynolds said, "we're still in with a chance. But we need to delay as long as possible."

As they turned again the President glanced at his wristwatch. "We'll have to hurry it up," he said. "I've got a meeting with the Voice of Democracy scriptwriting winners in ten minutes."

Reynolds said, "To help Massey delay things, I've instructed Gordon to leave a one-word coded message in his private computer indicating that he's sick. In other words he won't be able to supply the codes for that day for the Vandenberg central processor. The Russians will just have to wait and that will give us a little more time."

"They're going to love that," the President said.

"Then we'll give them their spectacular."

"When?"

"I figure we should be able to stall them until the New Year. If they make the critical contact on January first then they can have it on the second." Reynolds looked speculatively at the President through his plain glass lenses. "One U.S. satellite knocked out of orbit should keep them happy for a while, shouldn't it?"

"A satellite, George?"

"Yes, sir," Reynolds said firmly. "That's what they'll have at the top of their list, I'll stake my job on it."

"If this doesn't work you won't have a job to stake. And neither will I if anyone gets to hear the details."

"Time is everything," Reynolds said. "After they've zapped the satellite, then they'll want to clinch our final destruction. We'll just have to string them along as best we can."

"And if they postpone the launch after, say, the beginning of February?"

"We've lost," Reynolds said.

"And Massey?"

"We've lost him too."

They stopped outside the French windows of the Oval Office. "But surely," the President said, "Massey himself should know when they're going to launch the Dove?"

Reynolds identified the carol reaching them above the noise of the traffic. "Oh Come All Ye Faithful." "The trouble," he said carefully, "is that since making contact with the Ukrainian, Massey has been out of touch."

Massey had tried to keep in touch. He had walked to Gorky Park to meet Rybak. It had been a sunny day, gold and ermine, and the chess players had emerged. Despite the cold, they sat at the line of battered tables moving their pieces with mittened fingers.

Cherry-nosed children followed by sedate parents skated along the footpaths; the ferris wheel was still, frozen until spring. In the background, small figures skied down the Lenin Hills.

Massey felt Christmas. Heard it on the cries of the children and the swish of their skates. Except that here there was no Christmas, only New Year. But the spirit was the same, delayed a week.

It was midday. But of the fat Ukrainian there was no sign. Massey walked up and down the line of players, men of all ages, no women. Those confident of a tactical advantage leaned back in their seats sunning themselves, while their opponents brooded darkly.

Massey stopped at a vacant table. A small man wearing a leather hat with flapping earpieces and yards of gray wool scarf around his neck pointed at the board, "You play?"

Massey shook his head.

The man's tone hardened. "Today you play," he said, sitting down.

Massey sat down. The man produced a box of chess pieces from the pocket of his navy jacket and set them up; then he held out two fists. Massey touched the left. White.

The man, whose face was lined, bristles missed by the razor buried in the creases, said in heavily accented English, "You have the advantage, *Gaspa-deen* Massey." His eyes—like dark wet pebbles, Massey thought—were focused on the board.

Massey moved P-K4. He knew how to move the pieces, that was about all. His opponent did the same.

Massey cast his mind back to college when he had last played and, wondering "Who told him my name?" moved his king's knight.

"So far so good."

"Who are you?"

"It is a mistake to talk while playing chess." He moved a knight. "I like to play black. I enjoy being on the defensive."

Massey moved a bishop.

"Ah."

A brilliancy or a disaster?

His opponent moved his queen's pawn, glanced at the players on either side, and, voice lowered, said, "When playing white you are always one move ahead."

"I did know that."

"Which means you must always look behind you."

Involuntarily Massey looked behind. There was no one there.

His opponent stuck a *papyros,* a cigarette with a hollow cardboard filter, between his lips. He struck a match. Over cupped hands, he said, "In this instance, look to your right but take your time. First make your move." He extinguished the match, inhaled, and blew a cloud of smoke into the sunlight.

Massey moved his second knight, yawned, and glanced lazily to his right. His opponent murmured, "Last table, by himself."

A young man came up to the last table but the sleek-haired, powerfully built man sitting there dismissed him with a wave of his hand.

Behind Massey a little girl on skates fell on the ice, now glossed with water by the sun. She was picked up, dusted down, and launched again, wobbling, on the footpath.

Three moves later Massey castled.

His opponent nodded, coughing up smoke. "Perhaps a little premature?" And whispered, "Rybak says you must shake your tail off. He will meet you the day after tomorrow at *Dietsky Mir* toy shop. Same time. My move? I'm sorry, I wasn't concentrating." He moved his queen with a plundering swoop.

Massey leaned forward and, conceding defeat, turned over his king.

His opponent inclined his head and was gone, trailing cigarette smoke.

Massey stood up, stretched, and strolled toward the frozen river. Five minutes, later he turned to pat the head of a boy on skates who had cannoned into him. Momentarily he saw the man who had been sitting at the end of the line of chessboards, before he dissolved, like a melting snowflake, into the crowds.

Massey turned and headed toward the main gate. Ahead of him that day lay a series of fitness tests. And Phase Three.

The tests were carried out at the Gagarin Cosmonaut Training Center at Zvezdny Gorodok, Star Town, forty miles to the northeast of Moscow, close to Chkalov Air Force base.

Set in a pine forest, Star Town consists of a nucleus of high-rise apartments, well-stocked stores, and recreation centers adjoining the actual training premises. In the center of the apartment blocks stands a statue of Yury Gagarin and close by, in the Cosmonaut Museum, a replica of his study.

As Massey and Nicolay Talin made their way through the dusk to the old red Moskvich in the training center's parking lot, mist created by the brief thaw swirled around them.

"A good thing you had your tests this afternoon," Talin remarked. "By tomorrow you'll have pneumonia." He searched his pockets for the car keys. "What did they examine you for today?"

Massey began to recite. "Visual acuity, Neurocirculatory conditions, auditory function, water electrolyte balance. . . Do you want to hear more?"

"Disorientation?"

Massey glanced at him. "Not today."

They reached the car. With a plastic scraper, Talin scraped the frost from the windshield. "Did you pass everything?"

"You know perfectly well that they'd pass me if I had a wooden leg. They're going to make a showpiece out of me."

"Then we're both showpieces," Talin said. Sedov, he thought, is my tamer; Massey is the call of the wild.

He slid the key into the lock. It was already freezing and he had to twist hard. He eased himself behind the wheel, unlocking the passenger door from the inside. "Did you know," he said as Massey sat beside him, "they told me to buy a new car? Part of the image. But I refused, I like this little red devil and it would take months to tune a new engine as well as this."

The engine fired throatily; clouds of exhaust joined the mist.

As the Moskvich accelerated toward Moscow, Talin said, "I received good news today." He paused, negotiating a long, slithering bend. "They gave me a date for the launch. It was to have been February 23. But they've brought it forward. Apparently someone in the Ministry of Defense, possibly Tarkovsky himself, wanted to fire Sedov and me on New Year's Day."

"But that's much too early, you wouldn't have time . . ."

"So they compromised. January 14."

"Even that doesn't give you time to get ready."

"You forget, we've done it before. There aren't many differences. Not from the flying point of view. Only the return-to-orbit procedure if anything goes wrong when we reenter the earth's atmosphere. Do the Americans know about that?"

"Oh yes," Massey said, "they know about that, all right."

A red light loomed out of the mist. Talin braked, felt the locked wheels continue forward on the ice. They stopped directly beneath the light slung across the road.

Massey said, "What's it like driving in Siberia?"

"It's better by troika," Talin told him. "Except in the cities."

"You were born in Khabarovsk?"

"Just outside." Talin switched up the heat. "You once told me that you had read about me in the United States. But, although we've seen quite a lot of each other recently, you've never elaborated."

Massey was silent.

The lights changed to green. The wheels spun, gripped.

"Well?"

"I know you were born October the tenth, nineteen fifty."

"Some memory."

"I remember because we're both Libra."

"You believe in that stuff?"

Massey shook his head. "You don't believe in such things after you've been in space. You know that."

"What else did you read about me?"

"There was an article in *Aviation Week and Space Technology*. You seemed to be emerging as a personality; the editor was obviously intrigued, because that's not allowed, is it?"

"It's all right," Talin said, braking again as a set of rear lights materialized in front of them, "if you're a footballer or a poet or a cosmonaut." He remembered a conversation with Sedov in a bar when Sedov had stopped him from talking about the Cult of Personality within the Kremlin. "Did the article reach any conclusions?"

"They obviously dug."

"Dug?"

"They found out a lot about you. When you were a kid you were a rebel, right?"

"A lot of kids are."

"I guess it had something to do with your father."

Talin frowned. Why should it? "My father?"

"You were very fond of him?"

"He died when I was twelve."

"Time enough to get very fond of him."

"I don't follow you," Talin said.

"It must have been a shock, the way . . . he . . . died."

"The way he died?"

"Let's not go into it," Massey said abruptly.

"Let's. He died from pneumoconiosis, the miner's disease."

"According to the article," Massey said, "he died from radiation sickness."

"In a coal mine?"

"In a cobalt mine."

"You're crazy."

"Persecution didn't end in 1953 with Stalin's death," Massey said.

"Are you saying he was killed deliberately?"

"Many 'enemies of the State' were given the choice of immediate execution or slow death in a cobalt mine."

Icy calm, hands gripping the steering wheel, Talin asked, "What makes you think, what made this magazine think, that my father was guilty of a crime against the State?"

They were nearing the outskirts of Moscow. Tall apartments loomed through the mist.

Massey said, "The magazine seemed to have access to a lot of information."

"With sources?"

"I don't see why they should have made it up."

"And what was my father supposed to have done?"

"Protested, I guess. That was enough."

"Protested? Protested about what?"

"About overcrowding, bad food in winter, conditions in the coal mine where he worked before he was sent to the cobalt mine. . . . He was something of a rabble-rouser, your father. He was tried before No. 2 District People's Court in Khabarovsk on November 8, 1962, before Judge Zina Orlova."

"And sentenced to death for protesting? Don't give me that shit."

Talin spun the wheel viciously. The Moskvich skidded around a corner. Talin drove into the skid, righting it.

Massey said, "He was accused of embezzling government property. Stealing coal, maybe, who knows. Anyway they were determined to make an example of him. The charge carried the death penalty."

"And you took the word of a journalist about this?"

A pause. The mist was clearing. Talin could see an illuminated red star over the Kremlin.

Massey said softly, "No, I checked it out myself."

"Who with?"

"Contacts. It's all true, Nicolay."

"I don't believe it. Why are you telling me this?"

"You should know the truth."

"My father would have told me the truth."

"I doubt it, Nicolay. Would you have told your son such a truth?"

"I would have found out. Even if my mother hadn't told me the other kids would have done." *No, they moved us to Novosibirsk!* "I don't believe it," he shouted, jamming his foot on the accelerator as a motorcycle without rear lights cut across their path, as he braked, as the Moskvich skidded broadside across black ice and somersaulted over a snow-covered embankment.

Dyetsky Mir, the huge toy shop opposite Lubyanka Gaol and the KGB headquarters, was packed.

Gingerly, Robert Massey eased his way through the crowds. The rib cracked in yesterday's automobile accident throbbed with pain and his body ached all over.

He discovered that the areas nearest the counters were the safest because there some orderliness prevailed. The shoppers had to line up while a salesgirl calculated their bill on an abacus. Armed with the bill, they had to line up at the cashier, then again to collect their purchases.

Massey was conscious of the cuts and bruises on his face but few Muscovites, intent on buying New Year gifts for their children, took any notice.

Exactly where Rybak would make contact hadn't been stated. Massey skirted counters stacked with rag dolls, toy rifles consisting of a metal pipe, a slab of wood, and a trigger, model rockets as primitive as the real Soviet hardware was refined.

The toys were crude, but did it matter? If a child was unaware of the sophisticated playthings of the West he was happy with these. And if Santa Claus was Grandfather Frost in a silver robe and tinselled hat, so what?

"You look as if you've been through a combine harvester," Rybak said, materializing beside him. "What happened?"

Massey told him as the Ukrainian led him through the crowds; they parted before him like demonstrators facing a baton charge.

"And Talin, how is he?"

"A few bruises. We were lucky."

"He knows how to pilot a spaceship but he doesn't know how to drive a car. Strange, isn't it? What have you to report?"

Massey stopped at a counter and picked up a toy revolver, its butt jewelled with a plastic red star. "The launch is on January 14." He pulled the trigger, nothing happened.

"Is that all?"

"At the next penetration, they are going to program our computers for an ASAT attack on one of our own satellites."

"ASAT?"

"Anti-satellite device."

"Which satellite?"

"Elint 23."

"Anything else?"

"Tell them Phase Three has been accomplished."

First hit, with devastating revelation, preferably personal.

The car was turning over and over; excited voices, hands pulling him out on to the snow.

"Anything more?"

Massey shook his head. Nothing more except that I am destroying a man's past and his future.

Rybak's fingers gripped Massey's arm. "I said the next meeting will have to be in Leninsk. What the hell's the matter? Are you concussed?"

"Where?"

"There is a church beside the railroad, a mile from the station to the west. Next Saturday. Six in the evening. But shake off your tail again. Did you have any trouble today?"

"It was still misty. I lost him in Gorky Street."

"And now I shall lose myself, not an easy task when you're my size."

But he managed it easily enough.

One life destroyed but millions saved, Massey reminded himself—if, that was, everything Reynolds had told him was true.

Comforted, Massey made his way toward the main door of the store, reflecting that so far, road accidents apart, the campaign was proceeding smoothly. It wasn't until that evening that he heard that Talin had disappeared.

15

TALIN had to know the truth.

To find it he had to reach Khabarovsk, 4,000 miles east of Moscow, and to get there he had to employ both guile and arrogance.

First the arrogance to bypass travel restrictions. In his experience, Soviet bureaucracy was so cumbersome that it could easily be toppled.

If he had been a peasant, a clerk, or a factory hand it would have been difficult. But he was élite, a cosmonaut, a Hero, with the ID to prove it.

He went direct to the Aeroflot headquarters at 49/51 Leningrad Highway. At the booking counter, a stout woman with lacquered blonde hair regarded him phlegmatically.

He told her that he wanted to fly to Khabarovsk. She reached for various forms but when he added, "Tonight," her hand stopped over the papers.

"Impossible."

"No seats?"

She shrugged: It was impossible.

Knowing that Aeroflot would always throw a humble citizen off an aircraft to make way for a VIP or a tourist from the West, Talin showed her his ID.

She was impressed. Recognition flitted across her features. Nervously she patted her helmet of hair. "Even so, it is impossible, Comrade Talin, because there is a delegation of geologists on the scheduled flight. There is no room."

Fine, Talin thought, he had no wish to travel on the scheduled flight. He sighed—and switched to guile. "I might just as well be trying to fly to Mongolia."

She smiled, joining in the spirit of the thing. "Ah, there you would have no trouble. There are plenty of seats on the flight to Ulan Bator."

Talin pounced. "Then book me on it."

"But . . ."

"If I'm not mistaken Flight SU-563 to Ulan Bator stops at Omsk and Irkutsk. Book me to Irkutsk." From there it would be easy to pick up a connection to Khabarovsk.

She snatched his ID and disappeared. She returned with the manager who asked Talin why he was flying at such short notice. When Talin told him it was the wish of the First Deputy Commander-in-Chief of the Soviet Air Force, the manager retreated swiftly leaving the blonde woman to cope.

With dimpled fingers she fed his requirements into the desk computer. When the answers came back, she took his money and gave him a ticket.

So he was through their first line of defenses. But he could still be stopped at the airport. Finding him gone, Sonya would be worried—he had been told to rest after the accident—and might contact Sedov. Sedov, knowing that he was due at Leninsk the following day, would contact Aeroflot. Hopefully, they would check departures for Khabarovsk from the domestic airport whereas he would be taking an international flight from Sheremtyevo. There could be trouble at Omsk and Irkutsk, but he possessed deep reserves of guile and swagger.

It was 6 P.M. Three hours and twenty minutes until takeoff. He walked down Leningrad Highway and went into a clinical, neon-lit café. He sat down with a cup of steaming hot coffee, to rest his aching body. "I don't believe what Massey told me," he thought. "They can't have deceived me for twenty years."

Half an hour later he stopped a passing taxi and told the driver to take him to Sheremetyevo.

He didn't report directly to the check-in desk; instead, sharklike, he circled the departure lounge with its marble columns and silver ceilings. It was said that you could always identify a KGB agent by his smart new shoes (Sedov being the exception), but there was no outstanding footwear among the fur-clad Mongols and Muscovite officials lining up for Flight SU-563.

Just before the deadline for check-in, Talin presented his ticket. The dark-haired girl behind the counter raised an eyebrow. "Ulan Bator, Comrade Talin? It must be much the same as the moon," telling him that she had recognized him.

He was given a window seat on the Tupolev 154. The aircraft was only half full and the seat next to him was empty. The engines fired. The aircraft rolled forward, taxied to the end of the runway. The engines screamed. Talin stared through the window at the black and white film of the night flashing past. The aircraft tilted, and he was on his way back to his childhood.

The village near Khabarovsk was a poor place. With its wooden cottages, fretworked eaves painted pink and blue, it was pretty enough when it was washed by rain, but more often than not it was grimed with coal-dust and in the winter it snowed gray snow.

But its grubbiness emphasized the beauty of its boundless surroundings, the *taiga,* where among the forests of birch, larch, and pine shaggy tigers hunted spotted deer, beavers, and wild sheep; where, from the melting permafrost, the pale people from the cities dug edible roots to keep them young; where, from the River Amur on the border with China, fishermen netted gasping sturgeon fat with roe.

Nicolay's father was an overseer at the mine; his mother worked there too, sorting nuggets on the conveyor belts in between cooking meals in the *izba* they shared with another family, next to the village well. In the summer, food was plentiful, bloody meat from the *taiga,* berries, black bread, and fish; in the winter the soup course lasted from November till April.

Being the only child of middle-aged parents, Nicolay was spoiled. On weekends he went hunting, trapping, horseriding, and fishing with his father, who had black hair and black eyes and black crystals under the skin of his hands. In the evenings his mother, a plump, jolly woman who sang the sad songs of Siberia with great zeal, taught him to read and write so that when, at the age of seven, he attended Work Polytechnical School 14 in Khabarovsk he immediately impressed his teachers.

When he got home at night after a work-crammed day—he was an Octobrist at seven, a Young Pioneer at nine—he was exhausted. After a summer steak or a winter soup, he tied himself in his sleeping bag in the room he shared with three other children and listened to his father and his friends uncorking the vodka bottle and their emotions around the coal-burning stove in the living room. As he retreated into sleep he sometimes heard anger rasping their rowdy good humor, heard oaths spilling from their lips.

Where, they demanded, was the equality they had been promised in the October Revolution? Where were the fruits of the Great Patriotic War that they had won? Was eight in one *izba* a decent way to live? And while they caroused and berated, while the coal spat and flared, it seemed to Nicolay that injustice also had something to do with a mother who sorted the good coal from the bad and had to make do with the bad.

Nicolay liked all these white-skinned, carbolic-smelling men, save one named Konstantin. He was inward looking, always listening. Nicolay knew this because he rarely heard his voice, although none of the other men seemed to realize this, not when they were intent upon washing the coal-dust from their throats with vodka.

One late afternoon after the day shift had been hauled to the surface, his father didn't return home. Nor did his friends call that night. Next morning, although his mother stayed at home, the cottage had an emptiness about it that at first Nicolay, on holiday from school, couldn't identify; then he realized that it was her songs that were missing.

That evening Konstantin called. Nicolay and the other children were banished to the bedroom. He heard his mother crying. Then the sound of breaking glass. When he opened the door an inch he saw Konstantin, blood streaming from his cheek, facing his mother. On the floor was a broken vodka bottle. Then Konstantin was gone.

His mother told him that his father had gone to Khabarovsk to be trained in the use of new coal-cutting machines. When he returned three weeks later, he was different, all the fun squeezed out of him. He told Nicolay that he had been promoted, but he would have to go away for a while to another mine.

They went fishing that day in a hole cut in the ice on the Amur, and they caught big fish with tails that snapped like whip-lashes. For a while, as the wind from the *taiga* polished his cheeks, the fun returned to his father. All the time two men stood in the background; miners going north with him, his father explained.

Outside the *izba* his father knelt and hugged him and said gruffly, "Look after your mother, Nicolay. Remember those fish we caught and the other times in the *taiga*." He didn't follow Nicolay into the cottage and Nicolay never saw him again.

How can I have been so stupid all these years? Talin asked himself, waving away the stewardess with the plate of food.

Easy. At twelve you ask a lot of questions, you accept the answers, and they lodge as facts. "Why have we moved to Novosibirsk?" "Because it's nearer to the mine where Papa's working."

A cobalt mine! Bastards.

"When are we going to see Papa?" "When he's finished this new course . . ."

"Passed on . . . What do you mean, passed on?" "He became sick, a certain sort of sickness, it happens to a lot of miners . . ."

Radiation sickness, cobalt miners. Bastards.

But how—and why—had they persuaded his mother to suppress the truth about her husband's death? Talin could hear their voices, "Your son's bright, he has a great future, don't blight his chances. Keep quiet and we'll look after you both in Novosibirsk." When she was old they had given her an apartment back in Khabarovsk. "There's no point in telling him the truth now. You don't want to lose that comfortable home of yours, do you?"

Could the authorities really have predicted that I was destined for the stars when I was only thirteen? According to Sedov, yes. They could spot a winner at ten.

But none of this is true. I am flying to Khabarovsk to see my mother and she will tell me it's all lies and then I shall go back to Leninsk, face the music, and return to *Dove.*

"I'm afraid," Oleg Sedov said, sitting down beside him, "that I'm going to be that notorious travel pest, the talker."

It was from Sonya Bragina that Robert Massey heard that Talin was missing. Not missing exactly, she said over the telephone, but not where he should be—in bed recovering from the accident.

Massey guessed immediately where Talin had gone and he wondered if the story Reynolds had supplied about Talin's father had been wholly true. Or whether, having discovered that he had worked in a cobalt mine, CIA Dirty Tricks had improvised, inventing his crime and his punishment.

Surely not everyone who worked in a cobalt mine was a miscreant sentenced to slow death?

If Talin discovers the story is false, then Reynolds's spectacular is a flop. Talin will denounce me, the computer deception will grind to a halt, and I will be sentenced to death.

In a cobalt mine?

"How did you find me?" Talin asked dully.

"You were under surveillance," Sedov said. "For your own good."

"Did you think I might be kidnapped?"

"You're a valuable property." Sedov's tone was light, but his dark, Slav features were even tighter than usual. His eyes looked tired, and he needed a shave. "I didn't authorize the surveillance. The order came from the top."

"And you found out about it?"

"Of course, cosmonauts are my business."

"And you took over?"

"I wouldn't dare to do that. But one of the failings of the KGB is that it's so over-staffed that authority is confused. I merely told your surveillance team to keep in touch with me."

"Which doesn't explain how you got on this plane."

"It wasn't difficult. Your shadow at Sheremyetevo didn't intend to board it anyway. He was merely going to tell headquarters to advise Omsk and Irkutsk."

"But he'll report my departure."

"I told him not to hurry because I was going to be on the plane. There's great scope for pulling rank in the KGB."

"And when he does report?"

Sedov shrugged. "I can handle that. Why shouldn't we fly together? We go into orbit together."

"Why should we fly together to Khabarovsk when we're both supposed to be at Leninsk tomorrow?"

Sedov said quietly, "I'm not flying to Khabarovsk," and added, "Nor are you."

"You can stop me, of course." Talin touched the sleeve of Sedov's shabby jacket. "But I'm asking you, Oleg, not to. I can't explain why."

"I know why."

Then it was true! "How can you possibly know?"

"Because there's only one possible explanation—your father. Which is why I didn't take the easy way and just stop you boarding the plane. I wanted time to talk to you alone. Peacefully, without a scene at the airport."

Words shrivelled in Talin's mouth. Sedov beckoned the hovering stewardess, who knew that they both carried red passbooks, and ordered a coffee and brandy. Talin asked for a vodka.

"You should have told your wife," Sedov remarked.

"She would have tried to stop me. Just as you're going to. You can use physical force but there's nothing you can say that will change anything."

But there was. Sedov had brought a surprise with him. The Truth. It couldn't be anything else, Talin decided as he listened.

It was true, Sedov confirmed, that Talin's father had been convicted of embezzling State property, true that he had been sentenced to death, true that the sentence had been commuted to hard labor in a cobalt mine, the double-talk for slow death.

"Listen to me, Nicolay," Sedov said. "Listen!" Half command, half plea. "That was a long time ago. It was a terrible injustice, it can never be put right. Your father should be alive today . . ."

Remember those fish we caught and the other times in the taiga.

Talin's eyes stung.

"But things have got better since then. There is still injustice, true. Everywhere in the world there is injustice. But the Soviet people have never known such good times. For the first time in their history they have sufficient. That's what the West doesn't understand: for us sufficiency is a miracle."

Talin was silent: He hadn't expected a confession. The aircraft bucked in turbulence; they were over the Urals, the portals of Siberia.

The drinks brought by the stewardess had spilled on to her tray; she apologized. As she departed, swaying expertly with the turbulence, Sedov said, "And we have peace."

"Through force. *Nasdarovya*." Talin tossed back the vodka.

"Through strength. Peace has never been won through weakness." Sedov was painstakingly carving out his words. "And you are one of the men who will project it into space. You'll be in command of its flagship. *Dove*."

"There's nothing wrong with your sentiments," Talin said as the aircraft bucked again. "But I'm still flying to Khabarovsk."

A new note of urgency entered Sedov's voice. "Look," he said, "the car crash was bad enough, but Aerospace has accepted your explanation—black ice, a motorcyclist without lights. . . . If they get the idea that you're emotionally unbalanced, then you can forget the launch. Fly to Khabarovsk and you'll never see space again. In any case," voice softening, "you'd only upset your mother. Why don't you leave it till you come back? Then fly out there with Sonya."

He was right, of course, Sonya . . . Talin remembered the man in the fawn suit who kept materializing during their honeymoon.

Surveillance!

Belatedly, the stewardess told them over the PA to fasten their safety belts because of the turbulence. As she spoke the aircraft dipped like a plunging elevator.

Sedov said, "Who told you about your father?"

Remembering that Massey had also told him the truth, Talin said, "I received a letter from Khabarovsk."

The stewardess returned to the PA: "We are now beginning our descent to Omsk . . ."

Apparently satisfied by the explanation, Sedov said, "Which is where we shall spend the night with Andrei Dyomin, the retired cosmonaut we've always been intending to visit. Then we'll take the early morning flight to Tashkent where there's a connection to Leninsk."

Talin said, "But I've got a ticket to Ulan Bator."

"Yet another computer error," Sedov said, taking another ticket from his pocket and handing it to Talin.

16

IN his mind Nicolay Vlasov had worked out a timetable.

Today, New Year's Eve party with the President; possible showdown with Tarkovsky.

Jan. 1. Critical Vandenberg penetration.

Jan. 2. Proof that penetration has been successful.

Jan. 13. Definitive penetration.

Jan. 14. Devastating proof that final penetration has succeeded.

The last two dates weren't positive. But certainly the whole operation had to be concluded by January 14 because that was Tarkovsky's new date for the Dove launching, brought forward to impress the President—old men admire speed. And what timing: The dramatic Soviet step into space synchronizing with the destruction of all America's cosmic ambitions.

Or put another way, Vlasov thought, drumming his fingers on his desk, I have fourteen days in which to avert a holocaust.

But several suspicions, the crosses he had to bear, were already grouping to threaten the too-neat timetable.

Firstly Massey.

The seduction. Vlasov pressed the start button on the tape recorder in his office.

"Why did you come to the Soviet Union?"

"Because of what they did to me."

"Who?"

"The Company, the CIA."

Vlasov speeded up the tape.

"Who is the Ukranian, Robert?"

"They shot me full of drugs, those bastards."

Vlasov remembered the advice he had been given long ago, "Whatever form the interrogation takes, concentrate on a truth divorced from the questions."

Which was what Massey had been doing.

On the other hand what else could he say if he was genuine? If he didn't know who the Ukranian was? Careful, Vlasov, lest your suspicions wreck the whole operation.

The photographer was taking the pictures now. Routine—there might be a use for them some day. The KGB had the most comprehensive archives of pornography in the world.

Without emotion, Vlasov imagined the girl lowering herself on to Massey.

"The truth is that I wanted to share."

"To share what, Robert? Quickly, I'm so excited."

That was the trouble: She had been excited and she had finished the exercise too quickly. Peslyak had employed an amateur.

"The stars."

That sounded convincing too, tallied with what he had said during his initial interrogations. To all intents and purposes Massey was exonerated from any suspicion.

And yet everything he said was too pat. What, then, Nicolay Vlasov, is the point of these tests if you don't accept them?

Massey had smashed the microphone in his lapel.

An accident. He couldn't have kinown it was there because the drug they had used obliterates aural reception.

Unless Massey had been trained to take antisurveillance action after a compromise.

Impatiently, Vlasov pressed the STOP button. He was fast becoming paranoiac.

The Rybak lead had evaporated, as of course it would have done if Massey was genuine. *Which he is!*

But what about the meeting between Massey and the Estonian named Nosenko over the chessboard in Gorky Park?

Vlasov slotted another tape into the recorder. It began with a scream.

Then a reassuring voice, "Sorry, comrade, we were a little hasty. We won't switch on the current again if you tell us the truth."

"What truth? I don't know what you're talking about."

"What was the message for Massey?"

"Massey? Who's Massey?"

"Who won the game of chess?"

"I did . . ."

"Wasn't Massey any good?"

"He was lousy but what . . ."

"So you do know his name is Massey?"

"I don't know anything. I just played a game of chess with a stranger like anyone does in Gorky Park."

"With a foreigner?"

"Why not?"

Scream.

"Don't get smart, Nosenko, if these electrodes get overheated they'll burn your balls off."

Another voice, "Was the message from the Ukrainian?"

"What fucking Ukrainian?"

"You know what fucking Ukrainian—Rybak."

"Massey, Rybak . . . I don't know any . . . No, please, no . . ."

The scream was louder this time. Vlasov turned down the volume control.

"Now, Nosenko, what was the message?"

The first voice, "Hold it, Mikhail, I think we lost him."

"Shit."

Bunglers! Vlasov stopped the tape. They should have checked his heart before applying the electrodes. More ammunition to be fired in Peslyak's direction.

Quite possibly there hadn't been anything Nosenko could have told them anyway. Why, then, had Massey lost his tail the following day?

It could have been coincidence, of course—there was mist around that day. And Massey had only been lost for eight minutes. Long enough!

You've got to stop this, Vlasov, before they cart you off to a psychiatric clinic. Outside the sun was setting coldly over the white rooftops in plumes of pigeon-gray and pink.

Vlasov pressed the intercom and told his secretary to fetch his hat and coat and tell his driver to bring the Zil to the main intrance.

One last suspicion presented itself unsolicited to Vlasov before he left his office. The last contact with Vandenberg had been aborted because Gordon was allegedly sick. Was his indisposition genuine? Or am I being set up for the biggest intelligence double-cross since ULTRA?

He picked up his hat, straightened his back. To hell with it, he was going to a party.

Frosted snow crunched beneath the wheels of the Zil taking Vlasov and his wife to the President's weekend dacha near Zhukovka. Moonlight added coldness to the night, icing fields of snow, isolating the black pine forest.

Unlike so many Russians, Vlasov didn't like winter. Like Stalin, he was a scheming Georgian, and he loved the sun in which to hatch his plots.

Why Intourist couldn't promote the Soviet summer he couldn't imagine. July in Moscow with the river beaches packed, *kvas* vans in the streets, the scent of carnations (from Georgia) heavy on the air, parks full of families unfurled in the sun . . .

Guards peering into the Zil cut short summer. The driver showed his papers, the militiamen stepped back.

The Zil coasted down the driveway, past relays of guards and electronic warnings, to the presidential dacha, a magnificent anachronism, like a Loire château, with spires and balconies and terrances, its room lit tonight with a festive glow.

In the baronial living room, its walls lined with split pine from Canada, maids circulated among the guests with trays of drinks and *zakuski*. Like all Russian rooms in the winter it was sweating hot, the area around the log fire like a sauna.

Vlasov's wife, regal and distant, immediately joined the Politburo wives sipping sweet champagne and, between gossip, monitoring the alcohol intake of their husbands. One vodka too many, one indiscretion, and they might be transferred to a hydroelectric power station in Khatanga. Except, Vlasov reflected, that these days disgrace would probably be confined to the circle of power: old men had to stick together.

Vlasov, aware that, with his portfolio of secret lives, he was the least popular guest in the dacha, joined the foreign minister.

The President, oblivious to the heat, was standing in front of the fire talking to Tarkovsky who was trying to ignore the sweat trickling down his old, warrior face. The President, Vlasov thought, looked magnificent; his bulkiness exuding resolution, heavy features brooding—an old predator in his lair.

The President beckoned him over. "I want to have a talk with you and Grigory. We will adjourn to my study."

Over their glasses, other members of the Politburo and their wives observed their departure. A council of war on New Year's Eve?

Vlasov recalled his timetable . . . *possible showdown with Tarkovsky.*

The President poured them vodka, in deference to the New Year, and Narzan mineral water and stationed himself in front of another log fire. Now that he was in his den rather than his lair, surrounded by books and trophies and photographs of himself with heads of state including a clutch of American presidents, he looked benign. A deception!

He raised his glass, drank the vodka in one gulp, and quenched its flames with Narzan. "We are at the beginning of a new year, gentlemen, and I think we all suspect it is going to be an unusual one. Grigory tells me that the battleground of man is about to shift to the heavens."

He replenished their glasses. "I'm sorry to strike this somber note at a time of celebration, but we have important problems to solve. You've *both* brought me proposals for maintaining Soviet dominance,"—Tarkovsky looked hard at Vlasov over his vodka glass—"and I think it's only fair that at this time we share our knowledge equally. I'll wager that you, Nikolay, have already discovered everything there is to know about Grigory's plan."

The statement posed the question, and, with a nod and a flicker of a smile, Vlasov admitted it was so. Before Tarkovsky could turn to the KGB chief, the President said to him, "Perhaps at some other time, Grigory, you and I may speculate together on how Nicolay was able to obtain his knowledge when he certainly did not get it from you—or from me for that matter—and, as you've told me so often, you have not divulged your proposal to anyone else."

"Is this the time for humor, Comrade President?" Tarkovsky said.

"Probably not." Turning his head toward Vlasov, the President said, "Tell him about your plan now, Nikolay."

Vlasov suppressed his reluctance and began to relate the scheme Massey had brought them.

Tarkovsky ran his hand over his close-cut gray hair and touched the steel plate in his skull. It had begun to throb. It was his early warning system. "Has it ever occurred to you, comrade, that you're being double-crossed?"

"That is always the first thing that occurs to me, Grigory. That is why we are causing the Americans to destroy their own devices."

The President stood back, sleek and bulky in his well-tailored suit, drinking Narzan and listening to the two men argue.

"What you have destroyed so far, Nikolay, would not impress a lieutenant in one of my Siberian divisions. When is your next penetration?"

"Tomorrow."

"And what will you abort this time?"

"An American spy satellite," the KGB chief said silkily.

"Impressive, however . . ."

"Enough, gentlemen," the President said with one thick forefinger held up. He pointed at Vlasov. "You, Nikolay, have until the second week in January to offer unimpeachable proof that you have penetrated the United States military program in space to such an extent that it can be paralyzed. If not . . ."

"You will launch Grigory's plan?"

"We assemble it," the President said. "It would only be launched if we discovered that the United States was about to take a decisive military initiative."

"You mean attack?"

"It would be up to my advisers to decide what constitutes military initiative," Tarkovsky said with elaborate patience.

Looking past him, Vlasov saw caverns of fire, towns ablaze. The logs shifted, igniting fresh flames. "But they would be guided by you," he thought.

The President tossed back the last of his vodka and put the glass down with finality.

To Vlasov, he said, "It's up to you, Nikolay, to see to it that we need not consider Grigory's more extreme proposal any further."

And to Tarkovsky, "If he fails then I shall not oppose the preparations you must make."

As they walked toward the door, Tarkovsky said to Vlasov, "Are you sure you fully understand what I've proposed to the President?"

"Quite sure," Vlasov replied. "With the fleet of Dove shuttles you intend to build a series of platforms in space equipped with the latest beam weapons that can destroy every Western satellite in orbit."

"That's not . . ."

"Furthermore, you intend to use the Doves themselves to launch nuclear attacks on the United States, a course of action that would almost certainly lead to total nuclear war and the destruction of the world as we know it. Happy New Year, Grigory."

At what stage in adventurism did you judge a military leader to be crazy?

Was Napoleon crazy when he decided to invade Russia?

Was Hitler crazy when he decided to do the same?

Was Grigory Tarkovsky crazy when he considered arming Dove shuttles with orthodox hydrogen bombs to destroy the United States's military space centers?

Vlasov sank deep into the leather cushions of the Zil taking him and his wife home to Kutuzovsky Prospect. And stared without seeing at the moonlit countryside merging with the suburbs of Moscow. Instead, he saw the latest medical report on Tarkovsky supplied by the Kremlin Clinic. (The medical histories of all Kremlin VIPs eventually reached Vlasov.) According to the report, the combination of circulatory weakness and pressure from the steel plate in his cranium were combining to produce symptoms of schizophrenia.

Which didn't necessarily mean he was crazy. Many august leaders throughout history had been schizophrenic, meaning that they suffered occasional disconnections between thoughts, feelings, and actions. On the other hand schizophrenia wasn't a certificate of perfect sanity.

Two factors decided Vlasov against taking steps to have Tarkovsky removed from office: The old men would rally around him (who wasn't having circulatory difficulties?); his scheme, although it was cataclysmically dangerous, was so bold that it just might work.

Its strength was the military tactician's oldest weapon—surprise. The early warning system of the West was geared to detect and destroy missiles fired in anger, not shuttle spacecraft peacefully orbiting the globe.

Certainly the West would be aware of them and would be monitoring them, enviously but indulgently, from the NORAD headquarters deep inside Cheyenne Mountain at Colorado Springs and from NASA's Goddard Center at Greenbelt, Maryland.

Even as the first Dove plunged earthward, off course, there would be no undue alarm. The first H-bomb would be launched with pin-point precision on Vandenberg, which would be destroyed, and with it the United States ground-based military initiative in space.

Pearl Harbor once again.

In many ways, its concept was not dissimilar to the Orbital Bombardment System when a missile in orbit was slowed down with retrorockets so that it fell on a selected target. But that had been negated first by the Americans' OTHR warning system, then by the AN/FPS-85.

But no system could anticipate a Dove (Hawk?) being used as an instrument of annihilation.

After discharging its H-bomb, the Dove would fire its new subsidiary engines and return to orbit. A sitting target? By then the space stations assembled by Dove crews would be fully operational gunships equipped with beam weapons that could pick off any hostile U.S. hardware at their leisure.

While the U.S. reeled under this blow, other Doves would bomb Wallops Flight Center, and possibly—it all depended on the pressure of the steel plate in Tarkovsky's skull—the Johnson Space Center at Houston and Kennedy at Cape Canaveral. These second-wave Doves might have to be sacrificed, but they would be a means to an end. An eminently worthwhile end in Tarkovsky's view. From space, the Soviet Union would rule the tiny globe and its pygmy people.

Vlasov's wife said, "Soon we won't speak at all. Perhaps we should learn sign language. Do you realize we are one hour into the new year?"

"Yes, my dear," Vlasov said absently. He patted her hand.

Theoretically, Tarkovsky was right. Astonishingly, earth-based nuclear missiles would soon be obsolete, their teeth drawn by the balance of power, the fear of reprisal. With the perfection of laser and particle-beam weapons, missiles would soon be *conventional* weapons. They could, of course, still inflict appalling destruction; but the chances were that they would be detected and destroyed from space.

No, Tarkovsky's thinking was logical as far as it went: To rule you had to preemptively strike in space—no spatial arms races, no interminable disarmament talks, no balance of power. But did his thinking go far enough? In Vlasov's opinion the answer was a resounding NO. It was flawed logic that appealed to old and inflexible minds.

As the Zil swung into Kutuzovsky, Vlasov listed in his mind the arguments against Tarkovsky's conclusions:

(1) In 1980, GRU had estimated that the U.S. was five years behind the USSR in the development of high energy lasers, charged particle and neutral particle beam weapons. Well, by now the Americans could have overtaken Russia. Which led to:

(2) The conquest of space would not necessarily be the debacle envisaged by Tarkovsky. U.S. gunships in orbit might well have the capacity with their own speed-of-light weapons to atomize the Soviet space stations. Which would lead to:

(3) War in space, which would inevitably rebound onto the globe with horrendous results.

(4) Tarkovsky's calculations were based on the assumption that America's military space program on earth was concentrated in certain areas, notably Vandenberg. Like the old soldier he was, Tarkovsky should have considered alternative options. Such as:

(5) The San Marco off-shore launching pads close to the Kenyan coast; Japan's island space center at Tanegashima; and submarines equipped with long-range beam weapons. From Japan, Vlasov's thoughts switched to:

(6) China, possibly the biggest flaw in Tarkovsky's scheme of things—the menace which Western disarmament negotiators tended to forget when they accused the Soviet Union of hoarding excessive stocks of missiles. Russia was vulnerable from attack from the West *and* East. Which explains our persecution complex, Vlasov thought.

And it was perfectly feasible that, while the USSR was engaged in conflict with the West in space, China would attack from the East. You certainly couldn't dismiss the existence of their space center at Shuang-Cheng-Tzu, a thousand miles west of Peking: The Chinese had launched satellites from there—and IRBMs, which they had fired into a site at Lop Nor, 500 miles away.

To sum up, Vlasov told himself, Tarkovsky's idea is plausible but reckless to the point where it endangers Mankind. Therefore, anticipating the possibility of my own failure, it must be sabotaged.

But how? It came to Vlasov as the Zil pulled up outside the block in Kutuzovsky. It was the most awesome decision he had ever taken.

17

NEW Year's Day.

At 10:55 A.M. Sergey Yashin, getting hungrier and thinner by the hour as his worries proliferated, sat down at the computer terminal at Tyuratam.

Behind him stood Vlasov, Moroz, Peslyak, and Massey.

Today Yashin's hunger was a slavering animal. Here he was, a man who saw the computer as the agent of peace and plenty, using it as a weapon of war.

If this penetration succeeded, then an American satellite would be destroyed in space and worse would follow.

At 11 P.M. contact was made.

At 11:06 Yashin was dismissed. He went straight to the canteen.

At Vandenberg, Daniel Gordon also worried.

Not that the Soviet INPUT operation wouldn't succeed—nothing could stop it—but that one day it would happen for real and the Pentagon wouldn't know a damn thing about it until it was too late.

Partnered by the crew-cut Chuck Raskin who, as usual, said very little, Gordon was monitoring the INPUT which was much as they had expected it to be.

As he stood among the consoles, screens and tapes, Gordon furtively took his pulse. To achieve this he stood with his hands loosely clasped, forefinger of the right hand on the left wrist.

Slow and faint.

Ever since, as a delaying tactic, he had transmitted to the Russians the coded message that he was sick Gordon had felt sick. Nothing specific but today he sensed that his blood pressure was low rather than high.

He caught Raskin looking at him. Guiltily, he moved his finger away from his wrist.

When the operation was over Gordon drove quickly home and went straight to the bathroom. The do-it-yourself blood pressure apparatus was missing.

When confronted with this, his wife said calmly, "I know, I threw it away; it was driving both of us crazy."

He took his pulse again; it was racing.

Chuck Raskin also had problems but they were of a vastly different nature.

Because he had been born with inequality—a brain that planned incredible feats of sporting prowess and a body that couldn't obey it—he believed fanatically, but privately, in equality.

The man seated beside him at the basketball game in his home city, Louisville, Kentucky, between the Kentucky Colonels and the Indiana Pacers had talked about equality.

The Colonels were leading because their giant center kept scoring from impossible distances. "It isn't fair, is it," he said, "that one guy should be born with so much going for him."

Raskin glanced at the man beside him. He wasn't so deprived—squarely built and solid but, Raskin guessed, clumsy. He had sandy hair and a foreign accent.

After the game, which the Colonels won, the two of them went for a beer. By a lucky chance the man, whose name was Alex Melnik, worked in Los Angeles for IBM and they became friends—a rare relationship for Raskin—because, as Melnik put it, they were both "athletes posing as spectators."

After they had watched a game—football, baseball, basketball or whatever—they went back to Melnik's apartment where, as often as not after a few drinks, the conversation extended to inequality in general, particularly in the global context.

But it was three months before Melnik suggested sex. And another week until Raskin agreed.

Six months to the day after their first meeting, Melnik suggested that Raskin might like to do something practical about their debates on global equality by helping to ensure that the super-powers enjoyed parity in space.

How? Why, pass over to the Soviet Union some of the U.S. military space secrets, of course because America was demonstrably ahead in its shuttle orbits, the key to the future.

Raskin realized immediately that this was so much shit; nevertheless he enjoyed the feeling of power he suddenly possessed, not to mention his relationship with Alex Melnik.

Perhaps one day, he reasoned with himself, he could do something that would really establish the balance of power in space instead of tilting it in favor of the Soviets.

None of which solved the immediate problem facing him as, after the last Tyuratam-Vandenberg link-up, he drove toward Los Angeles, where he was supposed to meet Melnik at a bowling match.

He solved this problem by taking the Santa Barbara exit. It was, he realized, the most temporary of solutions. After being stood up, Melnik would be after him with pleas, threats, and blackmail.

Oddly, Raskin rather enjoyed anticipating such perils.

And anticipating the way in which he would deal with them.

In the light of the information received on the afternoon of January 1 from the American Embassy in Moscow, the President of the United States involved two members of his cabinet—the Secretary of State and the Defense Secretary—and the National Security Adviser in the Talin Conspiracy.

They met, with George Reynolds, at 6 P.M. in the Situation Room, the command post sunk beneath the West Wing of the White House. It was in this somber, secret, and economically furnished chamber that, daily, a picture of global and spatial developments was composed.

The composition was made up from thousands of fragments. Photographs from spy satellites, electronic pulses from radar stations, observations from SR-71 Black Bird surveillance aircraft, digests from the world's media, reports from embassies, consulates, intelligence agencies, spies . . .

As an aide had once vulgarly put it, "If a sparrow farted in Outer Mongolia its echo would reach the Situation Room."

Earlier that day, long before the President had decided to spread the responsibility for Talin, the Situation Room had been electrified by another item of intelligence—blown-up surveillance photographs showing the deployment of CPBs, charged particle weapons, in the Soviet Union. It had been known that the Russians had built a CPB generator at Saryshagan on the Chinese border. It had not been known that they were in a position to deploy the generator's products, far more deadly than lasers.

This disturbing information had been included in the black leather file containing the briefing that was presented to the President in the Oval Office at 9 A.M. every working day. Within fifteen minutes he had digested its contents.

The subsequent meeting in the Oval Office that morning had been dominated by the mushroom appearance of the CPBs.

President: How far behind are we, Bill?

Defense Secretary William Fryberg: Not too far, Mr. President.

President: How far's not too far?

Defense Secretary: Maybe six months. We've made good progress at the Los Alamos and Lawrence Livermore labs recently. We may be behind now but when we produce the goods we should go ahead. You know, the Soviets always like to produce in haste and repent in leisure.

President: You should have been a lawyer, Bill. Maybe you'll make Attorney General yet. (Consults chart showing deployment of CPBs). Any idea where they're aimed?

Defense Secretary: At us, I guess! And the Chinese, of course. And into space. As you can see they've moved them into their space centers. Into Tyuratam, for instance.

President: Could they have shifted them into space itself?

Defense Secretary: Could be. They've sure as hell got lasers on their killersats. But, as you know Mr. President, CPBs are way ahead of lasers: they don't just melt a target's armor, they sock right through it at the speed of light.

But all that had been before the coded message marked URGENT from the U.S. Embassy in Moscow that had prompted the five man emergency meeting in the Situation Room. It was brief and to the point:

> Russia's Dove shuttles are to be used to assemble an armada of gunships equipped with lasers and CPBs.

And if that wasn't enough:

> The Doves themselves are to be armed with conventional hydrogen bombs to be dropped on selected targets in the event of hostile action by the United States.

The source?

An informant.

At one minute past six, the President began to address his four confidants—the Secretary of State, Joseph Craig, a sleek, round businessman turned statesman, who exuded confidence and calm; Defense Secretary Fryberg, slim and canny with his head cocked like a listening bird; Henry

Fallon, the National Security Adviser, archetypal Washington, crisp but cautious; and Reynolds.

The President was backed by a chart showing the deployment of all known satellites orbiting the earth. The table at which the five men sat was flanked by steel filing cabinets. Security was maximum.

The three newcomers to the conspiracy had a ruffled, why-weren't-we-consulted-earlier air about them. They directed their hostility toward Reynolds, who fielded it adeptly—he had been in the field a long time.

The President, Reynolds thought, looked as crisp in a mature way as Fallon. White shirt with button-down collar, striped tie, dark suit, brown hair.

The President said, "I won't attempt to conceal the fact that this was originally a two-man operation." Three sets of eyes focused on Reynolds. "Or that you have only been enrolled because of today's developments. As George knows, this was to have been a spectacular aimed at upstaging the Soviets, with the bonus that this man Talin would bring us a whole bundle of space secrets. But today the implications have become far graver and, at the same time, far more exciting."

He glanced at his gold wristwatch. Reynolds knew why.

The President drank some water and continued, "We have today received conclusive proof that the Soviets have deployed CPBs. We have therefore got to speed up our own particle beam projects at Lawrence Livermore and Los Alamos. And then we've got to persuade the world that we, as well as the Soviets, have to deploy them *as a deterrent*," emphasizing the familiar last three words.

"A whole lot of people," Craig said, "were unimpressed in 1981 when we tried to justify the deployment of Pershing II missiles by publicizing the deployment of the Soviet SS-20s."

The President swept on, "We have also received information from an unknown source that the Soviets plan to build gunships disguised as space stations in orbit."

He paused and drank more water.

Fallon took the opportunity to point out, "There's nothing new about that, Mr. President. As you know, the Russians have been experimenting with laser weapons firing bullets of light from space stations for years."

"So have we," Fryberg observed. "Not to mention battle stations armed with antiballistic missile systems more than 1,000 miles high in orbit. What's more we'd be goddam self-righteous if we took them to task for launching killer-satellites."

The President said to Fallon, "They have been *experimenting* with laser-armed space stations. Now they've *got* them. And they're not armed with lasers, they're armed with CPBs. And they're going to build a whole armada of them to win the Battle of Space before we've got off the ground." He paused. "But we'll beat the bastards yet."

The spectacular, Reynolds reflected, had come a long way since last summer when the President had suggested a preelection coup.

The President said, "If Talin brings down the Dove in America, complete with equipment designed to release hydrogen bombs, then, gentlemen, we have all the proof we need that we must perfect and deploy death rays."

Reynolds spoke for the first time. "Supposing," he said, "that the Dove piloted by Talin is actually loaded with an H-bomb?"

Fallon said patronizingly, "Even if it was carrying the bomb, it wouldn't be primed."

The President consulted his wristwatch again and said, "In four minutes' time we shall know if we have succeeded in maintaining Robert Massey's plausibility. In other words, we shall know if we've successfully followed the Soviet instructions on zapping a satellite out of the heavens."

A shadow of a smile passed between the President and Reynolds. It said: *How's that for shutting them up?*

The President's hand reached for the telephone receiver linking him on a direct line to NORAD.

Apparently the Russians didn't know a lot about U.S. killer satellites because, instead of instructing a killersat to destroy an item of American spatial hardware, they had given the job to a jet fighter.

No ordinary jet, it was true. A McDonnell Douglas F-15, in fact, armed with a two-stage rocket that was itself armed with a Vought impact head.

The weapon, known as a hot-metal kill, was guided to its target by radar and heat seekers; it had so far blasted five exhausted scientific satellites out of orbit.

Today, instructed by Vandenberg computers penetrated by the Russians, the F-15 was intent on zapping Elint 23, an electronic spy satellite designed to record radiation from military maneuvers.

At 1811 hours, as the two-stage rocket fired by the F-15 sped toward it, Elint 23 was one of 3,483 satellites in space, all of them tracked by telescopic cameras and radars strung around the globe.

1812 hours. Rockets on target.

At that moment, Elint 23 wasn't high on the priorities of the majority space scanners on duty, and its disappearance would attract minimal attention except at a Soviet tracking station in Camagüey, the east coast province of Cuba, and an American observation post at Eglin Air Force Base, Florida.

1813. The telephone in the hand of the American President trembled a little, as did the telephone in the hand of the Soviet President seated in a chamber beneath the Kremlin, not unlike the Situation Room beneath the White House.

1814. Still on target.

1815. A fraction of a second passed . . .

Zap.

There was now one less satellite in space.

1816. The United States President spoke into the phone, cradled it, and, smiling, said, "Gentlemen, we're still in with a chance."

The Soviet President replaced his receiver and said, "Congratulations, Comrade Vlasov. You now have twelve days in which to bring the United States of America to its knees."

18

THE skates sung.

Swish, swish, they went, as, with Sonya at his side, Talin skated around the frozen lake ten miles from Leninsk. Songs that his mother used to sing to him resurfaced. He tasted summer berries, smelled the glowing metal of the stove. "Remember those fish we caught and the other times in the *taiga*."

Hands clasped behind his back, he skated away from Sonya, accelerating with lunging rhythms, the cold air polishing his cheeks.

He completed a circuit, weaving between skating families, and returned to Sonya with a flourish. On skates, wearing a pale blue ski suit and white boots, she lost none of her grace.

He took her hand and they skated together. Both in blue, they looked, Talin thought, as though they had skated together from childhood.

"You left me again," Sonya said.

"I used to speed skate at the university."

"I saw you skate away and I thought, one day he'll leave me forever."

He squeezed her hand. "Don't be silly."

"You won't ever leave me again, will you, Nicolay?"

"Only . . ."

"I don't mean in *Dove*. I mean in your spirit."

"You know why I flew away from Moscow."

"You should have told me. I would have understood."

Would you?

"I left a note," he said. "I was upset."

"But we should have been able to discuss it. You discussed it with Sedov."

"Only because he followed me. And we have discussed it since."

"And I told you that the past was filled with terrible injustices like that. But not any more."

Not inside the Bolshoi.

In front of them a plump woman with a woollen scarf around her face fell sprawling on the ice. Screaming with laughter, she was pulled to her feet by a husband half her size.

The sun had burned away the morning mist and polished the ice; the low hills and snow-mantled pine forest unfolded in its rays.

Talin began to skate faster, pulling Sonya along with him. "You mean there is no injustice any longer?"

"I don't mean that; of course I don't mean that. What I mean is that we don't live under a tyranny any more."

"We certainly don't have total freedom."

"I do, you do . . ."

With the implication that it was in the interests of the masses not to enjoy such liberty. Ironic how such thinking so closely resembled the philosophy of the rulers overthrown by the Bolsheviks.

". . . You could have got into terrible trouble. They might have stopped you from flying *Dove.*"

"I was saved by Sedov."

"Sedov! Always Sedov. I would have stopped you from going. Comforted you . . ."

Because it was such a beautiful day he compromised. He said, "I should have told you," and saw her smile and blink and heard her say, "Nicolay, if you're ever troubled again . . ." and interrupted her, "Then I'll come to you."

Letting go of her hand he said, "Now let's see you dance on skates."

And off she went circling, speeding, spinning, until she stopped in front of him with a curtsey.

He kissed her and she said, "And now a surprise." Standing back to watch his reactions, she said, "Don't worry, I'm not pregnant. Nothing like that."

"Why should I worry?"

"I'm going to dance in Moscow on January the fourteenth, the day you fly into space. *The Red Dove.* Isn't that marvelous?"

Talin said it was.

"So, in a way, we'll be together. And while I'm dancing, I shan't worry."

"You will the rest of the time?"

190

"Of course."

"No need," he said, stretching out his arms. "They'll take good care of *Dove* and me, we're valuable properties."

He held her close and looked at her upturned face and knew that he would never forget the conflict of joy and worry he saw there.

It is often assumed that the Church in Russia is virtually defunct. In fact, the Russian Orthodox Church boasts fifty million members (more than the Communist Party in the Soviet Union) and is one of the world's largest religious communities.

Where it differs from other such communities is that it is firmly controlled by the Communists. Its clerics are screened by the Party, its worshippers monitored. Despite such restrictions, it seems to be on the ascent.

One small outpost of Christianity in Russia is an old church a mile from the railroad station at Leninsk. It is built of stone, small, and sturdy, and wears its blue dome with cheerful assurance.

Cosiness, Massey thought as he approached it through the bleak dusk, was the first attribute that came to mind. Mellow light shone from within, luring you from the bitter wind driving powdered snow along the street. You smelled burning tallow and incense even before you reached its portals.

Inside, a few worshipers, mostly old women with autumn-leaf faces, knelt in prayer. Candles spluttered, lighting icons on the walls.

Rybak knelt in a pew at the rear. Massey knelt beside him. In their bulky winter clothes, the two of them occupied four places, the Ukrainian two and a half.

Massey greeted him, but, head bowed and hands clasped together, Rybak ignored him, and Massey realized that he really was praying. Surprising himself, Massey joined him.

Finally, Rybak said, "Well?"

Massey said, "The date of the launch is unchanged, January fourteenth, in one week's time. We mustn't meet again, we might blow the whole thing."

Rybak said, "I agree. But we're safe enough here. The KGB only mounts surveillance during services."

A tall man wearing a cheap *shapka,* long gray coat and felt boots came into the church, peered around, then left.

"KGB?"

Rybak shook his head. "A thief. Probably thought *we* were KGB."

Massey said, "So tell them to assume the defection is on and take all the necessary steps."

Rybak slid one hand inside his black parka. "I bring gifts," he said, surreptitiously handing Massey a gun and a grenade. "By the way, you did lose your tail again?"

"In a street lavatory, I'm becoming an old hand." Massey slipped the weapons into his coat pocket. "Have you got any bullets for the gun?"

Rybak pressed two packets into his hand. "A useful automatic," he said. "A TT 1933. Basic but lethally accurate. The grenade's an old fragmentation F1. It will blow a man into little pieces. An enemy or yourself if you don't want to fall into the hands of the KGB. And now the Good Book," he said, handing Massey a Bible.

A heavily bearded priest walked past them. He smiled at them. Two new members of his flock.

"What's this for?" Massey asked. "Last rites?" He fingered the soft leather and vellum pages.

Rybak said, "Inside it you will find the necessary papers for Talin to read. You will also find documents for yourself—red passbook, etcetera, exit visa, train ticket to Nakhodka—most of the journey will be on the Trans-Siberian—a ship ticket to Japan, which is the ultimate terminal for most travelers on the Trans-Siberian, and a fortune in roubles."

"Wouldn't it have been easier to try and escape westward?"

"Perhaps," the Ukrainian said. "But I figured the KGB would expect you to make contact with your people in Moscow. Either way your chances of escaping are about 80/20—in the KGB's favor. What you must do," he said producing another small package, "is shave off your mustache and hair. The best disguise is always the one you remove, not the one you adopt."

"Identity?"

"A nice touch," Rybak said. "Your new name is—wait for it—Vlasov."

"Nicolay?"

"Mikhail." He handed Massey the package. "This is for Talin. A way of dealing with awkward fellow cosmonauts in the *Dove* who don't want to defect. It was dreamed up by your Mr. Reynolds who, by all accounts, would cut his own throat for President and Country. Reynolds versus Vlasov . . . Who would you back?"

"This package, what's in it?"

Rybak told him, adding, "There are also decoded messages among the papers you're going to show Talin that will help your cause." He told Massey about the information that had reached the U.S. Embassy in Moscow relating to the H-Bomb and the function of the space stations. "Dynamite, eh? Even better than the stuff you were going to show him."

Massey shivered. "Terrifying," he said. He paused. "And what about you? Will you be around?"

"God willing. The KGB checked me out at the *banya* in Moscow but they didn't get the name I operate under."

"You're not known as Rybak?"

"Yangel. One of the best aeronautical engineers in the business. Which is how I got myself work at Leninsk Airport."

"And Tyuratam itself?"

"I'm working on it. They've got some electrical faults on a Proton booster. I met the chief engineer on the project in the Cosmonaut Hotel and almost persuaded him that I could fix it."

"I figure you could fix anything," Massey told him.

"One last thing—a message from Washington. Tell Talin to make his move as soon as possible after the launch." He gripped Massey's arm. "That's it. May God be with you."

And he means it, Massey thought as he watched Rybak stride out of the church, flames of the candles flickering in his wake.

Talin had sold the wreck of his red Moskvich—anything could be repaired in Moscow—and bought a new cobalt-blue Lada 1600 in Leninsk.

Today, Sunday, six days before the launch, he drove Massey back into the city after an intensive day's work at Tyuratam. Only later did it occur to him that Massey must have maneuvered him into offering him a lift.

Massey had also inquired when he had bought the car and, when he had replied, "Yesterday, why?" had followed that up with: "Has anyone had any opportunity to plant bugs in it since?" and had relaxed a little when he had replied, "No, I parked it beside *Dove* out on the pad today, and last night it was locked up in my garage."

Now as Talin drove through the darkness along the almost deserted highway to Leninsk, he realized why Massey had been so worried about microphones. Oddly, nothing that the other man was saying really surprised him. There came a moment when he understood the point of it all. Looking at the American, Talin said, "You're trying to tell me your defection was contrived?"

"Yes."

"You don't intend to stay in the Soviet Union?"

"No."

"Then you lied about everything else as well?"

"No, everything else I said I meant, especially what I said about space."

He continued to speak but Talin heard his earlier words: *I believe in Mankind. We are participants, you and I, in the greatest revolution man has ever known: He is stepping off the Planet Earth and establishing himself in space, in eternity. And he has a chance, this one chance, to share eternity in peace. To leave tribal warfare earthbound.*

". . . and I want you to realize, to believe, that those are the reasons why I am doing this . . ."

To share space, the superpowers have got to have access to each other's information. They've got to know if one or the other is planning a criminal act.

Talin gripped the steering wheel. "What are you hoping to achieve?" he asked.

Pointing at a lighted café, Massey said, "Do you mind if we go in there? I'm being followed and it would look suspicious if we stopped the car and talked."

Talin nodded and parked the car. They went into the café, which was shiny new and decorated in red and orange. Steam billowed from a tea and coffee machine that a sharp-featured young man handled inexpertly but with arrogant assurance, like a captain on the bridge of an ocean liner.

They hung up their coats, ordered tea with lemon and took the cups to a table isolated at the back of the café. Massey took a blueprint of the *Dove*'s vertical tail structure from the inside pocket of his jacket—"so we look as if we're discussing the shuttle."

From the same pocket he produced a photostat of an official document emanating, Talin noted, from the Science Policy Research Division, Congressional Research Service, Library of Congress.

"This," Massey said, "was to have been the damning evidence. Since then other material has come to light. But read this first."

He slid the photostat across the table under the *Dove* blueprint. Talin's initial calmness was now followed by a series of shocks as sharp as pistol shots spaced out by a marksman.

The photostat was an extract from a report on the Soviet Union's space program. The extract dealt with Doves. One paragraph had been underlined.

It is reliably understood that the stations constructed in orbit by cosmonaut craftsmen carried into space by Dove shuttles could be used to generate radiation onto selected areas of the earth's surface. In this way the Soviet Union, using equipment manufactured at Sarova, could annihilate the populations of hostile countries and, when the radiation threat had receded, occupy its unscathed cities and countryside.

Talin thought, "Doves of Peace used for genocide? Ridiculous. Laughable." Then he thought, "What was it about the *Dove* that struck me as different?"

He said to Massey, "You're a spy, of course."

"Not a spy. An agent."

"I think subconsciously I always knew."

"It's irrelevant anyway. What matters is our beliefs. That's why I came to Russia."

194

"And your masters, do they share our beliefs?"

"Not in the same way. But they do believe that power criminally used in space will destroy the future."

"Why should I believe this piece of paper?" he asked, sliding it back under the blueprint.

"I had no reason to fake it."

"But the CIA—I suppose that's who you're working for—they would have had reason."

Massey said, "Yes, I suppose they could have faked it. Anyway it's not that important now."

"Annihilating nations isn't important?"

"The document, not its import. These *are* important." Massey passed across the decoded messages from the U.S. Embassy in Moscow. "These could have been faked too, but I don't figure they were."

Talin read the first message. It told him that the stations the Doves were going to construct in space were to be adapted so that they could fire controlled particle beam weapons at the earth.

Belief and disbelief struggled with each other. Talin's head ached. Calmly, he sipped his lemon tea and said indulgently, "Now that makes more sense," but he couldn't quite manage the ironic smile.

"It isn't necessarily a contradiction. The platforms could be designed for both functions. Warships don't rely on a single weapon."

"Tell me something," Talin said with determined nonchalance, "would you have admitted that the CIA could have faked the radiation report if you hadn't come armed with this second . . . lever?"

Thoughtfully, Massey traced a pattern on the condensation on the window. A star, a porthole to the black night outside. Eventually, he replied, "I don't know, but I don't think I would."

His honesty reached Talin.

Massey said. "Now read the second decode." He stared through the star-shaped porthole, already dripping out of shape.

Talin picked up the other message.

Dove had been redesigned to carry a hydrogen bomb.

The young man behind the bar pulled a lever and steam whooshed past him.

"Hard astern," Talin said.

"How was that?"

"It doesn't matter." A hydrogen bomb. Was that all?

"Have you read it?" Massey was frowning, puzzled.

"Yes, I read it."

A hydrogen bomb. In my Dove. Nothing more?

NOTHING . . . MORE?

Another question expanded inside him, pushing at the inside of his skull: "What was it about the Dove that struck me as different?"

An H-bomb... Dove with a cuckoo's egg... a mushroom-shaped cloud... a Siberian village built around a pump obliterated ... a boy on a horse riding away pursued by death ...

The village became a great city, the boy a legion of youth fleeing.

He turned abruptly to stare through the star in the condensation, now a shapeless orb. As he did so he accidentally knocked his mug of tea on to the floor. The mug shattered. The other customers stared at him, then, losing interest, they looked away.

Talin said, "Do you believe this?"

"It was supplied to our embassy by a Russian. It has the ring of truth about it, though, of course, *Dove* wouldn't carry an H-bomb on a proving flight." Massey's voice was gentle. "Why don't you check it out? Ask Oleg Sedov."

Talin said, "Yes, I'll do that." And it wasn't until they were back in the car that, wonderingly, he said, "Do you realize that you haven't actually asked me?"

"To defect? Then I'm asking you now." And at last Massey gave him the details that he had memorized long ago in the presence of George Reynolds, adding Rybak's message, "*If* you decide to do what I'm asking, then don't waste any time up there."

"Time?" Talin glanced sideways at Massey. "But you and I both know that time doesn't exist—up there."

There was only one place to confront Sedov—in his own apartment where there would be no bugs.

Talin dropped Massey and drove there, belief and disbelief popping up and down in his mind like puppets, and with them relief and despair.

He now knew what it was that had seemed different about *Dove*: a modification to the cargo bay in addition to the fittings for the new mechanical arm.

Tomorrow, Monday, had been scheduled for final instructions about the new payload. Had they intended to tell him about the bomb bay?

Bomb bay? Who says it's a bomb bay? The CIA, that's who. Well, if that was what the CIA claimed, he would see what the KGB had to say about it.

Sedov had been watching television. The black and white set still flickered in the corner of the living room. A member of the Politburo wearing a gray fedora and a black topcoat delivering fraternal greetings to another Warsaw Pact leader wearing a gray fedora and a black topcoat.

Sedov greeted him with surprise and pleasure and clapped him on the shoulder. "Come in, have a drink, where's Sonya—ah, yes, back in Moscow, rehearsing, I'd forgotten." He took Talin's outdoor clothes, cut short the fraternal greetings on the television.

Talin asked for vodka. While Sedov, wearing an old green turtle neck sweater and baggy gray slacks, prepared *zakuski* and fetched the bottle of Stolichnaya from the refrigerator, Talin took in the familiar surroundings.

He had never liked the apartment. It was stifling hot but it contained no warmth. With its easy chairs covered with brown plastic, crooked table, bowl of desiccated fruit, never-opened books on the shelves, it was a stage set for a disorganized bachelor.

Sedov raised his glass. "To Saturday."

"To Saturday."

The vodka dropped, burning, into Talin's stomach. He didn't bother with Narzan, nor gherkins and cashew nuts. He held out his empty glass.

Sedov refilled it, the expression on his disciplined features questioning.

Talin explained, "I had an unpleasant taste in my mouth." He tossed back the vodka. "I heard some rumors today at Tyuratam."

"Rumors aren't allowed," Sedov said, smiling.

"About the Dove program."

"Ah."

As though he had anticipated the confrontation. But I mustn't be too sensitive, Talin warned himself. It was impossible to read features as controlled as Sedov's.

Talin said, "I heard that the platforms they're going to build in space are going to be armed,"

"Of course." Sedov replenished both glasses and sat down in front of Talin. "You must have known that. We don't stick them up there for the Americans to shoot down."

"With beams."

"With beams," Sedov agreed. "The Americans have got them, we've got to have them."

"CPBs?"

Sedov's expression tightened. "The weapons of the future. We can't be left behind."

"The rumors," Talin said, feeling for words, "say that the CPBs are to be aimed at the Earth. Had you heard that?"

"They're adaptable. They can be fired up or down."

"If they were fired at the Earth that would start a nuclear war."

"Or stop it. If the beams were aimed at the American launching sites."

"And their submarines?"

"I'm not a beam ballistics expert," Sedov said. "What was the source of these rumors?"

But, with cold frosting his soul, Talin kept at him. "The rumors also concerned *Dove* itself."

There was a new wariness in Sedov's voice as he said, "Really?"

Talin thought: *He knows.* "They say that *Dove* will be armed with a conventional nuclear bomb."

Deny it? Please God deny it.

Sedov took a mouthful of vodka, held it in his mouth for a moment, then said, "I think you deserve an explanation."

Hope withered.

Sedov said, "The Americans have orbital bombs in space . . . we have to make some sort of reply . . . we must always be ahead. . . ." For the first time that Talin could remember Sedov's voice had lost its way. ". . . a deterrent, no different in that respect to a missile armed with a nuclear warhead . . ."

Talin said, "Don't give me shit, Oleg." He held out his glass. Sedov filled it. "Something I've always wanted to do," Talin said. He drank the vodka and hurled the glass at the wall.

That night Talin dreamed that he and Sonya and their two blond children, a boy and a girl, sought refuge from a nuclear holocaust in a mine. But it was a cobalt mine and there they met his father. "Like me," he told them, "you have two chances—to die slowly down here or quickly up there." When he turned, Talin saw that the sockets of his eyes were empty.

Sonya took Lisa's hand; he took Viktor's They began to ascend through a tunnel toward quick death. "Where are we going?" Viktor asked. "Fishing," Talin answered.

On Friday the thirteenth, the eve of the launch, Robert Massey watched a gaunt-faced Sergey Yashin make the last computer connection with Vandenberg and, indirectly, all the military mission control centers in the U.S. Vlasov was also there, accompanied by Moroz and Peslyak, the three godfathers of Soviet espionage. Which was hardly surprising, Massey reflected, in view of the fact that, assisted by aerospace experts, they believed they were programming Vandenberg to destroy all American military and spy satellites in space, plus any on the ground that could be launched to replace them.

Occasionally Massey became aware that Vlasov's greenish eyes were staring at him speculatively. Wondering why he had twice eluded his tail? My presence here today, Massey thought, should convince him that it was chance; but Vlasov wasn't a man who readily accepted chance.

Tomorrow he will know just how right he was to doubt. And he will also realize that it wasn't coincidence that the Vandenberg penetration had coincided with the *Dove* launch. It had been planned that way as a means of creating chaos, a stroke of timing by Vlasov's only equal in the world, George Reynolds.

That evening Talin telephoned Sonya.

Breathlessly, she told him that she was in the middle of the dress rehearsal for *The Red Dove* that was to have its première at the Bolshoi tomorrow "while you circle the world."

He said, "I telephoned to tell you that I love you."

"And I love you. Perhaps when we're together again . . ."

Perhaps what he never knew because he cut the connection and closed his eyes.

PART FOUR

PREMIERE

19

BLAST off was scheduled for 10 A.M. Talin was called at six, but the call wasn't necessary—he hadn't slept. And still he didn't know what he was going to do.

His conscience said defect; his birthright said stay. He looked into the bathroom mirror and saw a saint, he looked again and saw a traitor. Indecision ebbed and flowed. He bent to rinse his face in the basin—and vomited.

He took his pulse. It was strong enough but too fast, so he took a tranquilizer in the hope that it would deceive the monitors at Launch Control.

A car arrived to pick him up at seven. The driver talked incessantly but Talin hardly heard him. He was glad that it was still dark, because he didn't want to look at the land, flat and dull though it was, in case he never saw it again. He hoped it would snow. The satellites had forecast a snow-free launch but they were frequently and dramatically wrong. Yes, snow would help. To keep him here or to store as a memory?

At 7:55, Talin, Sedov, and their two passengers, a scientist and a military observer described as a meteorologist, arrived at the floodlit launch-pad, wearing their red flight jackets, a far call from the cumbersome suits the space pioneers had worn. They carried their white helmets fitted with radio headsets under their arms.

Dove, Talin thought, looked peculiarly vulnerable, dwarfed by the two rockets and the fuel tank to which she was locked. Not until they were jettisoned after the launch, would she come into her own, a high-flying bird of infinite grace.

One day carrying in her womb a lethal egg. How could men perpetrate such a travesty?

As he stood at the foot of the skeletal access tower acknowledging the applause of the ground staff, Talin noticed another pool of floodlight in the distance: the complex where they had installed ground-to-air beam weapons.

A cold wind blew in from the east polishing the stars. Sedov took Talin's arm, and they entered an open-fronted elevator that whisked them to *Dove*'s entry hatch.

With the two passengers seated behind them—all of them now had their backs parallel to the ground because *Dove* was mounted on its tail—Talin and Sedov checked their life support systems and began their pre-launch checks. They tapped out queries on one of the spaceship's four computers. Immediately the answers flickered back, green and phosphorescent, on the two screens in front of them.

As the computerized countdown continued, the great tank clamped to the exterior of *Dove* filled with liquid oxygen and hydrogen.

Talin remembered his excitement during the previous countdown. Today it was rasped by an intrusive quality. Fear. Of what he might do.

Could they pick up this new tension on the monitors?

Through the headset attached to his helmet came the voice of the launch controller, "Any messages for the Russian people?" Like the first *Dove*'s maiden flight, this mission was being followed throughout the Soviet Union and Warsaw Pack countries on radio and television.

The public knew that this *Dove* was equipped with a steel-jointed arm to deposit and pick up satellites; they knew that it was capable of relaunching itself into orbit if anything went wrong as it reentered the earth's atmosphere. That was all they knew.

What I should tell them, Talin thought, is that this launch should be made from Plesetsk, the base between Moscow and Archangel from which military missions were launched.

He felt Sedov's stare.

The Launch Controller's voice came on again, "Do you read me, Comrade Talin?"

"I read you. Tell them I'm proud to have been chosen to represent them once again in space. That I'm looking forward to returning . . ."

To where?

"And your wife?"

This time he played it their way. "Tell her I love her."

After the confrontation six days ago, Talin had been scared that Sedov would make a report to his superiors.

But, perhaps because Sedov hadn't anyone in the world except the surrogate son now sitting beside him, no report had been made.

The launch controller said, "And you, Oleg, have you any message?"

"The same as Nicolay. I'm proud to be representing the Soviet people and the Party on this mission."

Sedov took off his helmet and headset. "You know," he said to Talin, "I meant that. Did you?"

"About the Russian people, yes. I didn't mention Party."

"That's the way they'll infer it."

"I don't care how they infer it," Talin said.

"Is everything . . . all right, Nicolay?"

"Everything's fine," Talin said.

In front of them the sky was glowing cold green and the stars were withdrawing.

They returned to the checklist. Letters and figures continued their ghostly dance on the screens.

Occasionally the scientist who was investigating the harnessing of solar heat and the "meteorologist" asked questions.

Then they were on the brink of beyond.

Ten, nine, eight . . .

The countdown was followed by two heads of state: by the President of the Soviet Union watching on television in Moscow and by the President of the United States listening on the radio in Washington, where it was the early hours of the morning.

The Russian leader sat in an ornate reception room in the Kremlin; the American in his living room in the White House with his wife.

. . . seven, six, five . . .

The heads of the two biggest secret police forces in the world also waited anxiously. George Reynolds in his soulless office at Langley, Virginia; Nicolay Vlasov in his well-appointed room in Dzerzhinsky Square, Moscow.

Paradoxically, the two Americans were much more interested than their Soviet counterparts. As people are when they believe that a rival's hour of glory may disintegrate into catastrophe.

The two Russians were more concerned with another countdown—the last hours before the previous day's comprehensive penetration of Vandenberg took effect. The debacle was timed for midday. After that the talons of the American eagle would be clipped forever. What could be more interesting than that?

. . . four, three, two . . .

If anything went wrong now, they would have to escape in shutes linked to bunkers 1,000 feet away.

. . . one, zero . . .

Talin thought, "It hasn't snowed."

Dove's three main engines fired, their 1,100,000 pound thrust momentarily bending her fuselage; then, resiliently, she sprang back into shape.

Three seconds later, with the engines straining at 90 percent power, the great rockets to which *Dove* was clamped also ignited, lending her another six million pounds thrust.

Simultaneously, the shackles holding the whole shuttle—spaceship, rockets, and tank—were unlocked.

It shuddered.

Talin said into the mouthpiece of his headset, "We have lift-off."

A part of him saw and heard the ascent as though he were on the ground. The great tail of white-gold fire. The billowing nest of gas. The majestic climb into the pale sky. The spectators, who had retreated to a stand four miles away, would hear a deafening roar. A little later there would be a sonic boom.

Gently, as intended, Dove rolled onto her back as she curved upward. For much of the mission she would stay that way without any discomfort to her passengers—free of the harness of gravity it didn't matter which way up you were.

As the messages flickered on to the computer screens, Talin glanced at Sedov. He was staring ahead and, with gravity pulling the flesh of his face backward, there was a desolate quality there that frightened Talin. *As if he knows about the decision I have to make.*

Talin moved his left hand toward the computer punch-out. With the gravitational pull, it felt as though it was encased in plaster.

When they were fifty seconds into their journey, the main engines throttled back to 70 percent power to cope with Max Q, the point at which maximum dynamic pressures were reached.

Upside down, Talin gazed at the mountains and plains of Kazakhstan.

Ten seconds later, the engines picked up full power again.

When she had been climbing for two minutes, when her speed was four times the speed of sound, when she was thirty miles high, *Dove* discarded her two rocket boosters. Their parachutes opened, and they began their descent to the Aral Sea.

Dove's main engines continued to propel her upward until, nine minutes

206

after launch, at a height of eighty miles, they shut down, having consumed 500,000 gallons of duel.

Explosives dispatched the external tank. *Dove* was alone.

Smaller engines fired. Then a last burn planted *Dove* into orbit, traveling at 17,500 mph at an altitude of 160 miles.

The time was 10:41.

Dove, scheduled to stay in orbit for four days, was tracked at seven land bases in the Soviet Union, and at stations in Fort Lamy in Chad, Khartoum in the Sudan, Mirny in Antarctica, Camaguey in Cuba and Kerguelen in the southern reaches of the Indian Ocean. It was also followed by tracker ships sailing the oceans of the world including the *Kosmonaut Yury Gagarin,* which boasted 120 laboratories and 100 antennae, and could be patched through by telephone to any part of the Soviet Union via Molniya satellite links.

The West followed *Dove*'s progess through tracking stations strung across the United States, including Hawaii and Kodiak Island, Alaska, bases in Britain, West Germany, Guam, and Australia, and from tracker ships. The pride of the U.S. observation posts was the AN/FPS-85 at Elgin Air Force Base, Florida; its radars set in a towering concrete hulk could sweep vast areas of space in a fraction of a second.

Today, January 14, had begun like any other day in these Western stations monitoring all the satellites and the debris orbiting the earth like riderless horses in a track race. The station duty officers were aware of the *Dove* launch and observed it take its place in orbit with casual interest.

Until 0300 hours Washington time, when each received a coded radio message from NORAD, nerve-center of the United States's early warning system: BE PREPARED FOR UNSCHEDULED MANEUVERS BY SOVIET ORBITER DOVE. AND BE READY TO RENDER ASSISTANCE WHERE POSSIBLE.

Even more urgent messages were radioed to beam and missile-launching sites deployed over the United States and other NATO countries advising them not to react to any message mistakenly reaching them that, if the Soviet orbiter plunged toward North America instead of Asia, its intent was hostile.

George Reynolds had said, "We need a spectacular, not a disaster movie," and the President had replied, "Holy shit, George, you had us all fooled — you have got a sense of humor."

Puzzled unit commanders only learned much later that the warning had been deliberately delayed in case Soviet cryptoanalysts decoded the messages and warned Tyuratam to abort the launch. As it happened, the Russians didn't decode the warnings until two and a half hours after their dispatch.

At 1145 hours Moscow time, Nicolay Vlasov joined the Soviet President in the red and gold, chandelier-hung reception room in the Kremlin. Tarkovsky was there, suspended between triumph and doubt. Together the three of them walked into the marble-floored hallway and took the elevator to the briefing room in the basement.

The President sat at the head of the long, mahogany table. On his right squatted a battery of telephones, behind him two maps, one showing the deployment of United States' missiles in the States and Europe, the other the location in orbit of U.S. military satellites.

At the far end of the room stood a computer terminal. The walls were painted schoolroom-green and were bare except for the maps, a photograph of the President, a television set, and a portrait of Lenin. Vlasov and Tarkovsky sat opposite each other.

The President poured himself a glass of water and said, "If that telephone," pointing at a black receiver, "hasn't rung within fifteen minutes, then I shall assume that Tarkovsky has won."

The telephone was a through line to Yevpatoriya in the Crimea, the deep space tracking station whose functions had been extended to monitor all satellites. It also housed Mission Control for *Dove.* If Vlasov's comprehensive penetration had worked, then, at midday, blips—American ones— would be leaving Yevpatoriya's screens like so many shooting stars.

Vlasov thought, "The phone must ring. When it does, when those blips go skating off the screens, then the United States of America is defenseless and we have won."

"I sincerely hope," the President said, "that it does ring."

Tarkovsky said nothing, which was a change.

They were over the Pacific, a glinting lake, and they were weightless. Talin took a pencil from his flight jacket pocket and let go of it. It floated where he had left it.

He unstrapped himself and walked in slow motion around the flight deck, inspecting the batteries of buttons, dials, screens.

Standing, he had a better view of the globe. Blue, green, and ochre, it was dappled with puffs of cloud.

Talin's gaze shifted beyond its arc to the realms where there were no dimensions. Didn't they understand that? If there was no weight, why should there be distance? Why should there be time? Perhaps one day, down there, they would realize that they were trying to assess space with false standards evolved from horizons, tides, night, and day. Perhaps one day they would stare into the firmament and discover that they were looking at themselves.

He helped the scientist, an alert, sun-tanned, forty-year-old named Vinnikov, to release his harness, leaving Genin, the "meteorologist," an unsmiling man in his thirties with cropped, prematurely gray hair, to free himself.

Genin said, "Do you intend to do any work outside the ship?"

"Maybe on the third day," Talin told him.

If there was a third day.

As arranged, Reynolds drove from his office in Langley to the White House while *Dove* was in ascent. He arrived as it went into orbit, long before there was any possibility that it could deviate from its schedule.

He was directed to the Situation Room to which the President had moved. Secretary of State Craig was there with Defense Secretary Fryberg and National Security Adviser Fallon.

The President, wearing a tweed sports jacket and open-neck cream shirt, looked tired. "We old men need our sleep," he said as Reynolds sat down. "When do you reckon he's going to move?"

Reynolds said, "He's been advised to make his break as soon as he can. When our codes are busted and when Nicolay Vlasov realizes that he isn't going to push us out of space, the game will be up, or near as dammit."

Rasping one hand over the stubble on his jaw—it was the only time Reynolds could remember seeing him unshaven—the President said, "What do you reckon they'll do when they figure it out?"

Craig answered for Reynolds. "For starters, they could try and hit *Dove* with a ground-based beam weapon."

By 12:05 P.M., Vlasov began to suspect that he had been the victim of the greatest confidence trick in history.

Picking up the black receiver, the President said, "We'll try calling *them*," and, into the receiver, "Anything?" Slowly, without replying, he cradled it. His great head sunk low. "We'll give it another five minutes," he said, his voice barely audible.

"Of course," Tarkovsky said.

At 12:10 the President called again.

It was then, from the expression on the President's face, that Vlasov *knew* he had been tricked.

A peaceful future dominated by the Soviet Union and achieved by brains instead of brute force, disintegrated, so much gossamer. The children on his study wall stared contemptuously at him.

Shaking his head, the President replaced the receiver. To Vlasov he said, "I'm sorry." To Tarkovsky a gesture with his hands—"You win."

So I, the old fox, have been outwitted, Vlasov thought. But why?

He was vaguely aware that, on the TV screen at the end of the room, the *Dove* launch was being replayed.

A telephone rang.

They all started, but it was the red receiver.

The President picked it up, listened for a moment, then handed it to Vlasov. "For you."

Moroz told him that intercepted coded messages, sent that morning to all tracking stations, early warning systems, and missile-launching sites in the West, had finally been decoded.

It was then that Vlasov finally realized why he had been duped.

He replaced the receiver without replying.

Without seeking the President's permission, he picked up another telephone and snapped, "Get me Peslyak."

When Peslyak came on the line he said, "Get Massey."

20

TALIN realized, ten minutes before Vlasov heard about the decoded messages, that the moment of decision was almost upon him. Massey had warned him to act as quickly as possible before the Russians got wind of American preparations to receive a rogue spaceship.

He had calculated that, *if* he went through with it, the critical period would be during the third orbit because that would be the best time to deal with Sedov and the other two passengers. They had now completed two orbits, had opened and shut the cargo bay doors, flexed the manipulator arm, activated the TV cameras and checked out communications with Mission Control at Yevpatoriya, which had taken over from Tyuratam.

Could he do it? From space came the call, "Cut loose, be free." But, without speaking, the implacable presence of Oleg Sedov said, "Don't betray your country." Sedov, the personification of Russia. Of honor. My mentor on his last flight. And the man who still commands me.

Sedov's voice intruded into the turmoil of his thoughts. "It's good, you and I up here. For me the last time. I wouldn't have wanted anyone else beside me."

Talin thought, "I can't do it," and said, "Yes, it's good, Oleg."

"You know I've been worried about you. Ever since that time in my apartment." Sedov, sitting in his steep-backed navigational seat, glanced behind him, but the two specialists were out of earshot, standing hunched over consoles of instruments. "I began to wonder if you would quit . . ."

Talin, separated from Sedov by a panel of controls, didn't reply. Below them was Asia. Russia. Ahead Siberia. To the south he could see a snowstorm. He imagined the soft coldness of the flakes on his cheeks.

". . . or if you had some other plan?"

"Plan? What sort of a plan could I have?"

"You are a Siberian. A wild one. In space a man can shed the inhibitions he has learned on earth."

"The inhibitions you taught me?"

"If I hadn't, you wouldn't have survived."

If I don't go through with it, Talin thought, the KGB will confront me; men who, unlike Sedov, will be impersonally brutal. Because soon they will know that the Americans expected a defection. That I must have been approached.

Talin's reasoning raced ahead. But they won't publicly denounce me, because that would be a body blow to the Soviet image. Perhaps they will project me as the supreme example of Russian manhood who contemptuously rejects the blandishments of imperialist agents of disruption.

But what of Massey? Surely, as soon as he realizes that he has failed, he will escape by some prearranged route. I will miss him, Talin thought.

Sedov's words reached him first as an interruption to his reasoning, then as its destruction. Seemingly innocent words that ripped through his patriotism like bullets through a national flag.

". . . so you have a wonderful future ahead of you."

True, if they let me return to space. And how could they not if they portray me as a gladiator who has sent the forces of corruption packing?

". . . a beautiful wife, children perhaps. . . . The best thing I ever did was arrange that meeting between you and Sonya."

Arrange?

The first bullet on target. Into his soul.

Talin tried to discipline his voice. Casually, almost nonchalantly, he said, "You mean at the Bolshoi that day?"

"Where else?" Space had dispersed Sedov's reserves of caution. "You were made for each other."

But surely that had been for us to decide. "I knew I was one of a troop of trainee cosmonauts invited backstage; I didn't realize you had anything to do with it."

A warning was sounding in Sedov's mind. Too late. "I suppose *arrange* is a strong word . . ."

"Perfectly apt," his voice miraculously controlled. "And was it arranged that I should stay behind when all the others had left? And that Sonya should stay as well?"

"Yes, but . . ."

"And that meeting in the Astoria Hotel in Leningrad two days later, was that arranged? I knew a touring company of the Bolshoi was playing there, but I never quite understood why six of us were suddenly selected to tour the landmarks of the Siege of Leningrad during the Great Patriotic War."

"Does it matter?" Sedov was pleading now. "You fell in love, you're happy together."

"I might have been happier if I had been allowed to choose my own destiny. Did Sonya know that it was all set up?"

"Stop it, Nicolay. Don't throw away what you've got."

"Did she?"

"She didn't care, she loved you."

Talin turned his head and smiled, actually smiled, at Sedov. "How can she have loved a man she had never met?"

Behind them, the two passengers paused in their work, sensing dissension.

Sedov said, "I meant after the first meeting." Then, rallying, "Not now, Nicolay. We'll talk about it when we get back to Russia."

Talin said, "I suppose I should have known. That day in the bar when you told me that the First Deputy Commander-in-Chief of the Soviet Air Force thought it was about time we were man and wife. Time we met, time we got engaged, time we got married. Time we slept together, Oleg?"

"I'm commander of this ship and I'm ordering you to stop this talk."

From behind them came Genin's voice, "What's wrong, Comrade Sedov."

"Nothing's wrong," Sedov snapped. "I suggest you get back to your instruments."

"I'm entitled to know . . ."

"You're not entitled to eavesdrop on conversations between commander and pilot."

"I shall make a report about your attitude when we return."

"As it's my last trip," Sedov said, "I'll dictate it for you."

Genin reluctantly moved away.

Talin said, "I remember that day in the bar you said, 'Our lives have always been arranged.'"

"And I said that it wasn't so different in the West."

And it was then that Talin knew what he had to do. They had *arranged* his father's death, they had *arranged* to transform *Dove* from an ambassador of peace into an instrument of destruction, they had *arranged* his marriage, and now was the time to find out if it was different in the West.

Odd that it was the last, least important, revelation that had finally decided him. Perhaps it was because it had been perpetrated by Sedov, the one man he had trusted.

Calmly he pointed at the digital clock among the flickering dials and said, "I'm going to have some lunch if that's all right with you?"

Sedov began: "You're not . . ." but Talin interrupted him, "I'm not going to do anything rash. I just want to think a little," he lied.

As he made his way to the galley in the middle deck of the crew compartment, he saw below them a river, its tributaries like tendrils. The Ob. To the west the Urals separating European from Asian Russia. From Siberia.

In the galley he went through the motions of injecting a meal with water to rehydrate it—vegetable soup, steak, and rice, followed by apricots, washed down with apricot juice—and heating it up. That way he would avoid arousing suspicions. Then he dropped the powder that Massey had given him, a concentrated barbiturate named amylobarbitone, into the water supply. To eat, Sedov and the two passengers would have to inject their food with the water.

Then, because he had no appetite, he washed most of his own food down the toilet, the slowness of his weightless movements giving the performance a macabre quality.

Ten minutes later he returned to the flight deck.

Sedov looked at him questioningly. "Everything all right?"

"Everything's fine. Why don't you three have your meal now."

Supposing they weren't hungry!

"Okay," Sedov said, "you take over." And to Genin and Vinnokov, "Follow me."

Then Talin was alone.

They had been in orbit for less than three hours. Below them was Japan. He planned to land at Kennedy Space Center on the Florida coast at dawn.

The radio bleeped. Talin put on his headset. The voice from Yevpatoriya was unfamiliar, a nasal twang to it. "Is Comrade Sedov there?"

"No," Talin told the voice, "he's in the cabin."

"Get him and put him on."

"You can talk to me."

"I'm ordering you to get Sedov."

Was there any way they could possibly know?

"And I'm refusing."

Silence, followed by the voice of the mission controller, placating, "Please cooperate, Nicolay, this is a private matter between Comrade Kovalenko and Oleg."

"And who the hell is Comrade Kovalenko?"

He was tasting freedom already and there wasn't a damn thing Comrade Kovalenko could do about it because, if he succeeded in defecting in *Dove*,

214

they would never be able to reach him and, if he failed, then he would kill himself before they got to him.

The controller, his voice far too calm, said, "Comrade Kovalenko works for the Ministry of Defense." KGB?

"Tell Comrade Kovalenko that Comrade Sedov is indisposed at the moment"—in the bathroom, comrade —"and will be in touch as soon as he returns to the flight deck."

"Thank you, Nicolay," the mission controller said.

If they knew what he intended to do, what action could they take other than enlist the help of Sedov and the "meteorologist," who so far had evinced no interest whatsoever in the weather patterns below? Through the computers they could maneuver *Dove* in orbit, but he could cancel any attempts to make her reenter the earth's atmosphere. So they would have to rely on assistance from within *Dove*. Hopefully, that would shortly be impossible.

Sedov returned with Vinnikov and Genin.

Vinnikov said, "Better food than you get at the Metropole."

Genin said, "I thought it tasted bitter."

They all sat down.

Sedov said to Talin, "Well, did you have a good think over your meal?"

"I calmed down a bit."

"And you don't have any plans for revenge?"

"You mentioned a plan before. What plan could I possibly have 160 miles above the earth?"

"Only one thing. You could plan . . . you could plan . . ." His voice was losing direction. Talin looked behind him: the two specialists were unconscious. "Could plan . . ."

"Don't try to talk," Talin said.

Sedov's eyes pleaded with him. Suddenly his voice strengthened and Talin thought: "He was acting, he didn't inject the water."

"Because," Sedov said in a strange, forced voice, "I have news for you. Why do you think we've got Genin on board? Because," voice fading again, ". . . because," picking up once more, "this is a dummy run," fading ". . . they had to test the weight factor, angle, reaction to lack of atmospheric pressure . . ."

Talin leaned across the instruments and shook Sedov. "What is it, Oleg? For God's sake what is it?"

Sedov said, "There's a hydrogen bomb in the cargo bay. When that red light comes on," pointing with one drooping finger, "it means it's primed."

His hand dropped and his eyes closed.

Behind Talin the radio bleeped.

Still stunned by Sedov's words, he replaced his headset.

Sonya said, "Nicolay, what's happening, I don't understand?"
Her voice pierced his senses.

"There's nothing to understand."

"They say you may do something terrible with *Dove*. They're crazy, aren't they, Nicolay?"

"Yes, crazy . . ." No, he had to be honest with her; he owed her that. "There's something I have to do."

"What are you talking about, Nicolay?"

He could smell her perfume, feel her hair, taste her lips, and he said, "I won't be coming back."

"But tonight, the ballet, *The Red Dove* . . ."

Sadly he thought, "Even now she can't see beyond the walls of the Bolshoi."

He said, "One day perhaps I'll be able to explain. Just remember that I loved you." Then, harshly, "forget me."

"*. . . so in a way we'll be together. And while I'm dancing, I shan't worry.*"

Skates sang on the ice around them. *He held her close and looked at her upturned face, and knew he would never forget the conflict of joy and worry he saw there.*

Her voice from far away said, "But that means you're a traitor."

Was she reading hastily scribbled words thrust in front of her? It didn't matter; her tone was hardening and, not wanting to take that hardness with him, he said her name softly and cut the connection.

This final blackout in radio communication between *Dove* and Mission Control was made at 1305 hours Moscow time, five minutes after television and radio coverage of the spaceflight had been mysteriously curtailed.

"Get Massey." That had been gut reaction. Now, as he realized the full implications of what had been perpetrated—why Massey had so assiduously cultivated Talin, why he had evaded surveillance on at least two occasions—Vlasov virtually took over the control room beneath the Kremlin.

Survivor's instincts alerted, he told the President and the Minister of Defense what he believed was happening and over the telephone, issued orders, their crisp authority overriding his own shock waves of panic. On his instructions, Sonya Bragina had been patched through from a telephone at the Bolshoi to *Dove*. He hadn't expected much from the connection and he had been right.

When his first burst of activity spent itself, he leaned back and made what was a brilliant comeback, considering the circumstances. Leaning back in his chair, he said to the two men who had been observing his performance, "This is just the sort of emergency I feared would be precipitated by Tarkovsky's plan."

216

Not bad in view of the fact the three of them had just learned that American Intelligence might be about to bring off an epic coup.

He attacked again. "With a rogue pilot at the controls of a Dove, there's every chance that he'll bring it down in America, providing the West with all the details they need of our strategy in space. And with a Dove transformed into a hawk, an anti-Soviet propaganda catalyst that could turn the whole world against us."

While he waited for Tarkovsky to assemble his forces, Vlasov wondered if Robert Massey would have been able to persuade Talin to defect if he hadn't been armed with the information about Tarkovsky's gunships and Dove's bomb. The information that he, Nicolay Vlasov, had leaked to the United States Embassy in Moscow, in the hope that it would be used to muster world opinion against such madness. But he hadn't anticipated anything on this scale.

One hundred and sixty miles above the earth, Talin manhandled the slumped bodies of Sedov, Genin, and Vinnikov into their antigravity suits and helmets. Without the suits their blood would drop to the lower parts of their bodies. The result, in their comatose state, would probably be death. Then he buckled them into their seats, donned his own suit and helmet, and strapped himself into his seat.

At 0140 hours Moscow time, he took over manual control of *Dove*, turned her tail-first and fired the orbital maneuvering engines. Almost immediately *Dove* began to slip out of orbit.

The premature move by *Dove* was instantly picked up by American and Soviet radar scanners. Within seconds the information was passed to NORAD and Yevpatoriya, thence to the White House and the Kremlin.

Reactions in the U.S. and Soviet capitals were vastly different.

Jubilantly, the American President replaced the receiver on the direct line from NORAD and said, "Here we go." At the same time he picked up another receiver and authorized the release of a statement to the media, which had been warned to stand by for an important announcement.

The White House Press Room, fully staffed for the occasion, was galvanized into action. So were spokesmen at NASA, the Pentagon, and all interested Government agencies.

CBS, NBC, and ABC interrupted their programs from coast to coast. Early risers on the east coast caught the interruptions and spread the word. Cities, towns, villages awoke prematurely.

At the same time the news blitzed across the world. In the morning, afternoon, evening, or night, according to the time difference, families took up positions around TV and radio.

In Florida, reporters, photographers, and technicians raced to Kennedy

Space Center, where the *Dove* was expected to land at dawn, followed by armadas of cars carrying sightseers. Nothing like it had been witnessed since the landing of *Columbia* in April 1981.

In the underground control room at the Kremlin the reaction was equally dramatic.

It exploded from Tarkovsky.

He said, "We have no alternative. We've got to hit *Dove*. With a charged particle beam weapon."

He looked inquiringly at the President. Almost imperceptibly the President nodded.

21

ROBERT Massey had risen at 5:30 A.M.

From the window box on the balcony where he had buried them, he had retrieved the gun, ammunition, grenade, and forged documents wrapped in oiled paper.

Then he had driven in his black Zhiguli from Leninsk to Tyuratam, because he had to see *Dove* launched, being as involved as anyone. And then? He would stick around to see if Talin went through with it. If he did, then he would have to escape immediately because his involvement would be instantly apparent. If he didn't, then the escape wouldn't have quite the same urgency.

And it wasn't until later that Massey realized that he hadn't heeded his own warning to Talin: that as soon as the messages warning American tracker and missile bases to stand by for a defection from space were decoded, then the whole operations was blown—and the KGB would be on the hunt for its instigator, himself.

Meanwhile, being a cosmonaut and a companion of Talin, he hadn't been body-searched for a couple of weeks. He hoped today wouldn't be an exception; it wasn't.

After breakfast, he was taken with the other cosmonauts on a bus to a box reserved for them in the spectator stand. As *Dove* roared majestically upward, Massey discovered that he was cleansed of guilt: If the information leaked to the American Embassy in Moscow was true, then surely there was no reason for remorse.

After the launch, they were driven, privileged observers, to the firing control room at Launch Control to watch *Dove*'s progress. What finer place than this futuristic chamber with its computer consoles, TV screens, and complexes to observe when things started to go wrong—or right, according to your view.

The Hunter didn't attempt to follow Massey into the firing room. Instead he parked the white Volga, provided by the KGB in Leninsk, fifty yards down the access road and settled down to wait. He checked his knife, running his thumb lightly down its saw-toothed blade, and the TK automatic in the pocket of his hooded, fur-lined hunting jacket, fashioned in white to blend with the snow.

Like any other bureaucratic structure addled with delegated responsibility, the KGB tended to lose direction in an emergency and the order issued at 12:24 by Vlasov to "get Massey" hadn't reached the Hunter on his radio set until 12:48.

Get Massey. It was almost too good to be true. The Hunter licked his lips. Then the qualifying message reached him. "Get him alive."

"Message understood," the Hunter said resignedly into the hand-set.

As he waited, it began to snow.

Which suited Rybak who, parked a further fifty yards down the road in the blue Moskvich, was beginning to feel conspicuous, although, having been enlisted to help cure the Proton booster, he was entitled to be there.

A voice came over the Hunter's radio.

"Do you have Massey?"

"Located in Launch Control."

"Take him as soon as possible."

Other cosmonauts were leaving the complex, heading on foot for the canteen. Rather than risk a chase and a shoot-out among the consoles in the firing room, the Hunter decided to overpower Massey as he emerged.

He inched the Volga closer to the complex and, leaving the engine running, crossed the road on foot. As he waited beside the entrance, he was an almost-invisible predator.

But not to the Ukrainian who had also approached closer and was peering through the switching blades of the Moskvich's windshield.

At 1 P.M., when TV and radio transmission was curtailed, everyone left in the firing room suspected that something had gone terribly wrong. Replies to queries through direct channels to Yevpatoriya were evasive. One reply, however, clinched it, "*Dove* has broken contact."

So it was on. Now, Massey thought, you're on your own.

He was about to head for the rest rooms when a young cosmonaut who had been standing beside him said, "If *Dove* looks as if it's going to land anywhere outside the Soviet bloc, then God help Nicolay Talin."

Massey paused. "What the hell are you talking about?"

"No way is the Kremlin going to allow it to land in the West."

With a terrible presentiment building up, Massey asked, "And what's that supposed to mean?"

"Why, they'll hit it with a beam weapon. A CPB—they've assembled them over there," pointing through a window. "About five kilometres . . ." stopping in midsentence. "Hey, you're the American, aren't you?"

But Massey was gone, hurrying toward the rest rooms.

At 1:20, a clean-shaven man with a bald head emerged from Launch Control and stood for a moment staring into the snow that had thickened into a blizzard. Then he put on his fur *shapka* and, head tucked into the driving flakes, headed for the parking lot at the end of the access road.

According to the Hunter's calculations, there should still be one cosmonaut left inside: Massey. But now he had to make sure. Showing his ID to the guard, he entered the lobby.

A cosmonaut he recognized walked briskly across the marble floor. It wasn't Massey.

The Hunter stopped abruptly. There had been something about the bald man who had just left. A spot of blood on his clean-shaven lip. Clean shaven? Just shaven!

The Hunter outwitted by his prey. He turned, pushed past the guard, sprinted across the road to the white Volga. Tires skidding, he made a U-turn and accelerated toward the parking lot.

Rybak gave him a second, then followed in the blue Moskvich.

Both of them saw the black Zhiguli pass them on the other side of the road, heading in the opposite direction, Massey crouched at the wheel.

The Volga slewed around and, swerving wildly, took off again. Followed by the Moskvich.

A hundred yards past Launch Control the road forked. There was no sign of the Zhiguli, and the falling snow was a white wall. From the glove comparment the Hunter took a map of the space center. The fork to the right led to the assembly bays; the fork to the left to nowhere.

The Hunter took the left fork because it was at "nowhere" that the charged particle beam weapons had been assembled.

While the three cars converged on the CPB site, *Dove* was hurtling toward the entry interface of the earth's atmosphere, approximately half way around the world from its chosen landing strip at Kennedy Space Center. Talin had calculated that this maneuver would take eighteen minutes thirty-three seconds.

He had, he believed, estimated the entire defection with precision, choosing an orbit that would give the West maximum tracking time. Once inside the earth's atmosphere, he intended to reestablish radio contact, but this time with Mission Control at Houston, Texas.

Inevitably he would be stripped of many of the safeguards programmed into the computers. And he had an H-bomb in the cargo bay. The cargo bay was on top of *Dove*—a pilot would have to turn her upside down to discharge it—and if the bomb wasn't primed, he comforted himself, it was quite harmless.

The Volga drew level with the Zhiguli a mile past Launch Control. With a delicate nudge it pushed it off the road into deep snow.

The little black car butted its way a couple of yards to the right before stopping, engine still running, a buffer of snow in front of the hood.

Cautiously, gun in hand, knife in belt, the Hunter approached it. Massey had cracked his head on the windshield. He was unconscious, his *shapka* had fallen from his head and there was a trickle of blood on his shaven skull.

The Hunter stuck the TK back in the pocket of his hunting jacket and pulled open the door. The sound of the Moskvich pulling up behind him was drowned by the noise of the Zhiguli's still-running engine.

The Hunter reached into the car and grabbed Massey by the lapels of his coat.

As two arms encircled him from behind.

He could feel the strength and the girth of the man and he said, "Rybak" before the air was expelled from his lungs.

A rib cracked.

Another snapped; he could hear the retort inside him.

To start with there wasn't any pain. Until the Ukrainian increased the pressure and more ribs broke, digging into the Hunter's lungs.

With his first gasp of pain, blood sprayed into his mouth and, peering through the falling snow, seeing the *taiga,* he remembered how cornered prey had fought back, snarling and lunging and he thought, "This isn't any way to die."

He went limp, letting his body slump forward. The Ukrainian relaxed his grip. When the Hunter turned, straightening up at the same time, the knife was in his hand.

They looked into each other's eyes for a fraction of a second before the

222

Ukrainian squeezed again, buckling the Hunter's rib cage entirely, as the saw-edged knife slid into his own heart.

When Massey regained consciousness he went first to the two bodies, sprinkled with bloodstained snow. Finding that they were both dead, he returned to the Zhiguli and tried to back it onto the road. But the wheels merely spun, spitting out snow.

He returned to the bodies and removed the Hunter's white hunting jacket and, after pulling out the knife, the Ukrainian's parka. He placed one garment beneath each driving wheel.

The wheels spun, gripped, and, with a jerk, the car was back on the road. Before heading into the blizzard, he peered into the driving mirror and wiped the blood from his shaven scalp. Then he replaced his *shapka*.

His head ached, he felt sick, and, for a moment, he imagined he was in space.

His mind cleared as the CPB site materialized in the falling snow. Its fortifications were only partly constructed, as though the beam weapons had been rushed here prematurely, poised for a declaration of war.

Weapons . . . an anachronism. Massey didn't know too much about CPBs but he understood that you couldn't bracket such devices, once the property of science fiction comics, with orthodox guns or even nuclear missiles.

CPBs, which would out-date military lasers even before *they* were perfected, were powered by Pavlovsky generators that converted explosive bursts into electricity, which dispatched beams charged with particles such as electrons and protons at the speed of light.

Blithely, the Americans had long believed that the Russians couldn't aim them into space; but they had reckoned without the adaptation of magnetic mirrors that could bend the beams onto their target.

The CPB's overwhelming asset, however, was that so far no one had come up with an effective countermeasure.

The sentries guarding the makeshift, sand-bagged entrance seemed to be disturbed. By now, Massey recognized their confusion as the state of mind induced in a totalitarian state by the arrival of a VIP. An Army staff car, an old-fashioned, khaki-brown Chaika, with a driver at the wheel, was parked outside.

Robert Massey parked the Zhiguli, and Major Mikhail Vlasov of the KGB identified himself to one of the sentries. Robert Massey marched into the compound.

He walked down a corridor, new concrete walls still damp. Builders' materials lay in heaps on the floor. At the end of the corridor stood a Red Army captain, bareheaded, wearing a flak jacket and webbing belt with a holster containing a pistol.

Hand on the flap of the holster, the captain told Massey to identify himself. He glanced at the ID, handed it back, one thumb unbuttoning the flap of the holster. "No one goes in there," he snapped. "No one."

"But I . . ."

"If you knew who my orders came from you wouldn't argue, Comrade Major."

"Well, look at his," Massey said, casually slipping his hand into the pocket of his topcoat and producing the automatic, "and now that you've seen it, turn around. Now!" jabbing the barrel of the gun into the captain's flak jacket.

As he turned around, Massey hit him beneath the ear with the butt of the automatic.

Gun in hand, he burst through the door. Two men, one a Red Army general, the other a civilian, were crouched over a console studded with dials.

He shouted to them to stand away from the console. The civilian stepped back, but the general lunged at a black button at one side of the dials.

Massey shot him through the chest as his finger made contact. The building trembled and Massey knew that the beam weapon had been fired but, hopefully, in the panic, without accuracy.

The civilian, a pale young man wearing steel-rimmed spectacles, stood motionless, staring at the body of the general. Down the corridor came the sound of pounding footsteps.

With the gun, Massey broke the glass in a window and jumped through it. In front of him was a half-finished brick wall with a steel door leading through it. He tried the door, it opened.

Beyond was a space fifty yards wide, cleared of snow. In the middle stood a sloping concrete platform; mounted on it was what looked like an elephantine telephoto lens. One end was attached to a power unit, the other pointed toward the sky.

Beyond was another wall and another door. Massey sprinted around the death-ray projector and crouched beside the door. He tried the door handle, the door opened.

He took the fragmentation grenade from his pocket and drew the ring as the two sentries who had been guarding the entrance burst through the door on the other side of the CPB. He released the lever and tossed it onto the concrete firing pad under the cylinder.

He ducked through the door and slammed it shut. The explosion shook the wall; debris thudded against it. When it was over he opened the door. The two soldiers lay among the wreckage. The CPB, hurled from the firing pad by the explosion, lay on the ground, its barrel ruptured.

If a grenade dating back to World War I could wreck space age weaponry, then there was still some sort of hope, Massey thought as he slammed the door behind him.

Ahead lay another walled area, empty. The door this time was to his left. He opened it. Outside was a path between two concrete outhouses. He turned left at the end, skirting the main compound in the direction of the entrance.

The entrance was unguarded.

He ran through it, spinning around and falling as a bullet hit him in the arm. As he fell, he fired at the driver of the staff car crouched behind the hood. The driver reared up and fell across the hood, blood pouring from his shattered jaw.

With one hand Massey pulled him off the car. On the ground was a greasy rag that the driver had been using before the shooting started; Massey used it to wipe his blood off the hood.

Then he climbed into the driver's seat and headed for the secondary exit at the far end of the space center.

He stopped once and took off his topcoat. In the glove compartment he found a clean rag and a flask of vodka. He poured the vodka onto the wound, gasping as it burned. Deciding it was only a flesh wound, he pressed the rag onto it and, using his teeth and his free hand, tied a handkerchief around it. Then he put on his coat and drove off again.

"Now, Comrade Major, we shall see what sort of stuff you're made of," he told himself.

22

DOVE lurched violently to one side when it was seventy-five miles above the earth.

A beam weapon, Talin guessed, gripping the hand controller—it was the only answer they had left. Not a direct hit but it must have passed within a few feet of the fuselage.

Dove began to turn on her side, shuddering.

Talin fought the manual controls. *Dove* settled again, then suddenly dipped her nose.

Talin pulled, coaxed, shouted; but his arms were as heavy as lead as the earth pulled at them and his reactions were as slow as a drunk's. Gradually *Dove* raised her beautiful, aristocratic nose. Talin grinned fiercely, loving her. And it was then that he noticed that the red light beside the unconscious body of Sedov was glowing red. The bomb in the cargo bay must have been primed by shock waves from the beam.

Down plunged *Dove*. With enough nuclear power inside her, Talin thought, to devastate a city. His brain froze; his head slumped forward.

When he came to, he could see the curvature of land below and snow-capped mountains falling away to plains. He concentrated on the clock nestling among the sophisticated dials: It was 1410 hours Moscow time.

If his calculations were correct, he should touch down at Kennedy Space Center in twenty minutes. But he had no idea if his calculations were correct because the dials, airspeed and altitude indicators, artificial horizon . . . all had gone crazy.

But, in any case, could he now risk putting *Dove* down on land? His mind leapt out of its icy lethargy: It was out of the question. He had two alternatives: to fire the new engines designed to put her back into orbit or to ditch in the ocean and hope divers would salvage her if the bomb didn't explode.

If he went back into orbit, assuming that the subsidiary engines hadn't been damaged, then he would be hit again by another beam and the whole operation would have been for nothing.

No, he would overshoot Kennedy Space Center and ditch far out to sea where, if the bomb exploded with the force of the impact, relatively little harm would be done.

Ahead the air glowed with heat, 2,500 degrees of it. If the beam had loosened the protective tiles, they would fly off and *Dove* would burn up.

He activated the radio, sweeping through the wave bands in search of a contact. Nothing. The CPB might have affected it; on the other hand it might be the usual communication blackout caused by heat on reentry.

Talin reckoned that his speed had slowed from 17,500 mph at reentry to about 6,000 mph. He was approaching terminal descent at about 250,000 feet. Gingerly he tried elevons, rudder, speed brake, and rudder controls. *Dove* reacted sluggishly, like the wounded bird she was.

The mountains receded, a plain, then lakes.

Talin tried the radio again hoping to contact one of the VOR beacons which could guide *Dove*'s autopilot just as though she were a conventional airliner.

The faintest crackle reached him through his headset. Faintly he heard a voice.

"Kennedy . . . Kennedy . . ."

Not knowing whether or not they could hear him he said: "Soviet shuttle *Dove* here . . . believed overflying North America . . . have primed nuclear warhead on board . . . attempting ditch in sea . . . please advise . . ."

He began to repeat the message, but before he had finished he had lost contact again.

The American President slammed down the receiver linking him to NORAD.

He said, "Gentlemen, the situation is this: The Soviet shuttle is at this moment out of control and out of contact somewhere over the Midwest. It is thought that it may have on board a primed hydrogen bomb, but radio reception was so bad that the message was unclear."

He paused. "We have two choices, and you all know what they are: We let it land or we blow it out of the sky with an ABM." He glanced at his watch. "Those who think we should hit it, raise their right hands."

Secretary of State Craig and National Security Adviser Fallon raised their hands. Reynolds and Defense Secretary Fryberg remained motionless.

"So I have the casting vote. Your indulgence, gentlemen, for one moment." He picked up a telephone set aside from the others. "The hotline. I prayed to God when I was elected that I would never have to use it."

The Russian President held the receiver away from him, one hand clasped over the mouthpiece. Nodding at Tarkovsky, he said: "The President of the United States wants to know if *Dove* is armed with a hydrogen bomb. Do I tell him?"

Tarkovsky looked at Vlasov; his face was flushed, his small gray eyes bloodshot. He hesitated, then said, "Tell him no."

In the White House the President replaced the receiver and said to the four men sitting around him, "We don't hit, but we do take evasive action."

To Fryberg and Fallon he said, "You both know what to do, move it." To Craig he said, "You might as well stay here, Joe, there's nothing you can do," and to Reynolds, "You too, George, the spectacular could become the disaster movie you talked about, and as coproducers we have to stick together."

He pressed his hands against his forehead. When he removed them, he suddenly looked his age.

Between them, Fryberg and Fallon, using the White House communications systems, rapped out a string of messages to the NSA (National Security Agency) at Fort Mead, Maryland, to NORAD, the Pentagon, and the FBI. Through them subsidiary coast-to-coast emergency services were alerted.

All commercial and military aircraft were grounded. Where possible, stacked aircraft were dispersed north to Canada and south to Mexico, Central, and South America. All airports were put on emergency. Vessels on the Great Lakes and the eastern seaboard were warned to stand by for a ditching.

In the visual control room at Chicago's O'Hare Airport, controllers scanned the skies through their tinted glass walls; in the approach control room, the controllers searched their radarscopes for an errant blip. Elsewhere, early warning radar antennae continued to track *Dove*'s erratic progress.

Across the central plains of the United States and to the east, people left their TVs and radios to search the skies. Until the media picked up the story about the bomb; then they took cover. And it was then that calls began to pour into the White House: "Hit it."

". . . Kennedy . . . Kennedy . . ."

At first the rusty little voice on the radio identifying itself as Kennedy had spelled out HOPE to Talin. But in his mind he had a relief map of what the distant approaches to the space center should look like; they were nothing like the map far below him at the moment.

Suddenly and sickeningly he understood: Kennedy Airport, New York. That was the signal he had picked up. And the sheets of water below were the Great Lakes. Beyond them lay low cloud.

Too late to even try the orbit reentry engines.

He was a glider, flying, he calculated, at about 80,000 feet and traveling at two and a half times the speed of sound.

Theoretically he should by now have been lined up with the land strip. Except that now all he could see beneath him was cloud, and his instruments weren't working, and he wasn't in touch with anyone.

Tentatively he tried the glider controls. Again the response was sluggish. And for the second time in his life he found he couldn't navigate to the right.

"I once had a car like this," Sedov said.

His voice was slow and thick. Beside him the red light glowed brightly.

"Are you all right, Oleg?"

"An old Volga. It looked like a tank."

"I'm sorry . . ."

"And I had a son once." Sedov closed his eyes again.

Dove sank toward the endless field of cloud. In front of it, a Boeing 747 sprang out of the crimped gray surface, like a primeval monster emerging from a marsh, and soared steeply upward. Talin caught a glimpse of the scared faces of the flight-deck crew and the puppet heads of passengers.

By now *Dove* should have been below 50,000 feet, poised for the final approach, landing on a twenty-two-degree glide slope.

Mist swirled past the observation windows. Behind Talin the solar scientist stirred. Sedov murmured some words but they didn't make sense.

All I have to do, Talin thought, is to get *Dove* as far over the ocean as possible.

The cloud thickened.

And the salvage crews will reach us. It can't all be for nothing.

With luck they were over the sea now. Which was when he saw the tip of a skyscraper probing the cloud and, a moment later, saw Manhattan below him.

In Rome, the Pope prayed, and in churches all over the world prayers were offered.

Maureen Kay
XL244

SKO

In Manhattan, traffic came to a standstill as the big red and white bird sailed silently over its skyscrapers, lower than the World Trade Center and the Empire State Building. It had adopted a south-southwest course and was gliding over the Hudson River waterfront.

It was the chief liaison officer of the Port Authority of New York and New Jersey, whose responsibilities included Kennedy, Newark, and La Guardia airports, who decided to try and coax *Dove* into Kennedy.

He said, "The sonofabitch is going to ditch in the bay. At that speed it will break up and, if there is a bomb on board, we'll lose downtown Manhattan, half of Jersey City, Staten Island, and Brooklyn—not to mention the Statue of Liberty."

He told his deputy to call the Control Tower at Kennedy on the direct line and, snatching up a telephone, called the New York and Jersey City electricity authorities. Seconds later lights went out all over Brooklyn, Queens, the Bronx, Yonkers, Staten Island, Jersey City and Manhattan. In the gloom of a winter afternoon, the landing lights on Kennedy's longest runway shone brightly and enticingly.

Pictures of the runway and the crippled *Dove* were recorded by TV cameras and relayed by satellite throughout the world.

Dove had begun to respond more positively to the controls. Talin glanced to his left—and saw that Sedov was gripping his hand controller.

Sedov said, "I don't know what happened up there, but I do know that if we hit water the impact will break *Dove* up and the bomb could explode."

Dove began to veer east across the bay around downtown Manhattan and the most famous skyline in the world.

At the rear of the flight deck, Genin and Vinnikov were regaining consciousness, staring through the observation windows in bewilderment.

As *Dove,* guided by Sedov and Talin, continued to turn, Sedov said, "You should build a shrine to that old Volga of mine, she's showing us the way again." He looked down. "I figure we're over Brooklyn now, but where the hell are all the lights?"

"There." Talin pointed ahead at Kennedy's jewelled pathway. "The ones that matter. Can we make it?"

"Radio would help. I had a radio in that Volga. Whenever it died on me I used to revive it like this." Sedov leaned back and hit the radio console with his fist.

A voice crackled into Talin's headset, "Kennedy here... Kennedy here... do you read me, *Dove?*"

"I read you," Talin said.

The runway at Kennedy Space Center is 15,000 feet long. The longest runway at Kennedy International Airport is 14,572 feet.

231

The chief controller at the airport's ten-story high tower, equipped to handle fifteen aircraft simultaneously, was a grizzled ex-pilot named Rooke.

Alternatively staring at the single blip on a radarscope and staring out through the green glass window, he said, "A DC-9 lands at 130 mph, right? This baby's coming in at 220 mph. If she overshoots and she *has* got a warhead on board, then goodbye JFK. Goodbye Queens."

Thousands of staff and passengers had sought shelter underground. Others, figuring that if you were this close to a nuclear explosion it didn't matter where you were, had massed on the observation platforms. Fire engines and ambulances hovered, ready to pounce. A bomb disposal unit stood by.

Rooke's deputy made an adjustment to his headset and said, "I have you at 2,000 feet, *Dove*."

Ahead, closing, Talin could see the threshold markings on the illuminated strip; he could also see the fire engines and ambulances.

Sedov said, "Once again, she's all yours."

Talin hauled up *Dove*'s nose. The altitude indicator still wasn't working.

From the tower, "A thousand feet . . . eight hundred . . ."

At 300 feet Talin threw the switch to lower the landing gear and, praying, told Control.

A split-second pause. Then from Control, "Gear down." Followed by, "A hundred feet."

He was over the runway.

"Eighty . . . seventy . . ." and finally, "twenty . . ."

The 500 feet fixed-distance markings were streaming past. He was going to overshoot . . .

"Okay, down," he shouted.

The tires squealed. Talin braked. *Dove* bounced. The wheels touched again. Talin could see the fire engines and ambulances starting to move. Another bounce. The tires shrieked . . .

Dove stopped five feet from the end of the runway and stood there in the glare of the landing lights, looking sublimely innocent.

But there was nothing innocent about the bomb that was defused and removed from her cargo bay later that day. It was calculated that it might have killed three million people.

23

NEWS of *Dove*'s safe landing, her deadly cargo, Talin's defection, and the revelations about the gunships the Russians planned to build in space with their shuttle fleet, dominated the media for several days.

Everywhere, that was, except inside the Communist bloc. But even there the propagandists couldn't simply ignore the disappearance of their revolutionary shuttle, and brief reports were circulated to the effect that, owing to a "computer malfunction" *Dove*'s mission had been aborted. (The Première of *The Red Dove* at the Bolshoi had already been cancelled owing to the "indisposition" of Sonya Bragina; instead the first-night audience saw *Swan Lake*.)

On the day after Talin's defection, the Politburo held an emergency session in the Kremlin. The resignation, owing to ill health, of Grigory Tarkovsky was accepted, and a younger man was appointed. He was only sixty-seven.

Nicolay Vlasov, anticipating a call for his own resignation, had taken the precaution of calling upon the President and several other Politburo members, carrying with him what he euphemistically called their biographies. He also informed the President he had received a report from Los Angeles, via the Soviet Embassy in Washington, indicating that the situation was not completely irretrievable.

Vlasov was not asked to resign.

One day, he thought, as he left the building and gazed at the Kremlin's golden cupolas riding high in the blue sky above the city's quilt of snow, he would write a book called *Survival.* And when they read it perhaps his children would understand. Who knows, by that time he might have been promoted to the very summit of power; the latest report from the Kremlin Clinic on the President's heart condition was ominous and, with his dossiers at hand, there was every reason to hope.

They faced each other outside a pale, clinical building at 136 East 67th Street, New York, the Mission of the Union of Soviet Socialist Republics to the United Nations.

Around Talin stood a group of Secret Service bodyguards. Behind Sedov, clustered around the door that had already swallowed Genin and Vinnikov, stood a group of Soviet officials.

Talin said, "Why did you do it, Oleg? Why did you allow them to put a bomb in *Dove?*"

"Because I was ordered to. And because I believe in a nuclear deterrent."

"Here on earth, perhaps, but not in space."

"That's only an extension of its deterrent potential."

Talin said quietly, "I know you better than that, Oleg. There was another reason, wasn't there?"

"Very well . . ." Sedov's voice faltered. "The mission was a proving flight for the bomb as well as *Dove.* Word reached me from Marshal Grigory Tarkovsky that, if I didn't agree to carry the bomb, then not only would you never become commander of the shuttle fleet, but you would never be sent into space again . . ."

Talin said, "You should have told me."

"And then you would have refused the mission."

Awkwardly Talin stuck out his hand. "I was going to plead with you to stay. But there's no hope, is there?"

Sedov took his hand. "None. You see I'm a Russian. I presumed you had the same blood; I was foolish. But I wish you good luck, as I would have wished my . . ."

But the last word wouldn't come, and Sedov turned on his heel and walked briskly toward the waiting officials. Talin noticed that even in New York he had managed to clothe himself with a shabby coat and shoes that were down at heel.

Talin turned and strode, surrounded by strangers, toward the waiting limousine. He turned once and stared across the street; but Sedov had disappeared, and the door to the mission was closed.

As he climbed into the car a few flakes of snow peeled from the gray sky. He wondered if it was snowing in Moscow.

In a bar in Yokohama, the usual arrival port for passengers completing their Trans-Siberian Express journey to Japan by sea, a crop-haired Mikhail Vlasov reverted to Robert Massey.

He looked haggard and exhausted as though he had been through a terrible ordeal, but, thought the barman serving him a Japanese whiskey, there was an air of achievement about him.

Massey swallowed the whiskey, ordered another, and made a collect call from the telephone at the end of the bar to a number at Padre Island.

"I should be home tomorrow," he said. "But be prepared for a big change."

"Change, Roberto?" fear visiting the happiness in Rosa's voice.

"I've shaved off my mustache," and, as he heard her laughing and crying, he turned away so that the barman couldn't see that he was doing the same.

After a while she said, "I don't know why you had to go, Roberto. But . . ." She hesitated. ". . . was it very bad?"

Very bad? Since his escape from Tyuratam he had jumped the Trans-Siberian Express and hidden from the KGB gunmen in a pine forest with −30 degrees of cold biting through his clothing. He had been shot—another flesh wound—in a midnight chase through the streets of Nakhodka, the rail terminal, and the port before the sea crossing to Japan. He had survived a knife fight on the ship, although the Department V operative who had doubted his KGB credentials hadn't been so lucky.

"Not too bad," he said. "Not compared with what's been achieved. You see," he explained, "we're going to be together—and I'm going to return to space."

The President of the United States swung his ax and said, "So, George, we did it. And if, by any chance, I lose the next election, then you and I will go into the movie business together."

A breeze blowing across the President's ranch from the Pacific ruffled Reynolds's fine silver hair. "And make a film about lumberjacks?"

"George, I've said it before and I'll say it again, despite what everyone says you *have* got a sense of humor." The President leaned on his ax. "We've achieved a lot, you and I. Before our spectacular, the Russians were way ahead of us in the military application of space. Now, maybe, with world opinion turned against them, we'll have a chance to pull in front. Equality? It will never happen, George, it will never happen."

"I'm not so sure," Reynolds said. "Let's suppose that Gordon quits his job at Vandenberg this year—hypochondriacs often will themselves into wheelchairs. And suppose an agent cultivated by the Soviets took over. Then the Kremlin could make the connection work for them."

The President began to speak, but Reynolds held up his hand. "Now suppose we managed to persuade someone in the Russian computer terminal to work for us. Yashin, for instance, thinks computers should be used for peace not war. Couldn't he arrange American penetration of the Soviet military program?" Reynolds smiled faintly. "Then, Mr. President, we'd have equality. And that, after all, is what deterrence is all about, isn't it?"